Mrs Carrington

Prince Fortune and Prince Fatal

Volume 3

Mrs Carrington

Prince Fortune and Prince Fatal
Volume 3

ISBN/EAN: 9783337170028

Printed in Europe, USA, Canada, Australia, Japan

Cover: Foto ©Andreas Hilbeck / pixelio.de

More available books at **www.hansebooks.com**

PRINCE FORTUNE

AND

PRINCE FATAL.

PRINCE FORTUNE

AND

PRINCE FATAL.

By MRS. CARRINGTON,

AUTHOR OF "MY COUSIN MAURICE."

" Marriage is a desperate thing.   The frogs in Æsop were extreme
wise.   They had a great mind to some water, but they would not leap
into the well, because they could not get out again."—SELDEN.

IN THREE VOLUMES.

VOL. III.

LONDON:

SAMPSON LOW, MARSTON, SEARLE & RIVINGTON,
CROWN BUILDINGS, 188, FLEET STREET.

1880.

LONDON :

PRINTED BY WILLIAM CLOWES AND SONS, LIMITED,

STAMFORD STREET AND CHARING CROSS.

CONTENTS OF VOL. III.

PRINCE FORTUNE AND PRINCE FATAL.

CHAPTER I.

SAINT SWITHIN.

Sing, young hearts, while still ye are—
While ye still are young and fair!
Songless age creeps on when ye
Shall despised and loveless be—
Be despised like flowers o'erblown,
Whence are scent and beauty gone—
Like sere lilies be despised,
Now no longer plucked or prized.

Tuscan Maggio.

ANOTHER farewell, another meeting, and another parting! How great their significance! And yet how
light their hold! how brief their day!

"It is the way with everything"—as Lorraine
said—helplessly enough.

Now, when he turns his back upon this meeting and
this parting, it is with the sensations of a man, who,
having been whirled violently through the air, stands

again on *terra firma*, with brain and senses vibrating
to the degree of stupor.

He is on his road to England. Why? Simply
because he cannot bring himself to the consideration of
doing anything else.

Two other courses are fairly open to him. Considering the afflicting loss in which Lady Laure holds
so great a share, without asking her to condone the past,
and without the risk of raising expectations, it might
seem natural—even humane, to follow the master's
suggestion,—to seek her out, and to do for her what Le
Brun and the master have so abundantly done for him!

To do Lorraine justice, the idea of this step could
never of itself—have been presented to his mind. The
thing would have gone by default,—as if, with a sponge,
Lady Laure had been clean wiped out. If Lorraine
had set up a tombstone to her in his memory, he might,
with much correctness, have inscribed upon it the word
" Effaced."

Effaced, so far as there was anything to efface. He
had said that she was simple, dignified, and faultless,
and courageous and constant. But it was a truth that,
with all her gifts and graces, Lady Laure had never
moved him; had never left her mark upon him; had
been no surprise, no enigma, no amusement, no excitement; had barely pleased his eyes—not greedy after
beauty, and from the moment that Lucie appeared, had
become wholly supplementary,—had subsided into a
sort of lay figure, and was, as if she was not.

In his *rôle* of lover, Lorraine, from first to last, was little better than a cardboard marionette. When the strings were let go, he fell flat to the ground. It can't be said that he ever deceived himself into believing that he was anything much else. He had fallen from the clouds unawares into this engagement; he got accustomed to it; it was just bearable as it was; pushed to its limits, it became unbearable,—and thereafter came the crisis.

So weak to get entangled! So wanton to carry it on! So wicked to break it off! It is the probable verdict.

Of everyday occurrence are these unpremeditated entanglements; and then the man, passionless and loveless—either through idleness, cowardice, compassion—or a sense of honour—goes halting long between the two alternatives that still remain. Rarely, indeed, he chooses with Lorraine. And yet it is a question whether there is not a grim kindness in inflicting the sharp pain—rather than in risking the lifelong drag; whether a blow once for all—is not better than the chance of a fatal rebound!

Lorraine, we know, thought he had done well,—as well as could be done under circumstances for which he held himself only very moderately responsible;— quite as well done for Lady Laure, as for himself.

He may have been mistaken in his self-estimate. Once in regular harness, he might have made a docile

sort of husband, like the rest,—what with *his* inertiæ,
and Lady Laure's charms. Yet there were just the
other possibilities, and they were ugly—especially ugly
for Lady Laure herself.

But all these considerations with Lorraine are
things of the absolute past—past recalling, past regretting, past remembering.

The smiling calm beside the blue lake; the mad
succeeding storm; the whirlwind of swift fate, that had
swept Lucie from the earth,—had placed the lapse of
ages between Lorraine and Lady Laure. In the perspective of his mind, she was a mere point, and scarcely
that.

But there is a nearer perspective,—and the picture
is in his heart. It stands out in full relief. It has no
tame shadows; yet it is soft and quiet. Bright and
warm it is too,—so bright and so warm, that Lorraine's
blood goes throbbing with its rich colouring still.

It is the picture of Valérie de Keradec.

Since he had broken away from the fair and gentle
lady of his buried past, Lorraine had come across a
woman who had avenged her sex;—who had put to
flight, without a contest, all his preconceived ways of
thinking, speaking, and acting in regard to women;—
who put it all to flight, without his so much as knowing
it; who had taken him by storm at a glance; who hit
his fancy to a nicety; who kept him always amused,
always pleased—pleased with himself and pleased with

her; who drew out of him all the good in him—all the softness, all the energy, all the earnestness, all the courtesy; who piqued him by her frankness; who touched him with her sentiment; who bewitched him with her curling velvety eyes, and with her taking little face; who exacted nothing, yet made him her most devoted slave; who had all sorts of pretty ways; who showed all her feelings, except her feelings for him; who made him believe himself safest, when danger was nearest; who called it Friendship, and made it Love; who, in the day of trouble, could forget the love-sick woman,—and be the friend in need, and in deed.

Yes, in Valérie de Keradec, Lorraine has found the very echo of his own heart. Why, then, after these sore troubles—why not fly to wake that sympathetic echo again? Why does he hold back from the second course?

It may be—these sore troubles that rule his conduct. —It is not lack of feeling or of memory; it is not caution or distrust; it is not weariness or satiety. Absent, she still stirs his heart, as it has never been stirred before,—his brave and tender Valérie.

She is always the Valérie of that first and last embrace. Fond as was the parting, he could go without fear to as fond a meeting, for Valérie has kept all chains out of reach of eye and ear.

And yet he does not go.

Yes, whether Valérie or Laure, he is as far from seeking the one as the other. He gives no account to himself of all this; he has no motives, no objects, no plans. As far as he can say, plus his title, and his large fortune, he is going back to England to take up the life, he left behind in it.

Loughmore—with its images of gloom, its deserted rooms, its dark waters, its misty vales, its lonely glades, looms in the distance. But—let Uncle Loftus sleep a little longer before his new-made heir comes brushing the dew off the sod. Wait a while, till the grass grows green over his head.

It was Saint Swithin's Day when Lorraine, his six months' leave nearly doubled, walked about dinner-time into the mess-room of his regiment.

In the morning he had come up from Dover, having slept at the Warden over-night.

The white cliffs the day before, had given him a dazzling greeting, and as he steamed into the harbour it struck him that these blue depths of sky and sea, rivalled the hues that had been wearying his eyes for months.

"It's all a sham, those Southern skies," says he to himself.

But Saint Swithin, who was well on the look-out, with his watering-pot, made him suffer for his slander of poor Lucie's new paradise, before he was twenty-four hours older.

By the time he got into London, there was no confusion of ideas as to skies and skies in summer weather; something near upon thick darkness prevailed at noonday. And the rain,—there was no mistake about the rain either. It fell as if it had never fallen before;—it came down with the force of a new sensation, or as if the clouds were in revolt, or as if a new Deluge was to be the upshot of the matter.

Hansoms—they were just coming in—cut about, over the crossings and round the corners, *fins et gaillards*, in all the pride and glory of their high-stepping screws and brand-new paint.

More than one unlucky pedestrian, taking his shower bath and wading up to the ankles, fell a victim that day to the victorious vehicles.

Lorraine got through the half-dozen things he had to do with little delay. It was his misfortune, being an idle man, that he couldn't dawdle over what he had to do.

Within something like a couple of hours—thanks, possibly, to one of the aforesaid two-wheelers, as much as to his own energy—he managed to report himself at head-quarters, go to the livery stables, choose rooms at the Albany, and call upon his banker and his tailor.

Then he looks at his watch, and looks all round. There is absolutely nothing more to be done.

He might go to the club. But no,—he wasn't up to gossip, smoking, and ecarté to-day.

As he is passing, he looks in at the Academy. It will soon be closed.

Looking at pictures!—the most bilious thing alive, and scarcely worth the suffering; but he gets through an hour or so, chiefly by sitting down with his eyes shut. Then he is off again, this time on foot,—it will spin out the time. Everything looks wonderfully secure, to be sure, and wonderfully wealthy. Security and securities; — yes, that is the Briton's boast. Chartism nowhere, except *en l'air*. There is a tinge of heaviness all about; but under such a sky the Venus de' Medici would look lumpy.

South-west by west he steers, till he finds himself inside the old circle of things again.

As he walks across the barrack yard, he thinks he never beheld anything so depressingly hideous in his life.

He turns into the stables; interviews his servant, who seems glad to see him. But what they have to say to each other is soon said.

The man has done his duty by the horses, and he gets a five-pound note. The horses seem to know their master, and make a low whinnying which is gratifying. The stable-dog leaps up; but he is a mongrel cur, and excites nothing but a sigh for the absent Mufti.

The dog's name is Mops.

"Down, Mops, down," says the servant.

This is aggravating;—it is so near to Mufti.

Like Mufti the faithless, and like Bijou the faithful,—Lorraine turns out of the stables,—yawning horribly.

Many a hearty shake of the hand; many a cordial "How are you?" and much friendly congratulation, make up Lorraine's welcome, as he walks into the midst of his old friends again.

In the van stands the doctor,—a single man, and not too rich, and never known to be absent at dinner.

"Better?" asks he, closing one eye, as if for a microscopic observation.

"I've had nothing the matter," answers Lorraine.

"Ah! I thought it was sick leave," says the doctor, as if correcting himself.

"So it was," returns Lorraine. And he begins to yawn again.

"Come, old fellow," says the friend to whom he had delivered his parting blessing. "This is too bad; you look as bored as ever—and yet——"

Lorraine cuts the "and yet" short. He detects a dangerous smile in the corners of the speaker's mouth.

"What would you have?" says he. "I'm dead tired; and the weather is beastly;—yes, beastly is the word."

"As for the weather, it's been splendid till to-day," says the doctor.

"Ah! well," returns Lorraine; "I suppose I've

brought this to you, by way of a change. You may look out for storms now I've come among you. I've caught the knack of brewing them;" and a grim smile follows the words.

"Faith," cries a fellow-countryman; "then you've come back somebody else, I suppose; for that's not you at all!"

"And yet," says his other friend, resuming his interrupted speech, "report says that you have come straight from a fair lady's feet. You didn't get your stormy habits there, did you?"

"Report is a liar," returns Lorraine, bluntly.

"Well, it's the talk of the clubs, and there's the lady's father for authority."

Lorraine cursed the lady's father in his shroud, for a gossiping old idiot. Then he starts round and says, with the look of an animal at bay—

"The lady's feet I do come from is the red goddess of the Paris mob."

Lorraine's tactics were not bad. He turned the talk right round. Half a dozen questions assail him.

"Were you in the thick of it?"

"Did you storm a barricade?"

"Was it really so bloody?"

"Did you see many shot down?"

"Awoke pretty often to the tune of the Paris Angelus, I suspect," says the doctor,—who had studied medicine in the emotional city, under some revolution or another.

"Angelus,"—repeats Lorraine, absently; and his mind flies off to a mixed picture,—a grey city of the dead, chill and misty;—and snowy little Sanctuaries, dotting the purple hills beside a deep blue sea.

"Angelus, to be sure," repeats the doctor. "'Tis another name for the din of their *rappel*. I remember we turned out every night for a week from our Quartier Latin, to its drumming."

"Ah! to be sure," comes from Lorraine.

The words are drowned in much laughter, at the doctor's new application. He was the wit of the party, and it was the habit to laugh at all he said, whether witty or not.

Lorraine escaped into the Park when the dinner broke up. What with "the lady's father," the doctor's jokes, his fellow-countryman's brogue, the pungent tobacco, the witless mirth,—he had had enough of this revival of olden days for a first dose.

But the other extreme that he has plunged into is equally distasteful.

As he skirts the Ride, and turns up by the water— though the nine o'clock guard has not yet been told off—he scarcely meets a soul. Round by the gardens it is still more dismal; the damp hangs in the branches, the rain drips from the leaves, and the wind sighs and soughs, as if each old tree held an imprisoned dryad.

"What a sponge of a country it is!" cries Lorraine. "No wonder we cut our throats periodically, and drown ourselves upon a system! And what a lot of kill-joys we are at the best! As for those fellows, of course, they can't help it; and there's no harm in them; but, one way or another, they've become insufferable to me. I suppose I've got out of the go of it all,— if I ever was in it! Anyhow, I can't stand it at present, —that's a fact."

Lorraine gives a shiver. "Here's a pretty evening for the middle of summer!"

Then he looks round him. "And here's a pretty desert for the middle of a city! in the middle of the season, too!"

Lorraine had altogether lost sight of St. Swithin and his watering-pot. But he hit the right nail on the head when he said he was "out of the go of it."

The earth and sky, the places and peoples, the ways and words, the habits and manners, the friends and the company, he had left behind him,—were too entirely opposed to this first night's home experiences, for him to take to the change right off,—without a growl and a grumble.

Those balmy nights by that deep blue sea! Those children of the sun, who slept so little and sang so much! That etherealized dulness,—so endurable, after all!

That gracious lady, at whose feet he had, in truth, sat bodily so many hours a day, in spite of his vindictive retort upon Rumour's false tongue!

And that friend—with the dazzling eyes, and the tender heart, and the far-reaching soul!——

And that other blue-eyed water! that moonlit lake! that island garden! those holiday folks! those silver trout! that ruby Rhein wein!

Good Heavens! What would he not give at this moment—his dinner digesting—to be taking a beating from the old moustache, with Mufti and Mufti's mistress within close reach of hand and eye?

Then in his mind's camera, rises the modest interior of the Rue Châteaubriand, with its fierce background, its fiery lights — life-stirring scenes — soul-stirring thoughts — the master's martyrdoms — Le Brun's heroism—Lucie's last rest—that last night's communings,—that last farewell!

It is too much for solitude. He hurries across the foot-track, comes out by the lodge, and passes through the gates. Here he comes upon the blaze of gas and the stream of traffic. Plenty of faces! But he may walk a mile without encountering a smile. Every one is in haste—every one intent, every voice under its breath. If some one would only seem to be out for his pleasure! If some one would only laugh! If some one would only sing!

One of the doctor's bad jokes would be a saving mercy, if it could only break the monotony of this lugubrious gravity.

Stop! What is that? Yes; he has got his wish. Lorraine throws back his head to listen. Yes, 'tis the human voice, pitched in a musical key. A smile crosses his face; he pushes on, as pleased as a child— as eager as a *dilettante* to catch the first note of a new *prima donna*.

It is no *prima donna*, though it is a woman.

A dozen paces up a private street stands a black figure; the bonnet hangs back on the shoulder; the dark hair falls loose; in the glare of the gas above it, the sallow and sunken face looks wan and wild.

The voice is a broken contralto, worn with rough usage and rude necessity; but it has been a voice once. The refrain rings out with the true artist touch—

> " Joli mois de Mai, mois de mes amours,
> Quand reviendras tu !—
> Jamais! ah, jamais ! "

This poor waif is a Frenchwoman then,—waking the echoes of the quiet street with her " *Jamais! ah, jamais!* "

Lorraine is inspired to go up to her. He puts a piece of gold into her hand.

The woman starts as the yellow coin glistens in the lamp-light. She takes a glance at his face; the face decides the wavering honesty.

" 'Tis gold ! " She holds it out to him. Her spoken
voice is low and hoarse, and it has its unmistakable
alien accent.

Lorraine puts it away. " Keep it, my poor creature,"
he says.

The woman turns her eyes full upon him; though
the cheeks are faded, the eyes keep their fires—soft
fires; velvety eyes, with the tears brimming over the
curling lashes.

Lorraine thrills as he stands. These eyes; they
are Valérie's!—the eyes of his brave and tender
Valérie ! More gold—still more gold—he presses
into the thin, brown hand.

" Go ! " he cries—" go back to your own happy
country ! "

" Ah ! never ! " says she. " They would not listen ;
—they would not give me this ! " And she holds up
the yellow gold in the dazzle of the gas.

Lorraine walks on ; he no more looks out for smiles
and songs. He is absorbed, like the rest. There is
still much to do,—much to be balanced, before he can
square things all round.

" I suppose I was a fool for my pains," thinks he,
as he nears his new rooms,—summing up the episode
of the quiet street.

"She had fine eyes, though,—Valérie's eyes, tears and all!" Yes, just that tearful glance that bade him adieu!

"*Mois de mes amours*," murmurs he, with his resonant baritone, well kept in. "She had a good voice. Poor creature! What will become of her?" He hums it again, "*Jamais! ah, jamais!* It's immensely pathetic. I wonder who wrote it. I'll try and get it."

And he did try,—and he·didn't succeed; but it was all one. To the end of his life, from time to time, Lorraine broke out with the refrain—with the plaintive pitch of the one high note, and with the dying fall, "*Jamais! ah, jamais!*"

"There's your old song again!" said his friends. Everybody knew it; everybody called it his; and nobody knew any more about it. "How does it go on?" "Where did you learn it?" "Who wrote it?" "Where did you find the air?" But Lorraine knew nothing,— so he said.

Some hearts sighed to it; some lips smiled to it. And as the years sped, these same hearts ceased to beat, and these same lips ceased to smile; but Lorraine sang—still sings on; sometimes sings, and sometimes smiles, and sometimes yawns, and rarely sighs.

Such, for him, is the life ordained!

The next day beholds a quite new programme for our hero. He puts his name down for the next and last *levée* of the season. Within a week he is duly presented, "on his accession to his title." He gets extended leave, upon the plea of pressing affairs; and, though St. Swithin has still fifteen days to run out, he bribes him to become a false prophet; and starts for Loughmore, with the south wind filling his sails, a blue sky overhead, and a sun worthy of the dog days.

CHAPTER II.

OULD IRELAND.

Three merry gipsies once I found
  Under a tree together,
Whilst my car, with a creaking sound,
  Slid o'er the sandy heather.

One delighting himself alone,
  Fiddle in hand, was seated;
And, as on him the sunlight shone,
  Rollicking songs repeated.

Another watched how the eddies curl'd,
  Smoking away at leisure,
Seeming sure that the whole wide world
  Had not a greater pleasure.

Stretched along was the third, and slept;
  On a branch his cymbal swinging;
Through whose chords, as the breezes swept,
  Dreams to his heart were singing.

Patched and torn are the clothes they wear,
  Little but rags and tatters;—
Devil a bit the gipsies care
  About such trifling matters.

Thus, thrice over, I've learnt to scoff
　Sorrows that e'er pursue me,—
To smoke, to fiddle, to dream them off,
　Should ever life be gloomy.

Onward plodding, I long looked back
　On the group from which I parted;
Those dark faces, and curls of black,
　Seeming so careless-hearted.

After LENAU.

NOTWITHSTANDING the aforesaid favourable auspices, Lorraine landed upon his ancestral shores with a predetermined disgust.

It was all in vain that Dublin Bay looked its very best. In vain that the Wicklow Hills shone crimson, tipped in the rising sun. In vain that the handsome terraced city, rose fair and white, out of its umbrageous surroundings. In vain that the western mountains hung soft and purple in the shadowy distance. In vain that the crested waves fringed the bold promontory with a line of snow. In vain, on this rare summer morning, that the air was as subtly clear as in a Southern climate. The only thing it did for Lorraine—was to bring up before him the Land of his Enchantments, and to give him a shudder like the echo of a bad dream.

They are soon alongside of the quay.

Now, it is not to be doubted that to step cheerfully from shipboard to *terra firma*,—to land pleasantly anywhere, requires a previous stock of hope and good spirits—a certain confidence in what you are stepping into.

This short voyage had been a somewhat longer one than usual; but Lorraine had not complained of this tardiness. He had the gift of patience; and he had another gift, which landsmen call—"being a good sailor;" and, moreover, the safe repose of these wooden walls, which shut out the strife, of crowding numbers of men and women,—was inexpressibly welcome to him.

But his landing sent him into the thick of it all again. His baggage was seized upon by a quartet of lusty tatterdemalions, and he himself had hard work to stand his ground as they pressed round him, pouring forth the national tongue in the most cajoling accents.

"It's me, Dick O'Malley, that's been on the look out for ye all this blessed night," says one.

"Git gone, ye rascal," cries the second; "and isn't it me the one, that's sent down express for the gintleman, by the guv'nor himself?"

"And whare will I have the pleasure iv taking yer honour?" inquires a third.

"And whare will this be going to?" asks the fourth, clinging desperately to hat-box, and carpet bag!

Lorraine positively sickens at the sound; he takes it as the type of the entire country.

But he survives the first brunt of it; and after that it comes easier to him.

The Capital did not detain him; he saw nothing in

it to attract. He pursued his journey to his possessions leisurely; there were no affairs to hurry about. At the present moment his life had not a single goal before it, except its end.

He travelled by cars, stopping here and there, as his inclination, or the time of day, decided. His way was west by south. As he advanced, locomotion became more and more arduous; but it was scarce a penance to move at a foot pace by these mountains and lakes, and these blue rivers;—these breezy moorlands, redolent of fresh fern odours and fragrant peat burnings,—issuing from some unseen cabin or secret whisky still.

Exquisite solitudes! which, with all his heart, Lorraine enjoys.

It was with these amended feelings that he arrived at dusk, with his one-horse car and its ragged driver, at the place which figured as the post-town to Loughmore.

The only building above the level of a hovel in it, was a small hostelry, built by his grandfather, for the convenience of arriving and departing guests. He had written to secure—till further orders—the one bed-chamber it boasted, in case he might find it convenient to wait there for the night, before going on to the Castle,—a distance of some six Irish miles or so.

Making sure of the empty bedroom, Lorraine was not inclined to announce himself by name. That was a moment much dreaded by him ;—a dread,—he was free to confess to himself,—if to no one else.

"For this night," thinks he, "I will still belong to myself. Heaven knows what nuisances are not in store for me to-morrow!"

So, hitting his hat against the low doorway of the house, he calls out for the landlord.

Now Tim Phelim, who at this epoch filled the important post of landlord of the Loughmore Arms, was a considerable respecter of persons. Making his observations out of the tap-room window, he at once decided that this arrival was one of no account. He had been looking for an arrival night and day, to be sure—anxiously looking; but that would come up after a very different fashion,—outriders at the least, if the exigencies of the roads impeded a carriage and four. So he took his time in presenting himself at the door.

"You seem to be all asleep," says Lorraine.

"Niver a bit iv it," returns Tim Phelim, coolly.

"I want a room for the night."

"Ye'll be in luck to get one, thin," is the reply.

"You have a room."

"Jist so," is Tim's curt rejoinder.

"Where is it?"

"Whare is it indade! Whare should it be but under the roof?"

Lorraine prepares to look for this room under the roof, himself.

But the landlord seizes him by the coat. "What wud ye be afther?" he cries.

"I am going to find this room."

"The Lord forgi'e us!—And what wunna, ane iv *yer sort* be goin' for next?"

Phelim has an undisguised contempt for the supposed nationality of the traveller.

Lorraine endeavours to shake him off; but mine host only holds on the tighter.

"I'll be obleeged to ye to guv up that!" says he. "D'ye happen to know who's inside that room, at this vera time? An' if ye don't know, I'll be afther telling ye, that it's jist his honour o' the Castle, arrived frae the foreign parts; it's jist Sir Claude himsel'!"

"Sir Claude!" exclaims Lorraine. The statement was sufficient to dumfounder our hero for a moment.

Could any one be persorating him? But no; there was a most inveracious look in Phelim's face.

"Nonsense," says Lorraine. "I shall be obliged to you to prepare that room, and pretty quickly!"

Then Phelim rises to the occasion.

"Divil a go ye'll get in thare this night!" Then he stops short. "An' if ye'll no be afther belavin' iv me word, I'll jist call a witness to the fore, though ye'd no desarve that I should tak' the throuble iv convincing iv ye—at all."

Whereupon Phelim retires with his injured innocence, and, seizing Barney, his Jack-of-all-trades, by the ear, whispers into it—

"Swar' for the life iv ye, that Sir Claude himsel' is in the bed up thar, or I'll sink ye pretty deep, and no mistake."

"I'll answer, niver fear!"

And so Barney goes to the fore. He is a person capable of all sorts of swearing—at the least; he can swear black or white, or both. It may have come of his vicarious offices—tapman, boots, and ostler in one.

Lorraine's petulance is subsiding into something like amusement at this first specimen of the trustworthiness of his tenantry.

Barney comes forward to where he is standing, with a fine swagger in his air.

"And isn't it for me to spak' out, and to tell ye the word that I know?—for didn't I tuck his honour in betwixt the sheets an hour agone by the clock, with these vera hands?"

Lorraine's gravity altogether gives way.

"If you did, he's got out of them again," says he; "for I am Sir Claude Lorraine. And now get me some supper, and put some candles in my room."

It was thus that Lorraine took his leap in the dark into the midst of "the nuisances." And it was, perhaps, the least harassing way of making his first plunge into them;—it made him laugh, at any rate.

But Barney's master has a word to say to him in private.

"Ye bould haythen," cries he. "An' what were ye

afther, sticking that big lie on to the tail of the thruth fur?"

"The thruth! the thruth!" cries Barney. "Oh, thin, ye riprobate. It's howld me tongue that I will afther this. The divil a taste iv it, if I lie agin fur ye, Tim Phelim!"

"And whar axed ye?" retorts Tim.

"Whar axed me! Didn't ye swar' by the Lord ye'd sink me, if I was not to the fore to swar' out my two eyes, that his honour was lying up thar in the bed,—an' he standin' thar, saft an' aisy, all the blessed time?" groans Barney.

"An' if I did, ye black varmint, am I to have me own mither's best linen put under the first ne'er-do-weel that comes up to the door?—an' iverything set out as fine as paradise, too?"

It is a clenching argument, and Barney, who is no sophist;—as he says "howlds his tongue." But it is as an aggrieved man that he gives in.

As for Tim Phelim, he is unacquainted with shame. He accepts the change in the face of affairs with alacrity; pushes Barney into the background; does the honours to Lorraine in his own person; and when he sets the grilled salmon before him, he remarks that his honour will not get it better cooked at the Castle itself.

Barney slinks off to the stables, and pours forth his woes into the sympathizing heart of the ragged car-driver.

" Musha ! " says he, " it's a pig that he is ! "

The—" he "—is the unabashed Tim Phelim.

" An' he in thar afther goin' in to his honour as
bould as brass. Ou—gh faith ! "—sighs Barney—" an'
I'll niver forgit it."

The home-coming of the succeeding heir is ever a
gracious event.   It is in human nature happily to have
more sympathies with things present than past ; and
although the world promises itself soon to have done
with kings, yet the proverb, " Le roi est mort ; vive le
roi," will still hold good here below.

Lorraine's stealthy advance had, indeed, in his case,
shorn his home-coming of its glories,—had put aside
blazing peat fires, triumphal arches, crowds and pro-
cessions, banners flying, and the like.

And even now that he was recognized, the most
enthusiastic were scarcely impelled to unharness the
poor beast that had brought him thus far, and to supply
its place to the one-horse car.

But this was a small matter with these warm-
hearted people.   They got no end of whisky, at any
rate, to drink his health in ; and that was the main
thing.

There was little ceremony amongst them, and, what
was better, no discontent.   They had had their own way
for many a generation.   It was not, perhaps, the best way ;

but it gave them all they wanted—whisky and potatoes, and wild game in abundance; fishing, too, by coast and lake and river; for the lands of Loughmore stopped only with the sea,—and the fishing, like the game, was to be had for the taking. If they had no specified rights over the one or the other, there was no one to say them nay.

Light rents, too, or no rents, as the law of custom had decreed ;—those who had always paid rent, paid it ; those who had never paid it, lived rent free. If the latter were too idle to be independent, the former were too proud to be dependent. There was room for all, and somehow, both in the Castle and the cabin, both ends did a great deal more than meet. It was not the most profitable way for any one perhaps, but it was perfectly patriarchal.

In these distant wilds, far away south by west, the race was pure—Irish of the Irish ; no mongrel mixture with either Saxon or Scotchman. If they swore by the Green, you must go beyond their boundaries to fall in with the white and the yellow—with Ribbonism and Orangeism. A free fight amongst themselves, without malice, and for their own personal pleasure, was their sole fisticuff enjoyment. The agent and the exciseman, born and bred amongst them, went with safe skins, and the noblest quarry that fell to their shots was a shy woodcock flying low.

Want was kept at bay—for if potatoes ran short— no one was without a pound to buy better food. They were not great at management,—they had yet to learn what can be done with a handful of grain, though sown on the top of a mountain ;—still, to all intents, they lived *by* the land, as well as *on* it.

Lorraine saw into things by degrees, and after his own fashion,—saw enough to wish to let well alone.

Sir Loftus had drained nothing out of the estate,—and, with his own peculiar difficulty of getting rid of money, he was not likely to drain it either.

"Some day or other," said he, "I'll see into those fisheries;" and that was his one idea for the present, of future improvement.

But if he took his responsibilities too lightly, and looked with too superficial a glance at the interests of his possessions, he surveyed with no indifferent eye their external charms.

The Castle, in truth, was gloomy enough. But these broad lands that spread beneath the sky ;—with what a charm did they strike him !—a charm too, as of something old, and of something very new.

It was full summer still, and the season was enchanting. Here there was no chained air, no breathless atmosphere.

The west winds came over the moorlands charged with the fresh flavour of a thousand miles of ocean. Here there was no stereotyped glare of unmitigated sunshine to bring up his cold shudders. All day long the inconstant shadows chased each other momentarily over mountain and lake. Here there was no strip of earth, narrowed betwixt shore and height, to make him chafe at prison bounds. Here water and land interchanged freely. The variety was endless, the stretch seemed boundless. The lakes lay with their black islands thick with yew; the fat green meadows spread seaward, awaiting only the fat cattle to graze on them; miles of brown bog and rock-strewn heather spread far and near; and in the midst, up-springing, rose the mountains, with their conical shapes and their fantastic distances, hiding many a dark cave and defile never touched by ray of sun, and many a rock-bound tarn, known only to the birds of the air.

Matchless, too, was the solitude in its safe repose; and yet swarming with life. Here, where for a generation, the huntsman's horn and the cry of the hound had never sounded, all wild creatures found their Garden of Eden. From copse and glen came the whirr of the winged game; under your feet scurried the rabbit and the hare; all unawares you came upon the grand red deer,—neither his race nor his lichens as yet uprooted by new men and new measures; all tribes of web-footed fowl peopled the lakes—the red plover and the curlew with its plaintive call, and even the solitary bittern's boom was still to be heard there. Such was the wild Eden that Lorraine found ready to his foot.

And all his own! It was not the sort of paradise he had left behind in the Land of his Enchantments; —and he thanked Heaven for it!

The great gap that divided him from his earliest

recollections closed up, as by a magic touch. With
unpremeditated feelings, he went straight back again,
through the years, to their very beginning. Even as
then he had roamed wild and free and happy, so now
came the same sensations of careless pleasure, as he faced
the fresh sea air from some breezy hill, or walked
through the mountain mist, or took his risk across the
bog, or lay stretched at noonday, between tufts of bog-
myrtle and heather, upon a bed of fern.

At times as he so lay, with half-closed eyes, and
senses lulled with the murmur of the insects, and the
mountain fragrance, and the stillness of human life,—
all that had intervened between those years, and these,
seemed to him but a tissue of visions ;—Lucie, Lady
Laure, Valérie,—they were none of them half so real—
as Uncle Loftus seated in his chair, watching the burning peat.

CHAPTER III.

Thus writes the cynic of his age
Neath Cupid's image on the page—
" Whoe'er you are, your master, know,
He is, or was, or will be so ! "

BUT all one's life cannot be passed dreaming away, under the sky, upon a breezy hill-side. Amongst other sufficient deterrents, skies may be drenching and hillsides damp,—a not unfrequent accompaniment to life in the open in this wild Eden. The alternative upon such days was to be sought, as Tim Phelim might have expressed it, "under the roof." But as the Castle stood, the alternative was rather a forlorn one.

The word "gloomy" scarcely expressed its condition. Something like a century—possibly you might make it two—had passed over its grey walls without a single *meuble* being altered or replaced, and for half a century or more these same *meubles* had hardly gone through the form of being so much as moved. It needs but little imagination to fill in the picture.

For a mortal endowed with the æsthetic tastes of

the present day, to come in for such a field as it offered, would be such an intoxicating windfall, as possibly to turn his craze into downright craziness;—the *gros lot* of the lottery tickets would be nothing to it. But unluckily for Lorraine, his mind did not take even mildly to these distractions. The utmost efforts of his genius in the way of restoration amounted to the brushing out two of the reception-rooms, and having the old rooms he had lived in as a boy fitted up for himself.

This done, there was little to do further, save to eat and sleep and look down into that black moat which had had such an ominous effect upon his worthy nurse.

But it is time, perhaps, to say a word about this worthy nurse herself,—still in the land of the living, and not less comely and flourishing, than when she first entered the grim portals of the Castle full five and twenty years gone by. Strong as were her first antipathies to the house and its master, she has still stuck to the spot,—out of love to her nursling, so she says;—but also because, for these last twenty years, secretly or openly, she has been the faithful spouse and better half of Mr. Burke. No more cogent reasons for overcoming the force of first impressions could possibly be adduced.

Even before young Claude was despatched to Eton, it had become a question with Sir Loftus what was to be done with this good woman.

"Give her money and send her off," said Sir Loftus to his confidant.

"But an' if she won't be afther goin'?" suggests Burke.

"Won't be after going!" cries Sir Loftus. "But she will be after going, and at once."

"It'll break the young masther's heart."

Sir Loftus heaved a heavy sigh. He knew all about broken hearts; and thereupon he fell into one of his long dreams.

"Sittin' thar," as Burke used to say; "a-thinkin' all about nothin'."

The next day, Sir Loftus put a sum of money into the honest Burke's hands.

"Put a bed," he said, "into the Lough Beg Lodge, and send the woman there; but mind you, I'll have no gates unbarred—no gates unbarred."

The sum of money covered a good many more household necessaries than the bed Sir Loftus considerately provided; and within a few weeks, nurse was standing, with her comely face, at as pretty a lodge doorway as heart could desire. How she was to subsist there was not a matter that Sir Loftus concerned himself about. But since this devoted woman, by the marriage tie, was already Mrs. Burke, there was no difficulty in the way of these two going shares with board as well as bed.

The society of the outer world—one of the paramount nuisances which Lorraine had pictured to himself—proved to be neither a nuisance nor the reverse.
It was too scattered for much intercourse. What there
was of it was well bred and well mannered and cordial,—
and, after all, Lorraine found nothing amiss with it,
except its scarcity. With all his imaginary dread of
his fellow-creatures, the actual man was of a sociable
and gregarious turn; and found himself more cheerful
in the company of the dullest heads in the world than
in no company at all. He was not hard to please
either. His tastes inclined always to the simpler side
of things—simple people, simple words, simple songs,
simple life.

What so natural, then, as that Lorraine should
bestow some of his vacant hours upon his second
mother, the tenant of the Lough Beg Lodge?

It was a picturesque exterior. Here the hand of
man had not been idle; the fairest of the floral
treasures, culled from bog and glen, bloomed here in
sweet luxuriance. Round the rustic porch, and
framing the low lattices, twined thick masses of green
myrtle;—not such myrtle as grows south, not such
myrtle as tries to grow north; but such myrtle as grows
only in the moist wealth of this Western Isle; no
withery, stunted sticks, no parched-up, dusty boughs,
—fragrant, succulent, exuberant.

The deep shade of the black yews—the tree of the country—fabulously old, shelters the low roofing. And a stone's throw behind lay the lake that gave it its name—a gem of watery beauty, wide, open, catching the sun all day and the moon all night. It was green, too, like all the rest; its clear waters reflecting its green banks with such a mimic truth, that as you looked down into its far depths, and beheld the growing trees and the grazing sheep, you were fain to believe in the fabled meadows of the fairy lore of the land.

In calm days this glassy lough scarce moved a petal of the water-lilies that floated upon its bosom; but in the fury of a western gale, it too grew furious,—fatally furious, it might be, to those who were caught crossing it at the worst moment.

The interior of this rustic lodge is also picturesque. Not too much light, but always the peat fire gleaming, and the door half ajar,—this last, the necessity of something too much now and then, of the smoke. But peat smoke is fragrant, and moreover, when taken in moderation, imparts to an interior a rich brown hue, reminding you of a Rembrandt or a Teniers' touch, thereby favouring also the picturesque. The space is roomy, the quaint old furniture somewhat scanty; but you see the better who is moving about: a central table, that does not change its place, fixed to the log floor; six chairs, all armed and easy; an

armoire; a small book-stand and table in one, with a
modern look to it, a mirror over it, and a rush chair
beside it; and everything rubbed up to the highest
degree of homely polish. There is another fragrance in
the room; it comes from the fresh rush mats which
stand in front of each armchair.

The hearth is wide, and the chimney wide too,
arranged for the smoking. On one side sits nurse;—
the name still clings to her; it is the name of all
others that she still loves the best. Beside her
stands her wheel; she has learnt to spin, like the
rest here, and she spins well too. On the other side,
in something more of a chimney corner, sits Mr. Burke
himself. No longer the active-stepping Mr. Burke of
former days. He looks now of great age, with a gentle
and venerable face, surrounded by long white hair. He
is feeble, and his hands continually tremble. His
voice is the firmest thing he retains of the happy
days of his prime, and he likes to use it. Mr. Burke
indulges more than ever in his glorious histories of
Cormac Lharhane and his peers.

The third figure in this interior is charming in
contrast, and charming in fact:—a young girl.

If you saw her for the first time, you must be struck
by her rare beauty. But you would be struck with
something more,—a candid daring, at once ingenuous
and resolute. Her clear grey eyes—clear as an eagle's
glance—meet yours quite honestly, and without a
blush. Her complexion, browned by the air, yet white

as snow at the roots of her auburn hair, has a splendid glow in it. And this hair, the gift of her Kentish kindred, has a glow, too, tinged with the gold-red of setting suns. It sits upon her head like a fine coronet, and she carries it with all the pride of a young queen. Tall, robust, and strong,—her figure is full and finished, and her bare white arms befit a young Amazon. .

This is Myrtilla—Myrtilla Burke,—a beautiful young woman in her eighteenth year, born under the roof of the Lough Beg Lodge, the very month which saw Lorraine an Eton boy.

As it happened, things could not have fallen out more opportunely.

The mother took the babe in her arms. "God is good," she cried. "He has sent me this in place of Master Claude."

The father planted a myrtle by the door. "She shall be called Myrtilla," said he.

In bestowing this name upon his daughter,—Burke looked both far forward and backward.

"Tak' gud care, wife, o' the darlint," said he to her mother, "an' we'll live to see the day yit, whan the gates 'ill be unbarred fur anither Sir Claude; an' our Myrtilla 'ill be the first to hand him the grandfather's sprig o' myrtle."

It all came true; only Burke's second sight didn't go so far as to see the new Sir Claude's look of amazed admiration, at the magnificent portress,—or the trembling wonder, rapture, and shame, that swept through the

young Myrtilla,—as that look of amazed admiration
sank deep into her heart. It was given in honest
innocence, in honest ignorance of the expression it
conveyed and the effect it produced. But it did not
fall harmless all the same.

It was Lorraine's first realization of what Irish
beauty—the beauty of the South—is in woman.

Those who know what that beauty is, in face,
figure, air, and carriage, will be inclined to absolve
Lorraine for his look of amazed admiration.

But there was yet a fourth to complete this rustic
interior. There was beauty here too—fine manly
beauty, but it was not of the soil. It was a youth
who stood six feet two without his shoes. He had
laughing blue eyes, and curly brown hair, and a mouth
that laughed as much as his eyes. He had a healthy,
florid colour, and a good bold walk. He had nothing
of the clod-hopper about him; yet he was a tiller of
the ground and a tender of the cattle, the son of a
Kentish yeoman of very low degree.

After " Master Claude,"—as was natural Mrs. Burke's
pride centred in her Myrtilla. As she grew day by
day to her womanly perfections, Mrs. Burke laid out
many plans, which for the most part she hid in her
heart.

She had, as she had proved, got over her local
prejudices as far as Mr. Burke went; but then, from
the first, she had found him affable—unlike the rest

of them, and she could understand what he said;—
she had understood it, in fact, to very good purpose.

But—for the rest of them! Well, they never got
nearer to her heart than they did the first day; to her
mind, they were always a rude, outlandish brood, more
to be avoided than conciliated.

It followed, therefore, that the most alarming bugbear in Mrs. Burke's eye was the possibility of this
wild brood furnishing a mate for her precious Myrtilla.
Many silent vows did she make to herself that this
climax of disaster should never come to pass.

It was to this end, therefore, that young Harry
English, the Kentish yeoman, appeared upon the
scene. It is needless to follow out the wary steps by
which she gained her point. She allowed her hand
only to be seen by degrees—and she played it skilfully—so that now, in the twelfth month of the youth's
presence here, he had been for the last three of these
months the affianced lover of the fair Myrtilla.

Myrtilla herself neither said nay nor yea. There
were no rivals on the ground, at any rate; and so,
without much persuasion or coyness, Myrtilla let herself be disposed of after her mother's heart.

Mr. Burke had little to say to the matter. Infirm
and partially blind, and with a fine respect for his
wife's prudent sagacity, he had only acquiescence to
give to all her proposals.

The young pretender, too, had something universally
winning about him. Frank and light-hearted and ready-

handed, and entirely without fear and without pre-
judice,—he fraternized with the youth all round, as if
he had been to the manner born amongst them.

The one drawback to the alliance was the staunch-
ness with which Harry stood to the determination that
he would take his bride across the seas, and settle
down with her upon his father's few acres. Mrs. Burke,
in her secret heart, acknowledged that he was right;
even more,—it was the thing she desired. And yet she
dreaded it. She wished both ways, as we often are
driven to do.

But to Myrtilla, it was the real attraction—the only
attraction in the affair. The girl's mind was not a
mere *tabula rasa*, upon which to write her maiden fancies
down. She, too, like her mother, had her ideas—her
secret plans, which she unfolded to no one.

She was ambitious. She wanted a wider scope.
She would see beyond these lakes and mountains.
She would hear people speak, one and all, in the
smooth speech of the gentry folk. She had sat at the
feet of her mother from her babyhood, listening to
her tales of the fine things to be seen, and the fine
ways people had of going on, in England.

Mrs. Burke often let her imagination run away
with her. As she talked on, it ran the faster, and the
stronger the effect it produced.

Sentiment had nothing whatever to do with Myrtilla's plans. She would like to be a fine lady if she
could. Once over there, she thought the way to this

fine-ladyism would come of itself. She knew that Harry was not a fine gentleman well enough ; but still, she took him to be a step to her own elevation. Beyond this, she had a burning stock of ungratified curiosity. As to any yearning of affection towards her mother's kinsfolk and country, she had not a shadow of it. Her father was dearer to her than her mother ;—at least, she loved him with a tenderer love ; and, what was more, she took from him and his blood, the qualities of her mind,—signally that quality, which combines love of country, and readiness to leave it.

Matters in the little household of the Lough Beg Lodge were precisely in this position when Lorraine one day fulfilled Mr. Burke's prophecy, and, in the character of the new Sir Claude, rode through the unbarred gates, and accepted from Myrtilla his grandfather's badge,—the myrtle sprig, giving her, in return, that which he could not take back again.

CHAPTER IV.

THE HERDSMAN.

"But Eunica alone loved not a herdsman."

THE southernmost half of Loughmore was a land of many waters,—waters of all varieties:—lakes, gloomy and gay, black and green;—rills and streams and falls;—everywhere the wild element was to be seen, reflecting the heaven above it, sleeping lazily among reeds and rushes, or dancing and dashing about, breaking up the earth with its silvery lines and curves, and giving to it, under the sun, a never-ending and ever-changing glory.

But Lough Beg lay high, and far outside this watery maze, though united to it in fact;——but the stream that formed the connecting link had a long way to travel,—first round the base of a great conical hill, that blocked the head of the lake, and then by many a mile of pleasant upland, before it encountered the serious torrent which bore it off breathlessly, and without reprieve, to a joint death in the black depths of the great mere beyond.

There were no waters on the estate which were

better for the white trout fishing than this stream which flowed out of the head of Lough Beg :—it was one of the boasts of the spot—and one of its prime pleasures ;—and when tired of this, there was the quaint conical mound for a more active sport. Its smooth-shaven form, which looked as if it had been thrown up from a mould, invited you to a slide down,—and half-way to its peaked summit, if you raised your voice, you could wake the echoes in a hundred glens,—wake them for so long—and with such a strange recurrence, that it was hard to believe that it was you only who first set them going.

Another pride of Lough Beg was its clump of old beeches—rare survivors of the timber of past days ;— these, together with a rich growth of thorn and wild ash, made an impervious shelter for the lodge to the north, and gave to the scene that woodland beauty which was the only charm lacking to the perfection of these broad landscapes.

No wonder, with its bright interior and its pleasant surroundings, that Lorraine, with his love for such simple matters, found plenty of occasion to visit Lough Beg Lodge,—besides the natural kindliness that led him to look in upon the good nurse,—and to listen awhile again, to the garrulous memories of Mr. Burke.

A change of clothes in case of a wetting, fishing tackle, and other matters, speedily found their way thither ; and Lorraine soon discovered the necessity of fitting up for himself a small room which had been used for the same purpose by his grandfather, and which Mr. Burke had turned to his own uses as a potato-house, tool-house, and cow-house.

A boat, too, was soon seen to grace the waters of the lake,—a little pinnace, with a mast and a sail, and a small punt to land in the shallows; and Harry English, whose Kentish home bordered upon the Channel shores, and who had almost as much of mariner as of herdsman in him, was appointed chief mate.

Lorraine himself pretended to the post of captain. It is a not uncommon arrangement in nautical government, where the responsible action rests with the second in command.—There remained only the name to provide for. Well, the fair daughter of the Lodge furnished this. The *Myrtilla*. What could be prettier?

And Myrtilla herself,—what was she doing all this time? She could not have told you, perhaps:——and yet, it was an absorbing pursuit,—nothing less than the perilous process of multiplying the effects of Lorraine's first look of amazed admiration, by that mathematical term, which represents things unlimited.

As for the look itself, it stood alone. There was no need of a second to stimulate the power of the first; but if there had been, it did not appear.

Lorraine was pleased, and friendly all round. He took his seat in an armchair, and lit his cigar, with his thoughts upon anything or nothing, and his eyes following also these two useful parts of speech.

When nurse and old Burke had struggled to

their feet at the first acquaintance, Lorraine had said cheerily—

"When you come to see me, you can stand up, if you think it proper. When I come to see you, we'll all sit down and be comfortable."

"The Lord bless him!" murmurs Mr. Burke; "and isn't he the vera mirror of his grandfather—the vera mirror?"

Lorraine took plenty of notice indeed of his pretty foster sister, as he called Myrtilla; but it was after the fashion of a grown man encouraging a growing girl. He commended her stature and her strength; he called her his *belle batelière*—a word, happily, she could not construe—when she took an oar with Harry across the lake. He turned over the books upon her little stand; they consisted of a thumbed breviary, a small print copy of the "Irish Melodies," a volume of saintly lives, a still smaller print copy of Irish songs in Gaelic, and an extremely old volume, with the date of 1619, printed in English and Irish, containing a singular essay upon the miracles wrought somewhere in the sacred isle, by the relics of St. Francis Xavier. Evidently the true Church had had the selection of Myrtilla's library, and Mrs. Burke, considering how she was situated, did wisely in putting her Protestantism in her pocket.

With a smile, Lorraine put aside one volume after another, and patted the girl on the shoulder, and said, "he was not much of a reader himself; but if she liked

the amusement, there was better than this to be had;
and that when he went to Dublin—which he must do
one of these days—then he would bring her back a lot
of new reading,—she might make sure of that."

It was all "saft an' aisy tigither," as Barney the
ostler might have said. "Saft an' aisy "—for every one
but Myrtilla, who went on steadily sowing the wind;—
the season for the reaping of the whirlwind had not yet
arrived.

So matters advanced, Lorraine finding nothing
that he could not very well endure in his life at
Loughmore.

Some duties he had to perform, some calls to attend
to, some slight acquaintanceships to keep up. But the
claims upon him were very impersonal; it was other
people's interests, and other people's lives that he had
to be troubled about; and as long as he was not
dragged with personal complications or implications
into such affairs, he was as little impatient of them as
his neighbours.

The winter was wearing away apace; but here,
where no frost is felt, and no snow lies lower than the
mountain-tops, it is not worth while, according to
northern notions, to speak of the season as—winter!
Sometimes it is a pure summer's day—and sometimes
an Atlantic hurricane. Lorraine takes both in friendly
part. He takes the whole life at Loughmore in friendly

part!—it is indeed the life of all others, just now,
most congenial to his feelings—most able to wean
him from the heart regrets, the jarring crisises which,
after a calm of five and twenty years, he had had suddenly to face, one after another:—and, as he always
said, none of his own seeking!—he stuck to that.

He is not a person to fight against the impossible,
or to refuse, after the first shock, to accept the irrevoc-
able. He chafes away at small things; but he is not
the one to break up his life for great ones;—and he
has not broken up his life. Still, whilst there is the
shadow of an association to carry him back, these cruel
memories—all these memories, so cruel, so tender, so
irritating, will come up, and come up! It is only
under the sky of his far-distant Loughmore that they
begin really to dissipate—not into thin air, but into
Time's softening distances.

It is true that he may be wrecked again in the
society that he has to mix with. There is no safe
guarantee for him as he enters his neighbour's draw-
ing-room against his encountering his fate again under
some pale, queenly brow, or some pair of bewitching,
velvety eyes. But Fate is merciful.

As he remarked to himself after his first small
round of visits—

"The young and the single seem improved away
out of these people. What a blessing it would be if
all the world could be married and middle-aged!
They'd be rather dull, but they'd lead up to nothing."

It was all very safe and true, as far as the visits were concerned. But there was always Myrtilla to represent youth and possibilities at the Lough Beg Lodge.

But these possibilities were as far from Lorraine's mind as the poles; further, in fact, since they had no place at all in it.

What he had in his mind was a genuine desire to please the young girl, and a very cordial sympathy with her matrimonial prospects. Harry he took to be a capital fellow; and he was only sorry that the pair were not to settle down and marry on the estate. He was full of kind deeds to both of them, especially to Myrtilla; and as the months wore on, the little book-shelf in the corner became gaudy with brand-new covers, from Dublin book-shops. And when a forced visit to London about regimental affairs took him over the Channel, the result of it to Myrtilla, was a chain of gold for the wedding-day.

The girl took it all, and said nothing. But she began to say less than nothing to Harry English.

"Mother," said that youth to Mrs. Burke—it was the word he had begun long to call her by—"Mother, what's the matter with Myrtilla? She won't speak to me and she won't look at me. She passes by me as if I was the leg of the table."

Mrs. Burke, when the night was quiet, and the others were in bed, took Myrtilla to her knees again.

"Sit down here, my child," said she, "and tell me what's amiss."

But Myrtilla, as yet, was only sowing the wind.

"Why d'ye ask, mither?" says she. "And what's Harry English after throublin' ye about?"

So Myrtilla put off the whirlwind.

It was now full spring again! How green and fresh, and what sweet odours everywhere! And what nosegays of violets and sweet asphodels, and bright May gowans, filled with their dainty spring perfumes the Lough Beg Lodge!

Lorraine had been visiting first one and then another of his middle-aged married friends,—paying visits of some length. He had presided at some spring races; the sport was good; he enjoyed it excessively. In fact, Lough Beg Lodge had seen very little of him of late.

But one day he went down there betimes. The wind was westerly and a little gusty, but delicious in its soft motion,—it stirred his hair as he walked along, and gave him that sensation of quiet exultation which such a day in spring,—where spring is really spring,— has the power of exciting.

At the door stood Harry English, leaning against the post, with the door itself half closed, as usual.

The young man's accustomed brightness was so shaded that even Lorraine, not prone to observe, stopped and made a remark upon it.

"Why, Harry," he said, "what's this?"

Harry does not pretend to deny that he understands what the "this" was.

"I am thinking," says he, "of returning to England."

"We must prepare for the wedding, then," rejoins
Lorraine, briskly.

Harry gives him a singular look—lost, however,
upon Lorraine, and then turns away with a very
audible sigh.

But Lorraine calls after him. "Stop, Harry!" he
cries. "I came down to have a sail. There's just the
wind for it. If you'll get out the pinnace, I'll be
down directly; and Myrtilla shall steer for us. I feel
too lazy to-day to do anything much;"—and so
Lorraine goes into the lodge.

Mr. Burke is asleep;—it is a weakness which often
overcomes him now. Mrs. Burke is in the inner room,
attending to her household affairs. Myrtilla is standing in the middle of the floor, with an attitude of
arrested attention. She had been listening, perhaps, for
Harry's explanation in reply to the question, "What's
this?" which a moment ago she had heard put to him.

As Lorraine entered, she sprang forward, going out
by the door. In a moment, she is in again, holding in
her hand a myrtle spray, with the tender green buds
opening down the stem. She offers it to him.

"He wanted to pick it," says she, pointing in the
direction of Harry.

As they round the jutting point of it, the wind, without a note of warning, rises with a great swirl.

Lorraine's eyes are half closed to the scene;—it is possible that the silent lull of this watery motion has sent him into one of his old siestas. But he rouses to the freshening of the wind, and then he speaks.

"Put up the sail, Harry; we shall get along a little now." Still, he scarce opens his eyes.

Harry shakes his head more ominously than ever.

Myrtilla's eye is upon him.—With a look of killing scorn, she throws round the rudder, and, with her arms "so white and so strong," raises the mast as if it had been a reed, drops it in its rest, and begins to haul up the sail.

"Stop, Myrtilla!" cries Lorraine. "What are you about? Where's Harry?"

The pinnace was small, and the full figure of Myrtilla hid from Lorraine's awakening eyes the recalcitrant body of Harry in the background.

But it so chanced or it was so predetermined that no opportunity was given for a deliberate reply to Lorraine's startled inquiry. In fact, before shock number one was over,—shock number two set in. The rudder was loose, and the sail was loose, and the wind, equally unstable, took another sudden shift with a double violence, and sent the little craft over by the beam,— sending also these two unprepared ones, Lorraine and Myrtilla, over with it.

Harry, his eyes calmly about him, has time to seize

III.   ✛

the rudder, and wrenches it round with the vice of a giant. He knows what he is about full well. Nor does he rely upon the powers of the pinnace in vain. The obedient creature, like a thing of life, answers to the appeal; and on the very verge of its catastrophe, rights itself for all safety.

But safety is not the word at this moment for these two in the water. All that Harry can do for them is to steady the pinnace. For one desperate moment he loses sight of both; but with the next they come up again. Myrtilla's head scarcely clears the keel of the pinnace. Aghast at the peril, Harry flings himself half out of the boat, and, seizing her as best he can, drags her up to him;—but with a shriek, she breaks from him.

"Where is he?" she cries, and, throwing up her arms, plunges back into the water.

Lorraine by this time has got into a serviceable condition.

The best of his Eton accomplishments was his swimming, and he had never lost it.

It was with no faint confidence in his powers, that in days gone by he proposed that swim for rescue, to Lady Laure.

A yard or two ahead of him he perceives Myrtilla borne up by her full skirts, yet near to sinking. It is the work of a moment to put one arm round her, and to strike out with the other.

Myrtilla—petticoats and all—is no slight weight to

bear along in this swelling water. And she is restive. Possibly she has an idea that his life is risked to save hers.

But in this matter at least, Lorraine soon brings her to order. There is no mistaking the sternness of his command.

"Be still, Myrtilla, or you'll have the pleasure of dying—not for me, but with me!"

Probably other people would have worded it differently. But this was Lorraine's way of speaking for Life and Death.

It all came to a good ending as far as lives were concerned; a shallow estuary was close at hand, and it took no very long effort for Lorraine to put himself and Myrtilla barely knee-deep in water,—and after that they waded to land singly.

Harry, with a beating heart and strong oar-strokes, followed them with the pinnace; and pushing in, takes them on board it again.

Then he makes an attempt to turn the sail to the safer use of wrapping it round the dripping Myrtilla.

The water seems to have had the unusual effect of rekindling her flames. She pushes away the forgiving hand, and applies herself to Lorraine's drenching coat-tails.

"Let it alone, Myrtilla," says he, laughing. "We must be wrung out—entirely, as you say here, before we're dry again. No doubt, we present a pretty picture; but there's only Harry here to laugh at us; and we're better off anyhow than if we were playing the parts of merman and mermaid at the bottom of the lake."

Harry's face has not the shadow of a laugh upon it. He sees nothing even hopeful in the situation ; but he devotes himself with all his nautical skill to prevent further mischance.

The wind was still skittish, but their upsettings were over for the day.

In spite of Myrtilla's unceremonious objurgations, Harry proved himself to know a good deal about the practical navigation of Lough Beg.

Now and then he looked askance at the wet skins of his freight, but it couldn't be helped. Slow and sure must be the order now, and so, with the oars only, and skirting far round under the lee of the banks, Harry lands them at last pretty well dry—to the eye, at least—at the stage behind the lodge.

CHAPTER V.

DEEDS, NOT WORDS.

Oh, soft, brown eyes!   Oh, glances turned away!
Oh, burning sighs, and tears so often shed,—
Dark nights in vain awaited,—vainly fled!
And oh, the vain returns of shining day!

Oh, sad complaint!   Oh, longings nought can stay!
Oh, useless toils!   Oh, time all vainly sped!
Oh, thousand deaths, in thousand nets outspread!
Oh, still worse woes, for me, their destined prey!

Oh, hand, arm, fingers,—laughter, forehead, hair!
Oh, voice and plaintive lute and viol rare!
So many flames one woman's heart to burn!

I blame you of so many fires possest,—
Which from so many sources scorch my breast,
That not one spark upon yourself you turn.
From the French of Louise Labé.

Let us suppose Lorraine departed, and the inmates of the lodge settling down for the evening, after the agitation of this eventful day.

Myrtilla is crouched between her father and the hearth,—with dry garments, and a smoking glass of the national beverage in her hand.

"Let it be Phadrick Lanaghan's potheen, mither," directs Mr. Burke, addressing his wife, when she pre-

pares to make the brew. "Ye'll find it 'aneath the bed,
whar he pit it this marnin'. It's no sic murdher as Tim
Phelim's pisin,—it's jist as saft as silk, an' as yellow
as crem,—mak' it het an' strang an' swate, fur the
jewel," says he, touching the glowing cheek lovingly.

Then the old man subsides again into the tears
that had been flowing more or less ever since he got
knowledge of the matter.

"Me darlint," sobs he; "an' ye had niver kim
up agin,—what wud the pore father hev bin afther
doin' widout ye?"

Harry sits at the side of Mrs. Burke; his cheek
is not glowing,—for him it is almost pale; and the
young man has a look of quite unusual care and
thought.

"Now it's your turn, Harry," says Mrs. Burke,
holding up the remainder of the potheen she has
drawn out of the keg.

But Harry shakes his head. He declines the
private whisky. He is in no mood for its inspiring
charms.

Mr. Burke makes a sign to his wife to pass the
horn over to him. As he sips and sips, he drops the
lachrymose for the cogitative.

"I'll niver know the rights o' it," says he, with his
eyes on the silken cream. "The wind was no sae vera
high this day!"

"It was poor Myrtilla's fault," says Harry, all
innocently speaking the truth.

"An' it was pore Myrtilla's fault!" cries the girl, firing up again. "An' it wasn't the pore Harry's fault that we werena drowned entirely, the twa iv us!—was it? And the blessed masther in the water, and Harry English setting as dry as a duck in the boat all the time,—the pore pittiogue!"

"Pore pittiogue!" That is an untranslateable expression. It is neither cursing nor swearing,—Myrtilla was not given to these accomplishments; and when she pleased, she could speak fair English; but when she raged or rejoiced, she was apt to relapse into her mother tongue.

Pittiogue!—Well, the nearest approach to it may be taken to be "pitiful fellow;" but that is not it either,—it combines every possible contemptible quality, that is not exactly vicious.

Harry had not taken many lessons in Irish,—he saw no need for it. He meant that his Myrtilla should speak English with him, when they were man and wife. Still, the scorn in the voice and eye gave him a pretty clear interpretation of the meaning of this word which was applied to himself, and had just then fallen from the lips of his betrothed.

He made no reply,—though upon this word turned the whole fate and future of every soul present.

Half an hour afterwards, Harry English got up and left the lodge.

"Myrtilla," cries Mrs. Burke, "why did you call our Harry a pittiogue? And didn't Sir Claude say that he behaved like a man through it all?"

Then Myrtilla got up, and, kneeling down by her mother, she hid her face in her knees, and sobbed as if her heart would break.

"Mither, mither," she murmurs, "I'll niver marry Harry English; I'll niver marry him!"

Myrtilla was a good girl, in spite of all. She was full of duty to her mother, and of tender devotion to her father, making his age and his weakness as light a trial to him as she could.

She never wandered from home or spent the day lazily. It was she who kept things bright and spruce within the lodge; and who was up the first, and to bed the last; she was less friendly than she might have been with the lads and lasses about; she held her head a little high;—it was laid down to English pride, bred in her by her mother.

It was one reason—the only one, perhaps—that Harry English started with no rivals in the field.

Mrs. Burke went to her slumbers this night sorely perplexed as to what course to pursue. She loved Myrtilla too well to make her unhappy; but yet, to see at one stroke all her prospering plans vanish and pass out of reach,—distressed her bitterly.

Harry, too, poor fellow, after all this time, what should she do with him?

"There never was a truer love than Harry's for Myrtilla!" cries she. And so she leaves it.

Lorraine had taken greatly to Harry English. This honest manliness, and these simple yet not boorish manners were entirely congenial to him. Allowing for the difference of rank, and some other differences, Harry was a reflex of himself. If you had seen them walking along together,—as far as the physique went, and at a passing glance, you would not have found much to choose between them. Upon closer intimacy, indeed, you would have discovered in Lorraine a grace —a nameless yet most expressive grace, which the other lacked, but still, the common verdict would have been that they were a couple of very fine young men.

As a consequence of this kind of *rapport*, Harry's appointment to the post of chief mate of the *Myrtilla* did not stop there. He was as much at the Castle as at the lodge,—always the one applied to in any small need of the master; in fact, he became a sort of henchman. If Lorraine had gone in for valets, no doubt he would have been the valet,—but this anomalous appendage was quite outside his notions of personal comfort.

Lorraine was out betimes on the morning after the lake disaster, and none the worse for the " triflin' wettin'," which, as it had had no ill consequences, was treated something as a joke by his faithful followers below stairs.

Outside the Castle, he came across Harry English,—still pale, with his hair somewhat unbrushed, his erect air gone, and a disordered look ; in fact, he had not even made an attempt to sleep all this night,—and Harry's first experience of not sleeping had a very serious effect upon his outer man.

"I have been waiting to speak to you, sir," says Harry.

"All right, Harry," returns Lorraine. "But how done up you look! And yet you didn't get into the water as we did yesterday ! "

"No, Sir Claude ; and therefore I am a pittiogue."

"A what?" says Lorraine, staring at him full in the face.

"A pittiogue," replies Harry. "And that is the reason that I shall be glad to speak to you."

"Of course, Harry ; but certainly you've taken leave of your senses."

As Lorraine said this, he looked more closely into the young man's face.

Now, Lorraine's readiest solution to anything peculiar in his fellow-creatures was mental craze. As long as people kept their senses, he could not conceive their conducting themselves in an out-of-the-way manner ; and looking at this moment closely into Harry's face, and listening to the strange jargon he has got in his head, Lorraine thinks to himself, "Here's another of them going mad ! There's no safety for any one ! "

"Well," says he aloud, awaiting what more of Harry's eccentricities were to come out.

"I am going home," says Harry.

"Ah!" replies Lorraine, "I wonder how Myrtilla is this morning. I was just going to see about her; but, as you're going down, you can do it as well."

"My home is not there," returns Harry, with a stolid air. "My home is in England, and I am going there."

"Well then," rejoins Lorraine, still obtuse, yet truly not wilfully so—it is his nature never to be digging for motives—"Well then," cries he, briskly, "we must look sharp about the marriage, as I said the other day. But I shall be sorry to lose you, Harry—to lose you both. Can't you think better of it, and settle down at Loughmore? I'll make it worth your while, Harry."

There is persuasion in every syllable of Lorraine's words.

Harry's face wears a smile of a very unusual kind. "Neither here nor there, Sir Claude. I am going to England alone; and never, please God, to return here, at any rate."

Harry fires up with his last utterance.

"Harry!" exclaims Lorraine, stopping still in the path.

They had been walking leisurely forward till now.

Harry draws himself up to his full height. When he stands as he does now, he tops Lorraine by an inch.

" Sir Claude," says he, " I'm nothing but a Kentish herdsman. I am quite well aware, sir, what I am." Harry gives something of a gulp. "And I can only speak in plain words, Sir Claude; and so here's the truth—Myrtilla is not in love with me; and she is in love with you."

" Harry !" cries Lorraine for the second time, and with a good deal more vehemence.

" You look as if you didn't know it, sir; and I've no reason to doubt that you're a true gentleman. But it's plain enough to my eyes, and I should have thought to yours."

Lorraine grasps the Kentish herdsman's hand.

" Harry, I swear to you—— "

" Don't swear about it, sir," says Harry, sadly.

But Lorraine takes no heed to that.

" I swear to you," he cries, " that neither by word nor deed have I injured you with Myrtilla! Neither by word nor deed," he repeats.

" You can't help your looks, sir," says Harry, still more sadly this time.

" My looks !" returns Lorraine. " What folly all this is ! Lift up your head, my dear fellow. Your looks are a match for mine any day."

Harry shakes his head. It is a way he has—a way with many people who are poor in words.

" Listen to me," says Lorraine. " The thing can be put into a nutshell. Here's Myrtilla. She is an Irish girl. You've not been here long enough to know the race. It's as proud as Lucifer. Well, you two quarrel. She won't give in. Her temper is tremendous; her tongue, no doubt, the same. She gives vent to a hundred things,—merely the outburst of her passion, and, I suppose, calls you by that name—whatever it was;" and he stops.

"A pittiogue," says Harry.

"Ha! Well, pittiogue. Have you an idea of its meaning?" asks Lorraine.

"No, sir," says Harry, briefly.

"Well," returns Lorraine, cheerfully, "for aught you or I know, it may be a very complimentary term."

"It don't sound like it," says Harry, gloomily.

Harry was right. It didn't sound like it. In these ancient forms of speech, savage or classic, sound and sense are wonderfully together.

"Now, Harry," begins Lorraine, taking up again the consolatory strain, "leave the matter in my hands. I'll speak to Myrtilla myself; and I suppose if she's willing, you won't hold back from the bargain."

Harry shakes his head again. As he felt yesterday, so he does now; he sees nothing hopeful in the situation.

But Lorraine walks away from him in the full confidence of his persuasive powers and his diplomatic skill in the matter of bringing two true lovers together again.

But first, for a moment he goes back into the Castle. He has just the very convenient sum of money

in hand to-day upon which he much reckons as a
supplementary argument with the fair Myrtilla. As he
remarked to himself, "None of these people are indifferent to money."

Thus armed, and armed also with the most honest
good intentions, Lorraine takes the road to the lodge.
But he has not walked half a mile before he meets
Myrtilla herself.

There is nothing downcast here. She comes joy-
ously forward to meet him ; her face is radiant with its
fresh beauty, and as she steps along, it is with the
spring of an unclouded spirit.

Lorraine is a bad hand at opening a subject. He
takes the girl's hand and turns her back with him.
Then he lets it go,—and, looking at her, says with a
laugh—

" Well, my little mermaid, are you ready for some
more fishing to-day ? "

Myrtilla is quite ready. She springs on before him.

Lorraine calls her back.

" I'm afther findin' Harry English for the boat,
yer honour," cries Myrtilla, scarcely slackening her
speed.

" Stop," says Lorraine, again. " You'll not find him
that way."

Myrtilla does stop, and looks straight at Lorraine.
Her eyes are full of last night's wrath again.

" The pittiogue ! " she cries. " And what's he out
o' the way now for ? "

"Who are you calling by this name?" says Lorraine. "What do you mean by it?"

And he takes his stern look, which makes her flinch.

"Oh, an' wud I be afther usin' iv it to yer honour, whan I wud die for ye, if it plased the Lord to let me!"

"Nonsense!" says Lorraine. "Don't let us have that again! It brought you no good yesterday, did it?"

He has an idea that he might appeal to the superstitious side of her nature.

"No good!" cries Myrtilla. "And was no that the swatest day to me of all my life before and afther?"

There have not been so many days since; but Myrtilla must be pardoned for this national imagery.

"Let it all alone now, and listen to what I have got to say."

Then Lorraine takes out a small pocket-book.

"Look here, Myrtilla," he says; "here's a hundred pounds. I give it to you for your own. It will furnish up your rooms nearly when you get to England, and the best thing to be done now is, that you and Harry should make a match of it at once."

He hands her the pocket-book, and she takes it—without hesitation, and with complete deliberation, holding it in her hands. She fixes her eyes on the ground, and so stands, perhaps for a minute or two. To Lorraine naturally it appeared many minutes.

"Well, Myrtilla," he says at last.

Not even then did she lift her head and eyes——
when she does, wrath and joy are both gone. She
is a shade paler, perhaps; her eyes are cold and
clear. Something seems to quiver round her mouth,
—but yet she speaks with wonderful composure and
self-control.

" You wish it ? " she says.

" I wish it," replies Lorraine, "and with all my
heart, Myrtilla ! "

She stands with her eyes chained to his face.

" With all my heart," repeats Lorraine.

" With all yer heart," echoes Myrtilla.

And then she turns back the way she had been
coming. But again she comes to a stop, and he, still
standing looking after her, calls her by her name.

Obedient to his voice, she looks round,—and, with
the natural action of untutored passion, she raises one
of her white arms to heaven.

"And when I'm gone," she cries, " if I niver see ye
agin, Sir Claude—if I niver see ye agin—the Lord
above be wid us both."

And then she turns and goes.

Lorraine turns too. He walks with slow steps and
a thoughtful face, revolving in his mind Myrtilla and
her fortunes.

Lorraine is given to summing things up in his
mind. He is rarely without a decided conclusion.
This was what he said now to himself—

" Harry may be right. The girl is full of all sorts of

wild passion,—that's clear; and she'd as soon slay you as love you, I suspect. But she has taken the money, and that clenches the affair, as I expected it would!"

And then he quickens his pace; but again he relaxes it; he even looks back, as if he might expect to see the subject of his thoughts coming running towards him. He can at this moment recall her perfectly to his mind; her glowing cheeks, her eyes in their grey splendour. He can see the half-haughty, half-tender quiver of her perfect features; and he sees the very swing and spring with which she bears her bold, supple figure on to meet him.

His gaze is still fixed upon the vacant distance. "There is something grand about that girl," says he, half aloud; "and if she's got a temper, Harry will anyhow have the handsomest wife in Kent. I'd lay a wager to it!"

Lorraine was at fault if he expected Myrtilla to fill again that vacant distance. Not even once did she slacken or stop till she reached the door of the lodge. It stood, as always, half ajar. Here she laid one hand upon her breast,—as if to gather up her spent breath. And yet she was not breathless. It might have been to gather up her strength for her resolve. She goes at last in quickly; and Mr. Burke, who is dozing as usual, awakes with a start.

"Poor father!" says the girl. "Did I wake you?"

"And isn't it a glad wakenin' from ye, me darlint?"

says the old man. "Ye let me sleep too much all day."

"It's gud to sleep, father," says Myrtilla; "then we are no thinkin'."

"No thinkin', jewel! Ye don't be afther thinkin' too much wid yer bonny face. It's alane for ane euld sick crater as yer father to be afther thinkin'," says the old man, sadly.

"Yes, father, yer right," is the answer, and then she comes tenderly up to him, turning the subject. "Ye have no had yer parritch broth this mornin', father."

"The mither is gane to the town," says he, "and ye have been takin' the air, and it's jist what ye shuld do, acushla."

"It's jist what I should no do when yer wantin' the parritch."

And then Myrtilla sets to work to stir in the meal, and boil the mess.

"It is gud, father. But wait," she cries, "where's the bit o' butter?"

. The bit of butter is added, and the old man at last well engaged with his breakfast.

Myrtilla slips away, and in less than a quarter of an hour she is back again. She has changed her dress. This one has a plain black stuff skirt, full and pleated; and a dark jacket that covers up her white arms; and upon her head is a little scarlet hood, which is almost too simple a *coiffure* to become her proud face.

Moreover, she has a little bundle in her hand, and, as she passes the book-case, she stops to look, and taking one of the brightest-covered volumes out of it, she slips it into the bundle. Then she goes up to the old man's side; she pushes his grey hair apart, and kisses his wrinkled brow.

"The mither 'ill soon be back now," says she; "but you'll hae the time to tak' another nap, father; and ye'll tell the mither, when she'll be comin' hame, that Myrtilla is gane aff to see Honor Magrath and her famelee; for it's to-morrow that they'll all be down to Cork for Americay."

"And ye'll be back this night?" says the old man, still supping his porridge.

"No, father, I'll no be back this night. 'Tis lang way there and back; 'tis a lang—lang way," says Myrtilla, saying the words with a slow and low utterance.

"Give me your blessin', my father," says she, and she kneels down at his side and takes the porridge basin from him.

"And won't I bless thee, me darlint?" cries the old man. "I'd be blessin' ye day an' night if I had me own gait. But it's no much worth, the blessin' iv an ould sinner like yer pore father. It's the Man above that must bless ye, an' may the blessin' of this same Man rest upon ye, an' may the marciful Queen o' heaven look down on ye, me heart's darlint!"

The old man has exhausted himself with his unwonted energy. He leans back, and closes his eyes, his trembling hand still upon his daughter's head.

"Take the parritch now, father;" and Myrtilla rises from her knees, and gives him back the bowl.

But the old man gently puts it back. "Not awhile, darlint. I'll jist sleep a bit agin, I'm thinkin'."

"And the mither 'ill soon be back, father."

And with this last word, Myrtilla goes away with her bundle. She does not stop on the threshold, nor falter, nor weep. She goes away calmly and quickly.

Mrs. Burke was soon back, as Myrtilla had said, and her husband rouses up again as she comes in at the door.

"And where is Harry?" asks she; "and Myrtilla, father,—where is she?"

Mr. Burke has a puzzled air. "I was to tell ye summat," says he.

"Has Sir Claude been down, then?"

"Nae, nae; 'twas from the darlint. Ah! now, it's to me mind. She's gane over to Honor Magrath; they'll be off to Cork to-morrow fur Americay."

"It's a long way," says Mrs. Burke; "and she'll never be back to-night."

Nor to-morrow.

It was about the sunsetting on the day after this one that Mrs. Burke, standing in the doorway watching for Myrtilla's return, sees Barney of the Loughmore Arms limping in through the gate.

He has anything but a cheerful countenance.

It may have been later troubles, and it may have been that injury to his feelings, done by the audacious Tim Phelim on a well-remembered occasion.

As he comes up to Mrs. Burke, he hands her a letter.

"It's an hour and mair that I hae 'ud been here, bit fur this limb o' mine," says he; "bit it ud a' bin all the same. They'se aff all tigither this lang gane."

The speech is dark to Mrs. Burke; but the letter throws light upon it.

It is from Myrtilla; it begins—

"DEAR MOTHER,"

(There had been "dear father" after the "dear mother," but the "dear father" is crossed out.)

"You'll be afther wonderin' no to see me hame, but I've somethin' to tell ye, and this letter will spake to ye fur me. As I tould ye, it's no marryin' Harry English that I can; and it's no staying at the Lodge fur me anny more, and sae I've jist gone wid Honor to Americay. Ye have no need to goan into anny perticklars to the pore father; he's no so sharp as he wer', and ye can jist pit him aff wi' ane o' yer tales. Tak' care o' yersel', mither; I'll be afther seein' ye agin ane o' these days; but the father, niver again. An' doan go to frit aboot me, fur I'm jist goan off to see what's goin' on, away fram the Lodge.

"Yer lovin' daughter,
"MYRTILLA BURKE."

Nothing could be more prosaic.

Except the one touch about the father, there is not one regret.

If Myrtilla had her feelings, she hid them, and did not work upon the feelings of other people.

CHAPTER VI.

THE SEA! THE SEA!

Lovers twain on a summer's day;
And this the burden of what they say,—
All for love! come what, come may.

Parting in tears on a summer's day,
Breaking their hearts in the regular way,
With a—Never forget! come what, come may.

East and West on a summer's day,—
Some to work and some to play,
With a—Fate to follow! come what, come may.

Times are hard on a summer's day,
Knocking about and the devil to pay,
With a—Fight for your hand! come what, come may.

Smiles suit best on a summer's day;
Life goes well, if hearts are gay,
With a—Never say die! come what, come may.

Lovers twain on a summer's day;
And this the burden of what they say,—
Better late than never! come what, come may.

IT would take more time that can be spared to write
the history of the next few days, both at the Castle and
the Lodge.

Much that is sad and piteous might be set down,

—the father's misty misery, Harry's crushed heart, Lorraine's unpleasant enlightenment.

As for Burke, his eyes soon closed altogether on the scene. No one told him his child was gone,—he was put off, as she had said, with one tale after another. But he was restless,—he missed her,—and when she did not return, he cried out in the confusion of his distress, that they had drowned her! And so he died. The loss did not kill him, but it helped Death's hand, which was already upon him.

As for Mrs. Burke, this blow takes all the pride out of her life. Even the charm of "Master Claude" is gone. She says, she will go back and live amongst her own people.

"I shall feel it less, Sir Claude," sighs she, "if I am with them." There is no violence in her grief; she has always been a quiet woman, both in her good fortune and her bad. When her first trouble fell upon her, her tears fell fast,—but she had hope; now she sheds few tears,—and has no hope.

"But Myrtilla will return to you, nurse," cries Lorraine.

"I think not," says she.

But it is for young Harry, perhaps, that Lorraine feels the most sympathy.

"Come, Harry, cheer up," says he. "There's always a home here, and if you'll throw in your chance with mine, where I am, there'll always be room for you."

But Harry is silent.

"You'll wish to take nurse over, no doubt," says Lorraine again.

Harry is still silent.

"Tell me what is your mind," says Lorraine, with patient persuasion.

Then Harry finds his voice.

"You are very good, Sir Claude," says he, "and I feel it very much, and I should be glad to serve you"—here the poor fellow begins to break down—"I should be very glad to serve you"—his voice is husky with his smothered anguish, as he stammers out—"but I didn't know my heart till she was gone. I can't live without her, and I must go after her,—and if I never find her, I'll go on looking for her till I die."

They are all gone: Burke, and nurse, and Harry, and Myrtilla. The door of the Lough Beg Lodge no longer stands ajar,—it is tightly closed, its windows are dull and dusty; there are no bright faces, no bright fire flashes behind them; the winds have torn the myrtle down, and there is no hand to nail it up,—it is all gone into a wilderness again.

Once more only, does the master of Loughmore ride through that way. He stops to look and to think; then, as he passes on——

"Bar up those gates,"—he says.

Yes—bar up those gates;—it is a spot, not for the

traffic of strange feet ;—a sacred spot, for here too, his
life has seen some happy hours—begin and end.

Whatever was Lorraine's share in turning the sunny
lodge of Lough Beg back again into a silent wilderness, nobody laid any blame to his charge,—neither
Harry, nor another,—nor himself. As he had sworn to
Harry, neither by word nor deed, had he sinned in this
matter. Had he so sinned, it would have been a much
simpler problem for him to solve.

For a month he took to silence—took to sitting
with his eyes cast down, fixed upon the smouldering
peat, like Uncle Loftus. No catastrophe of his life—
or rather, no catastrophe of the last two years—had
taken a stronger hold upon his mind, than this, the
latest.

The solution of the problem which at last he
arrived at, was not calculated to lighten the weight
upon his spirits.——

"There's nothing new in it now ; " so he thinks to
himself. "It's not the first, nor the second time only ;
and I'm neither a vain fool nor a blind idiot, nor I think
vicious ; but it's a fact, that, in regard to women, there's
something baneful that goes to and fro between them
and me,—something which is continually breaking up
my life,—and doing them no end of mischief."

This was Lorraine's solution to his problem, and not a satisfactory one.

But he rouses himself at last ;—there is very little of Uncle Loftus in Claude Lorraine,—and he spends the next month after a different fashion. He goes again amongst the married and middle-aged ones. But this does not answer as it had done before. The dulness is oppressive, and their society gives him no distraction from the effects of this new mental jar,—it is, in fact, quite the reverse. He becomes nervous; he thinks of Harry's artless words——

"You can't help your looks, sir;" and he grows afraid to look even the middle-aged ones in the face! — It was neither pretence nor affectation — it was physical. Perhaps—the result of sitting indoors for that month, after the breezy life abroad under the sky, which went before it.

The wise man says, "Consider the end, and you will never do amiss." Lorraine had no particular wisdom above his fellows; he had the practical sense which kept him from extremes, and which taught him also to take care of himself where it was possible. He could perceive, too, the advantage of considering the end ; his difficulty was, that he could not for the life of him discover—what sort of an end, humanly speaking, he had got to consider.

He must live,—and he has no one to live for, still he must do something with his life—but to be bandied about as he has been, tumbling from one shock on to another—no sooner out of one pitfall, than into the next—and all with no seeking of his own—this is a condition of existence that he will go to the poles, or to the middle of the earth, or to any other neck-or-nothing distance, to avoid.

"What's the matter with things?" cries he. "I wonder if it's the same with every one else?"

But no man thoroughly puts his mind to a matter without turning something or other out; and Lorraine, thoroughly in earnest, at last found a saving idea,— more than mere saving. He hailed it as a drowning man does the rope thrown to him in his last extremity; he seized upon it with unfaltering confidence.

"It will be my salvation!" he cried.

This redeeming idea—occurred to him after a hard day's ride through an autumn drizzle, as he stood, pretty well soaked to the skin, wind-blown, and with the salt spray dashing hundreds of feet up to his eyes, upon the sheer edge of an Atlantic precipice. Before him stretched the great ocean; and at his side gaped a huge sea chasm, where day and night, with deafening roar, the mad breakers beat against the barbed rocks that pierced its black depths;—and round and round deep down in the awful gulf, circled the chough and the sea-mew, glancing like snow-flakes in the darkness.

It was a stormy standpoint for a resolve, but Lorraine's was taken then and there.

The bluster of winds and waves had never come

amiss to him, and he laughed aloud now with the excitement of the wild scene;—it filled him with a new life.

"Water," laughs he, "water everywhere;—it's the best thing I've come in for—for many a day." One minute more and the resolve comes.

"The sea for me! I'll take to it altogether. There at least," he cries, "I shall be safe, and I need not fear my looks!"

The winds did not hear his vow, for the uproar in the chasm drowned all lesser sounds; but it was registered all the same,—and it was kept.

In another month he was launched. His "trim-built wherry" was not just such a floating palace as the world steams round the world in nowadays, but it was tidy and taut, with plenty of beam, a safe concern, in fact, in all ways. He called it the *Timon;* he thought the name well chosen. When he came to take his crew, he looked back to Harry English with a keen regret.

"If it had not been for all that," thinks he, "what a time of it afloat, we should have had together!"

Thus once more Lorraine goes forth a world-wanderer!—and once more, his Fatality sends forth from an exploding elysium, two other wandering souls, upriven from their safe joys!—And by one of those coincidences which Chance seems to take a reckless pleasure in adjusting, they are all three launched bodily, yet singly, upon the same stormy ocean.

Castle Loughmore and the Lough Beg Lodge stand now alike. Gone back to silence!

The spirit of Sir Loftus may return in peace to brood over both. Mayhap it has never departed;—unseen, yet not unfelt, it may have lingered, to infect his heir with its own morbid estrangements.

P.S.—We must take leave of our hero for the present; but let no one be alarmed about him,—he is always Prince Fortune,—not born to be drowned.

CHAPTER VII.

UNDER THE PORTICOES.

Sarà l'Italia—edifica
Sulla vagante arena
Chi tenta opporsi—misero!
Sui sogni lor la piena
Dio verserà del Popolo:
Curvate il capo, o genti,
La speme dei redenti,
La nuova Roma appar:
Non deporrem la spada
Finchè sia schiavo un angolo
Dell' Itala contrada;
Finchè non sia l'Italia
Una dall' Alpi al Mar!

GOFFREDO MAMELI,
fell defending Rome, 1849.

IT is much more than time, if we would not have her drop altogether out of mind, to seek again the gentle company of our Lady Laure.

We have been following too exclusively the steps, and the example, of her recreant knight. She is all but effaced from our pages,—but not from our memory! —It may be a question, if even from the memory of that recreant knight—she has ever been truly effaced.

We know, when brought to the point, with how

III.

much spirit he could speak up for her "courage and constancy."

In *her own way*, Lady Laure made her mark,—and that mark was borne in more than one human heart—borne through life to death.

But in regard to that other, who left her so easily; who lived out of her sweet presence with such apparent satisfaction. What can you say? Can you do more than repeat that which the prophet said long ago?—

" Can the Ethiopian change his skin, or the leopard his spots?"

There is the fatalism which underlies everything in it!—And yet what profounder truth exists? Exists for those who cannot forget, and for those who cannot remember; for those who cannot be comforted, and for those who cannot mourn. Exists under a thick veil, or a thin one, in ourselves;—and in everybody else.

To find Lady Laure, we must turn again toward the land of Lorraine's enchantments; and to the skies of poor Lucie's new paradise. It was she, who, for all of them, made the first discovery of this enchanting Eden,—she loved it from the first, and she loves it to the last.

And the safe retreat which shelters her sorrows is none the less soothing to her,—that it is beneath those skies which beheld her in all the forlornness of her desertion and bereavement;——which look down on the land that saw her happiest and saddest.

To find Lady Laure, we cannot go direct as the crow flies, nor take our flight with the far-wandering swallow,—though, considering that we travel on the wings of thought, it might be allowable to us to do so. But it would not be convenient, for we have some notes to make by the way; and we are in the happy position to choose. Therefore we make our first stage only as far as the gates of a little city that once was called "Il giojello d'Italia."

A little city which in times past, from the traveller's point of view, was better appreciated than it is now,—now that there is the demand for all in everything. But to some it is a jewel still. It has fine streets and piazzas, and statues, and palaces, and porticoes; and fine gardens by the side of a fine river. And one step across the bridge, and you are into the midst of the mountains, the green hills, and the sylvan woods, and the slopes dotted with villas and with a fine palace —and crowned with a Royal mausoleum.

Under the clear skies that rule here, all through the day from high windows you may see, in their glorious freshness, filling the cloudland, the white peaks of the

great Alpine giants. There lurks a disabling fascination in this for the stranger, new to such phantom
realities,—he forgets to run about the city for its
sights; and stands gazing and gazing, taking clouds
for Alps, and Alps for clouds.

On summer evenings, as you stroll across some open
square—or quitting the porticoes, walk down the
broadway to the fine river—you may catch the tinkle
of the cow-bell, in sight of the gas-lamp, and even hear
the rustle of the leaves in the woods of the near hills.

It is a pleasant place to find yourself in, when you
are aweary both of crowds and solitude, for you can
have town and country,—you can be gay and quiet.

But at this moment there is but little gaiety in
this pleasant city. A cloud is on every brow, and a sore
sorrow at every heart. Upon some faces there is the
pallor of despair, and upon others the red flush of an
anger that is akin to shame.

A grievous trouble has come upon its loyal people
and its Royal House. High hopes have fallen, and a
King is gone forth from their midst, with broken fortunes and a broken heart! And yet—in all his life he
has never been so honoured by his people, so dear to
their hearts, as in this moment of his defeat and self-
abasement.

In a café under the porticoes sits an Englishman,
revolving in his mind all these things and many
others; nor did he look much gayer than the rest.

The single cup of coffee with which he has broken his fast, seems to have satisfied his appetite ; his white truffles, his Asti, and his grissini—all delicate specialities of the place, stand before him untasted. Now and then he crumbles, now and then he nibbles one of the long bread pipes,—and that is his best attempt at this midday meal.

This is not his first visit to this little city. He has been here a year ago—a year almost to a day—twelve long months of anxious, impatient, weary waiting.

He sits with his eyes fixed upon a statue in the Piazza, of which he catches sight through the arch of the portico. It is of heroic size. The uplifted arm is in the act of sheathing a sword, that is never sheathed.

It has the force of a cruel truth for him.

In his turn, he is the object of observation. The head waiter of the café has been considering him attentively—and even anxiously, for the last ten minutes and more.

" Inglese—sicuro ! " says he to himself.

If he had spoken to any one else about him, he would not have used his good Italian,—for here there is little good Italian to be heard. If you would have wished to be understood in those days, you would have done well to speak in French, or in the dialect of the country.

As for our head waiter, he would tell you with pride that here he was born, but, like the rest of them, he had bided about, first in one city and then in another, till he has forgotten his dialect, and learnt his good Italian;—as for French, he will not speak it to you, except under compulsion.

He has taken to our Englishman, because he can not only understand, but reply to him in good Italian. It is this interest, in this meditative Englishman, which is at the bottom of his anxious looks.

" English ! " thinks he again ; " not to be doubted. What other country could send here a man who would sit staring out of doors, with a dish of white truffles before him served *à la fonduta!* "

The café is getting empty. The natives take this meal earlier by an hour.

The head waiter retires into a corner, throws his table napkin over his shoulder like a weapon in rest, and, putting one foot over the other and leaning against the corner of the buffet, he takes out a tattered volume. This is his hour for reading it, only his time has been abridged by the conduct of this infatuated Englishman.

It is a copy of the " Inferno." Nothing wonderful in that ;—not more wonderful than that an Englishman should neglect white truffles, and that English waiters should not know their Shakespeare by name—that is, the English waiters of that distant time.

English waiters of this present time are mostly not English at all.

Giuseppe—such is his name—can bear it no longer. He turns to the buffet, pours out a small glass of liqueur, and, marching with the air of a commander to the table of the dreaming Englishman, he cries—

"Drink, and eat!" Then he sets down the glass. "It is vermouth," says he—"for the appetite— Drink, and you will eat!"

The Englishman's conscience is aroused as well as his mind. He is well acquainted with the sensitive feelings which burn or smoulder,—or are smothered,—in the length and breadth of this much-divided land. He loves it well,—he loves its people,—he loves its tongue. In the midst of his own troubles he could sit down and weep with it, and for it. He does his best to atone for his exasperating conduct,—he takes the dose with an apology, and drinks it down.

The outraged Giuseppe touches the neglected dish with the tips of his fingers—and shrinks back dismayed.

"Freddo," he mutters; "freddissimo!" And he whisks it off for a *réchauffé*.

"Eat, then," is the command that accompanies the second appearance of the dish of white truffles—"good —buonissimo!—fit for a king!"

Then Giuseppe stops. He is clearly of the country.

He turns away to his corner—and he murmurs to himself, "Ah Dio! povero Re—povero—infelice— infelice."

And surely that is a tear that Giuseppe is brushing away.

But when one has to work, one cannot stop by the way to weep—at least, not stop for many tears; and recovering himself—but still with the pitiful face upon him, inspired by the nobler and sadder theme—and altogether softened and subdued, Giuseppe advances, and begs that the dish may be at least tasted!—at least tried!

The Englishman thanks him, and always in his good Italian—and he has a surprisingly sweet befitting voice ;—this, with a pair of wonderfully kind eyes, are all the bodily charms he has to boast of.

Giuseppe starts.

"Italiano !" cries he.

"Ma no."—

"But no" is the safe second thought. No ;—speak Italian as well as he may, he is "English, not to be doubted."

And when this one gets up to go, and gives for his *douceur* four times as much as Giuseppe hoped to get from him,—from the natives he gets nothing at all perhaps—

"English, and not to be doubted," comes over again.

There is no particular advantage in this excess of liberality.

As a foreigner once remarked : " You English

go about the Continent spoiling all the places and the people—for the rest of the world. You have made masters and servants uncivil—you have turned the children into beggars—nobody will do anything except for money;—and then you complain yourselves of—our exactions!"

Well, to be sure, the Americans, in their turn, have helped the English in these results.

Happily, all the places are not yet spoilt; and there exists still, many a quaint and comfortable little inn, in remote valleys and out-of-the-way towns, where it is a pleasure to live on your few francs a day,—where you will dine well and sleep well, and receive at all moments the gracious smiles of a contented host, and still more contented hostess, and the untiring assiduities of all the household.

Giuseppe was perfectly correct in his verdict of " English, not to be doubted."

There are other indications which mark this stranger to have come from the British Isles—beside his neglect of white truffles, and his open purse.

There is the cut of his hat and his coat—and his high-low boots—and his walk, which is so inexpressibly different to the rest of the world about here.

For the rest, he has sandy hair and whiskers; extreme height, broad shoulders,—and extreme ugliness.

But it is an ugliness so set off by a pair of large benevolent eyes, that, after the first ten minutes, you forget all about it. It is the ugliness of ungainly figure and features,—not that of expression and vulgarity.

As for the eyes, they might have been framed for a portrait, both when they beamed forth in all their active benevolence, and again, when not in observation, they opened larger and wider—with a vast unconscious look, which might have made you believe the owner to be a dreamer,—but for the power of intellect which went along with it, and which seemed to be on the stretch with some mighty abstraction of the mind.

They were the eyes of a man, who loved his neighbour better than himself, and who placed the severities of study, before the attractions of ease and pleasure.

The owner of these eyes now, however, appears absorbed in the mundane occupation of staring eagerly into every shop window that he passes. Up and down under the porticoes he goes searching evidently for something which he is slow to find.

First, he draws up before the shops of mixed curiosities,—and then the carved-ivories attract him, —and then it is the jeweller's, and then the fans.

Such fans! Of all sizes, of all lengths, of all colours,—simple and gorgeous. Then he goes on to the great magazines for the silk and velvet tissues. And then he falls back again upon the fans.

"I must take her something," says he—"something to speak to her a little of the world,—the world, thank God! I am going to take her back into."

So he goes into the shop, and he buys his fan. As he walks away, he gets nervous about it. "I hope I've done right," thinks he;—"it is useful."

Just then, he is crossing the open piazza, and he meets four ladies, and each lady holds a fan high between her eyes and the sun. They walk well, and have fine handsome faces; they wear the veil of the country, which sets off both their carriage and their features.

"Yes," says he, growing more satisfied with his purchase—"a fan is useful; it is not a worldly ornament. And yet"—thinks he, with the four ladies in his eyes—"a fan seems to me full of the witchery of a woman's face, and it is a woman's most bewitching ornament."

Now this Englishman knew that this little city had once held the title of the "jewel of Italy;" indeed, he knew most things simple and profound,— for he was a scholar—and a reader—in all tongues.

"It is a little jewel of a city," thinks he, as he stands under the porticoes at the entrance of his hotel. "It is rightly named!"—and his eyes follow the figures of the people as they cross from every angle the Castle Square—

—Peasants from the mountains, with their short petticoats and mules and broad flat-crowned hats;

Bersaglieri, with their raven plumes that sweep their shoulders; fine-made women, poor and rich, all with their fans; cautious-treading townsmen, with their look of North and South in one; and the *jeunesse dorée*, with their dash of pride and their air as much of the camp as of the court; and black-frocked priests; and brown-cowled friars,—and of these our Englishman thinks—

"They would be a loss to the picture,—but no loss anywhere else! They were at the bottom of this mischief!—of all this patriotic failure!"

This is our Englishman's private opinion,—which, Heaven knows, every born Englishman believes he has a right to hold and to declare!

As for our friend,—the truth of it is, he is not in love with priests just now; he has been chafing at, and fearing them for twelve whole months!

It is enough to put a man out of conceit with his dearest friend.—

As he thus stands making his comments, close under his eyes pass two men. They walk as simple citizens, but every one makes way for them.

The elder man looks for all the world like one of the cautious-treading townsmen. He is thick-set, and under the middle size. But the second impression corrects the first. His face is thoughtful and wary. He is speaking calmly,—but he smiles, and now and then rubs his hands sharply; but the smile and the

gestures are more shrewd than gay; the mouth has no
lines; the face is smooth-shaven; the lips often tighten.
The spectacles he wears do not hide the astute fire of
his quick eye. He has the look of a man who cannot
lose hope.

The younger man—younger by many years—has
all the dash, all the haughtiness, all the pride of the
jeunesse dorée, with none of its graces, and more than
its martial air. The head is thrown back, the chest
open. He walks the street with the fierce earnestness
of a man in the *mêlée* of a battle. He has the look of
a man who can never lose courage.

Behind these two follow two others—one with the
romantic air of a painter or a poet; the other with the
carriage of a military martinet.

These four cross the square to the homely-looking
royal house that bounds it. As they pass out from
under the porticoes, the younger man looks over his
shoulder and says, "Massimo." And at the word, the
four close up together.

Behind the Englishman stands the concierge;—
in any other land, you would have called him above
his station. But here, the people—like their songs—
partake by nature of the cultivated.

He touches the Englishman on the shoulder.

"There," cries he, with a tremble in his voice—
"there they go; and there goes the hope of our
unhappy country!"

"I know," says the Englishman; "and if the outside look of men goes for anything, your hope will not fail you ! "

Let us use our privilege—and survey the years as they pass forward in this little city.

Still these four figures go to and fro to the homely palace, and still the good concierge watches them— still points them out for Hope—and then for Pride— and then for Triumph !

But one day follows another, and men move on and move off,—and man's life is but a shadow, and here, more than anywhere, the mighty changeful Hand makes itself felt :—and one by one the figures of this Band of Hope pass out of the ken of the watchful concierge. Time has not forgotten to streak his black locks with grey ; he has left his youth behind him ; but still it is with a smile to his sigh, that he talks to you of all the changes,—and as the night falls, he will draw you out of the court, under the porticoes, and say with the old pride—

" Look across to that little window ; the lamp burns there to-night ;—He is there ! "

But there comes a day, when the head of the con- cierge—it is white now—is bowed to the dust.

No lamp burns in that little window ; there is no

cheer in the long frontage of that homely palace,—only
a line of closed shutters.

Just then a traveller comes that way. In many a
year gone by, he has stood chatting with the friendly
concierge; he is acquainted with all his hopes, and all
his pride, and all his triumph.

But this year they meet in silence. The traveller
respects the grief of the old concierge,—he even
shares it.

" He is not there ! " cries the old man, with a burst
of tears.

" Nor there ! "

And he points his trembling hand to the gorgeous
chapel on the hill.

" My friend," says the traveller, " take comfort !
Man cannot live for ever. This one has fulfilled all your
hopes; he has made a Nation; and won for himself a
grave in the Eternal City."

A grand and moving drama ! Worthy of all
regard.

But our Englishman stands only at the opening of
it. He beholds only these four manly figures crossing
the Castle Square, in all the strength of their lives,
and of their purposes. The web in which the great joy
of it, and the great grief of it, are to be so inextricably
woven up, lies as yet, a mass of indestructible threads :

—coming events indeed are so strong that by all eyes, the willing and the unwilling their shadows are to be seen; but our Englishman is a stranger fresh to the land;—he sees only a little way into these shadows; he does not fathom the fateful histories going on around,—the threads of that web, waiting to be fully woven.

But he has his willing eyes, and his sympathetic heart, and he turns off down the porticoes with the verse on his lips of a young hero-poet, who like that hero-prince of the homely palace, has been claimed in death by the Eternal City, as unalienably her own.—

A claim that could not be disallowed! And yet, like all the rest, made up of grief and joy:—a crowning pride, and a crowning pang to the cities that gave them birth.

As for our Englishman he knew neither the name, nor the birthplace, nor the heroic story of the young poet of his Song of Liberty—he had bought it that morning on a broad side off a vendor in the streets, and he murmured to himself this immortal,

"Fratelli d'Italia"

because its words took hold of his mind, and stirred his feelings,—as they have stirred the souls, and fired the blood of many a son of Italy since that day!—and of many a true heart besides!

Yes!—whilst Freedom is cherished, and her patriots and martyrs are remembered, the fame and the fate of,

> " ———— *Mameli, his young breast silenced*
> "*from Song*"

will not be forgotten!

CHAPTER VIII.

SHRINES AND SOLITUDES.

"The knees are weak, the race is long,
The battle hard, the foe is strong,
Narrow the gate, and strait the road,
The cross to bear a heavy load ;
And faint and fearful, oft I sigh
For rest, and for security.

"Think not of rest ! But deem thy life
A struggle and a deadly strife :
Toil, watching, prayer, alone can be
On earth thy soul's security !
A rest indeed the saints shall know,—
But 'tis in heaven, not here below ! "

H.

ONCE more by the blue sea !

Here again is the sweeping coast-line, with its bold
beauty,—with its towns and villages, crowning the
cliffs, or nestling in their clefts, or bordering some level
creek or promontory,—each various, each a little picture in itself !

Here are the rocks set six fathoms deep in blue
water, and the coral caves, where the waves may hide
when a-weary of tossing their white foam along the
shore.

Here is the wealth of the earth in gold and grey and green—citrons and olives and vines.

Here is the perfumed air; and here are the chamelion lights that tint a glassy sea, lilac and rose and amber sheen,—lovely as the pearly shells that lie below it.

Here are the light shallops that skim the surface; and here are the ships that seem to sail into the sun; and here are the white crests that chase each other in an endless race.

Here is the shelf they call a road; and here are the blood-stained rocks, and the dark gorges; and here is the river, a foaming torrent again.

And up there is the village on the rock,—and up and down go the peasant folk as of yore—some for the sea, and some for the hills, with their orange kerchiefs, and their red caps and sashes, their sunburnt cheeks, their light fare, and their lighter hearts!

Yes; and here is the white-fronted house, with the garden gate ajar, and the gay oleanders, and the green jalousies, smiling as ever, under the rule of the new tenant.

And there, too, stands the Villa Grimaldi.

Closed and cheerless,—the myrtle hedges meet, the magnolias are all untrimmed, the verandah has broken down; the curtains hang in splits behind the dust-stained windows,—they are bare and blindless, they stare at you with eyes of blank desolation; a ghost looks out from every vacant pane ;—it cries aloud that it is empty,—and yet no one cares to hire it. It has none of the snug comfort of the white-fronted house.

It is a doomed place,—doomed altogether, and its owner will pull it down, and set up two little villas in its place,—little villas on the plan of the white-fronted house; and then the ghosts will be put to flight, and human faces and human footsteps will bring it into the life of the sun again.

Why it has grown so forlorn no one can say. The rock shuts out the blast securely as ever, the waves keep up their sweet murmurings, the citron grove is still full and fragrant, and the purple hills stretch away behind it with their old seductive charm of sun and shadow, of mountain path and mountain wilderness.

All unchanged, too, are the stars of these hills,—the snowy shrines and sanctuaries, which stand out from their lovely heights, safe and secure—cynosures for prayer and pilgrimage, where wandering angels perforce must tarry, till they leave a blessing for their ransom! Safe and secure,—the storm and the thunderbolt pass them over, rarely the scath of the tempest comes nigh to them. So they stand all the years round, —never shaken, never forlorn, never forsaken,—with no ghosts looking out of their uncurtained windows.

To such a shrine must we go; for it marks the way we are to take to find the retreat which shelters our Lady Laure.

But first, if only for the sake of contrast, let us seek a ruder Solitude.

The way to it is arduous,—beyond these near hills, and their encircling heights, and along the falling ridges, to a wild valley stretching between pine-clad steeps.

Its broken level is a moraine, the glacier bed of a past age,—it lies under the sun, the Gehenna of these mountains, the hoary giants of the forest, hurled down by winter blasts, like bleached skeletons, lie rotting year by year, upon its imperishable *débris.*

It is the very type of desolation! But still, it lies under the sun,—every inch of it is lit up from dawn to dusk:—it is a smiling garden compared to the black defile which breaches it northwards.

A huge and gloomy cleft, tortuous and long, and lofty and narrow. No golden ray has ever cheered these Stygian depths,—no life, but the torrent of stormy water;—this has life, and to spare! It turns the head giddy with its wild caprices—now flashing through the abyss like a white ghost, now becalmed in strange black pools, which bewitch you to gaze into their stealthy quiet,—now hissing and hidden between the confused boulders which block its course.

It is dark down here; the yawning rocks hang close and high, they look as if they had been split apart but yesterday, and seem to strain to meet again above you, in a terrible embrace.

It is a place of awe and loneliness, nevertheless, it

is a path to an inhabited abode. A path with a tumble
and a scramble to it, for venturesome feet to follow ;—
but then, you may break your neck upon a kerbstone !
—and down here, as elsewhere, if your steps are sure,
you will reach your goal at last, and stand high and
free, the black defile lost in the distance below, and
above you a black shadow against the sky.

A fortress raised by the hand of man, upon a fortress
of Nature's raising. It stands alone, on its defence
against all the storms, defying all the powers of darkness, whether they assail the body or the soul.

Here live the Grey Fathers, with their many privations and their one pleasure—the matchless panorama
that Nature provides for them.

Here, from their narrow slab, they behold—morning,
noon, and night—all that earth and sky and sea have
best to display.

East and west spreads a boundless upper region,
peak beyond peak. Below, stretch the lesser heights,
sparse and bare, and lower still slant the green forests,
covering up valley and glade ;—the delusion to the eye
would have you believe that there is but to slide down
these green roofs, to reach the blue sea, which, far-
stretching to its dazzling horizon, bounds this enticing
picture of a world, to be seen—but not enjoyed.

Behind them rises a different world, which they
may enjoy if they please,—the upper world of virgin
summits, untrodden by the foot of man, sublimely
calm and still.

What dawns are theirs! What setting suns!

And what nights, when the myriad stars hang low in the purple darkness, in an atmosphere the dullards of the plains have never dreamt of! Or when, with a stranger beauty still, in the sudden twilight straight up above, upon the solitary towering snow-peak, sits the one star of evening, large as a moon, red as a flame; it is hard to think, that beacon light is not a fire kindled by human hands—by some benighted wanderer of these Alpine solitudes!

Solitudes,—God-given, and glorified.

But it is not among the Grey Fathers that our Lady Laure must be looked for.

A thousand, and a thousand feet, below this monastic fortress,—round by the sweeping valley, and between the undulating hills, cradled in a nook which catches every ray of this Southern sun, and holds it in fruitful possession,—with nothing to see but the olive wood before and behind, and the trail of the vine gardens to the right and to the left,—stands the companion Solitude,—the shrine of Our Lady of Consolation—the sheltered convent house of La Stella.

Up above there, the poor monks must face the icy winds, with neither tree nor slope to shield them. Here below, the favoured nuns breathe a joyous and

sunny atmosphere.   Up there, winter with all its frosts;
down here, spring with all its flowers.

Up there, the scarred branches of some solitary fir;
down here, the growth of the fig and the olive, festoon-
ing vines, and pasturage for cow and goat, and all the
cultivated treasures of orchard and flower garden.   Up
there, they will eat their crust, but they will lack the
handful of herbs to season it; down here, we shall
make up our dishes,—salsify and haricot, spinach and
asparagus; and what gatherings and dryings of figs
and of plums!

Down here, we will take our noontide rest, upon
our banks of blue violets.   Such violets,—large, pale,
double, intensely scented blossoms, which the world of
folly loves to see crystallized, and in their *bonbonnières!*

What flowery carpets in crimson, and white, and
yellow, and blue! What berceaux of roses, loose-
blossomed, thornless, creamy,—all sorts, all kinds, and
how they perfume the air!

What graceful evergreens! what pointing cypresses!
what aloes! What a stem of bloom, as tall as the
cypress near to it! And what a shrubbery there is of
the spiky leaves! Up and down you may go by terraced walks and flights of steps,—only the model lawn
is wanting;—in these lands the planner of pleasure-
grounds has no notion of that.   Where all is in
Nature's profusion,—shaven grass, would be out of
place!

There is water too, but no torrent,—a single silver

fall, coming down without a splash into the brimming tank below it. No gates, no walls,—a simple modern house, closed round by olive groves and vine gardens.

Here dwell the sisters of the Consolation, with their pension, and their orphanage, and their *dames pensionnaires*.

They are full of godly vows and godly works and godly recreation. They are the human lilies of the garden,—here they flourish safely and serenely guarded by their two good angels—their Virgin Saint, and their watch-dog Féroce.

It is as enticing a Solitude as the bounty of the earth has to bestow; and maybe it possesses one charm the more,—that it is a Solitude within close hail of the outside world. A zigzag cut through the thick olive wood, with a fall of a hundred feet, comes straight upon the mountain road. The Consolation is hid behind its impervious veil,—but sound can burst through prison bars; and as the white-hooded nuns glide with their noiseless steps in the wood,—breviary in hand reading their office, or with eyes on the ground making their daily meditation,—the crack of the vetturino's whip, the jingle of the mule-bells, the songs of the trudging peasants reach their ears, and perchance their hearts, and speak to them of the busy world they have done with for ever !

And here we shall find Lady Laure.

But surely—we see her now—upon that terraced walk !

She is not so changed in that strait robe, and that white head-gear, which shades her face, but that we can know her again.

To look at her, her attire varies but little from that sister who is walking some few paces on before her,—but still it varies.

Lady Laure has not assumed the habit yet.

She does not walk alone;—beside her is another figure to be recognized. . .

Grave and with a lofty brow, with calm and far-seeing eyes,—and a presence to inspire hope, and trust, and unto some—awe. With a voice also to match the presence,—the very echo of all it tells of.

He is speaking,—and the large blue eyes turn to him, with all the confidence of their first look in infancy ;—not a doubt—not a fear—not the shadow of a distrust, or of a thought kept back.

What is he saying ?   His hands behind his cassock, his look fixed upon the ground he treads.

His words fall like the dropping of water,—calm even,—distinct and low.

" Have trust ! You are taken from the world,—you are delivered from its snares. Do you think that the Divine Hand that deprived you of all your friends in this world—laid on you these grievous trials to no end? Was it not, think you, to perfect the graces of your soul, already so abundant,—to lead you to walk in the right and perfect way, which conducts to all good?"

But it is now Lady Laure's turn to speak—

"Abbate," says she, "our Father in heaven is so good, that He must love all that is good,—and there must be many kinds of good—many ways of seeking it. I cannot think there is only one way—only a few who find it."

"Only a few who find it." It falls from the abbate like an echo, with the key-note changed;—a plea changed to a sentence pronounced.

"Strait is the way and narrow is the road;—have you not been taught that? If all can go in,—what is the meaning of this strait and narrow way?" and he bids her stop and answer.

"Ah!" says she, "I was thinking of all the good people. I know that there are bad people as well as good."

"What do you mean by good?" asks he.

"How can I tell you all the ways there are of being good?" There is a tearful reproach in her eyes.

"There is," says he, "but one way by which good can be sanctified for us."

"I know that we must believe," says she.

"To believe aright—we must be taught aright."

The abbate's voice has its most inflexible tone, and Lady Laure feels it to her heart.

"Ah!" cries she; "it is that, it is that, abbate! I can only believe as I have been taught. I can only walk in the way that I have always walked in. I cannot walk in yours, abbate, because—because I do not understand it."

Then she clasps her hands with all her gentle fervour. "But you know—you know that I love and reverence you all. You cannot doubt that."

Once more the abbate bids her stop and listen.

His eyes leave the ground,—they meet hers with the fullest compassion. All the inflexibility of his voice is gone,—and in its place is the soothing and kindling solemnity of the office that is his.

"My child," says he, "you say that you do not understand,—but if you had the love that you lack, you would then not lack the understanding. To love and to understand are words which express each other, —only love must lead."

Again the abbate's eyes fall to the ground. "The love that is part of the Divine," says he, "consists in the submission of the heart, and of the will. Its source is in the heart,—it has nothing to do with the knowledge of the human understanding. In the pursuit of human wisdom, knowledge excites love,— but in the wisdom of the saints, love produces knowledge. He that loves most—knows most. We must all be as little children!" cries he; "we must all begin as little children!"

The abbate pauses, as if lost in thought. Then once more he speaks, and with a more exalted tone. "What," he exclaims, "are the lofty, the ambitious, the fruitless conceptions of the unsanctified human mind in its highest flights,—but the dust and ashes of vainglorious conceits,—the dead bones of a body without a soul? In what does it all end? In discord, in detraction, in disappointment, in depression,—in dismay it may be;—and it may be, in defiance. Is that a better state for the soul? By faith and works, so we must live; not by a faith of our own inventing, or by works of our own selecting. We must find a guide. It is the gift of Heaven to choose our guides aright. But let us suppose the soul in safe hands,—and then, this faith, and these works, will unite her to her Creator, and instruct her how to love Him."

"Abbate," sighs Lady Laure, "I do not think that it is love that is so wanting in me. It is only that I cannot change. So many changes—so many hard things to bear, have come upon me. So much do I owe to my life here,—so much to you,—so much have you helped me to say—'His will be done.' But yet—I cannot change. I am the same as I was before it all began. If I could think it a fault, I would say so;—you know I am not proud in my heart. But I cannot think that I am wrong. Something tells me that to-morrow, when I go from this dear shelter—and

these dear friends,—when I go from you, my best and
kindest friend, still in my old mind,—that I shall do
what is right, and not what is wrong."

Her voice is troubled—and the tears stand in her
blue eyes. But she has courage. She is constant.

"So near to all safety!" murmurs the abbate—
"so near to it!"

And he strikes his breast with the bitterness of
baffled hope. Then once again he turns the full power
and searchingness of his commanding eyes upon her.

"What is that something?" says he. "Are the
spirits of darkness less active than ever?"

"Ah! abbate," cries she. "Do not frighten me;
for I cannot change!"

"Cannot change!" he repeats. "Is it to change,
to rise higher,—to advance a step in the ladder of
holiness,—to see the angel at your side,—to take his
hand,—to be so helped onward and upward? This is
not change! It is but to move nearer to the safe road
which we should all seek,—which, if we saw clearly,
we should have no doubts, no hesitation about. It is
but to bring the beautiful twilight of the soul into the
full sunshine of heavenly light."

Lady Laure meets those commanding eyes with her own, brimming with tears and tender gratitude and regret.

She sees how vain are all these words. If they reached to heaven itself, could they move by one iota the standpoint of either of them?

She lays her hand upon his arm.

"Come with me," she says—"there!" And with the other hand she points into the distance.

"I must go there—once more with you."

She half leads the way, turning her head with a look of gentle entreaty. But he does not hold back,—he is soon at her side;—then, with slow steps, and silent lips, and eyes cast down in pressing thought, they leave the boundaries of the Consolation.

A slant of steps cut below the olive wood, takes them down to the level of the mountain road; once upon it, they follow its line upwards.

They are still silent,—for to-day, there are to be no more of those fruitless words—and to-morrow—will see Lady Laure beyond the reach of their renewal.

CHAPTER IX.

SAINTS AND SINNERS.

He has burst from many a tether;
 She is pure as angel bright.
As they take their way together,
 To them comes a priest in white.

On their brows their lives are written,
 And the priest can read them well—
Read that sinner sorely smitten,
 All her graces he can tell.

Sheep without a shepherd wandering,
 He and she go up and down.
Pious priest! these souls from foundering,
 Save! and win the ransom crown.

Stops the priest that smitten sinner,
 Holds him in his pious clasp;
But he fails to touch or win her,—
 Like a cloud she leaves his grasp.

Safe, poor sinner! take thy rest, then!
 She must wander on alone;
All her graces still unblest then,—
 Cannot save her or atone.

WE left Lady Laure and the Abbate Faa di Bruno,
with a silence between them, that came of a tacit
consent.

As a usual thing,—there would have been nothing

forced in their walking side by side with voiceless lips,
—for they were not talkers.

The abbate was a man who never opened his
mouth but to say the thing that had to be said; and
Lady Laure had the happiest sort of taciturnity, which
neither weighed upon herself nor on her companions.

But to-day it was neither the lack of a momentous
topic, nor the repose of happy silence, which closed
their lips,—it was rather, as Lady Laure said sadly to
herself, because to speak was vain.

They are mounting the spur of a projecting cliff.
The ascent is sharp,—the cliff is steep,—and the fall
is fenced off by a parapet of stone.

As they near the crest, they behold two objects: a
white-washed shrine, set into the parapet,—and opposite
it, on the more level ground, the four low, white-washed
walls of a small enclosure. It stands bare and treeless,
—the iron gateway fastened with a single ring. Inside,
sparsely scattered, are a few rudely carved wooden
crosses.

It is the Campo Santo of La Stella,—and it is here
that Mr. Mildew, his troubles over, found his rest at last.

These two who knew and loved him well, who had
some guess of what and how keen those troubles were,
—stand together now, to take another last farewell of
him,—and of each other.

In the happy days of poor Lucie's new Paradise,
poor Mr. Mildew dropped out of mind.

But in the Purgatory that followed so swiftly upon it, Mr. Mildew came up again;—came up with a still tenderer tie for Lady Laure, since the safe shelters kind Heaven granted at last to both of them were near unto each other. To Lady Laure, at first, it seemed but a small thing, the difference between his retreat of death and her retreat of life;—to her they seemed once more together.

Day by day she stood beside his grave,—she brought to it the flowers that he loved, and she loved,—she opened all her heart to him, and it seemed to her that he heard her and replied.

Yet not all her heart. She talked to him of the father she had lost,—of the brother she had loved,—of the friends she had found,—of the peace that was entering her heart;—but not one word of the lover who had forsaken her,—not one word does she say to this dear dust of that disdainful scorner.

She breathes no word of all the broken-heartedness —of the quick fulfilment of those prophetic fears. And if she could have spoken, it would have been with the same halting words as in the old days, when her sighs were the foreshadowings of her abandonment. She could neither have blamed nor justified,—for she was still herself—still unchanged.

As she said with her sweet appeal to the abbate— "I cannot change."

Not in any chosen spot—in truth, in this narrow space, there is no chosen spot to take—but with its wooden cross, just like the rest—is the grave of Mr. Mildew.

"Spes—Fides—Caritas." So runs the legend, roughly cut in a sort of nimbus, on the three arms of the cross, with just his dead name in the middle, joined to these three living words.

Lady Laure's tears are flowing,—she is touched to the heart with all the pathetic thoughts of this last interview.

She takes the hand that has been the hand of a father to her, she looks through her tears at the green grave at her feet.

And—"Ah, my friends!" she cries; "if I could but once more hold a hand of each! My friends,—my friends! in what world shall I find you again?"

But the hand of another Friend—of another Father;—the Will of that other Power, which has overruled all her destiny,—which has not quitted her for an hour,—unseen—unfelt—unknown,—but always beside her, with its resistless sequences, its silent forces, its secret springs, its halt, and its advance,—is here at this moment, strong, prescient as ever:—here with its mighty shield, and its mighty stay,—and it brings up for the next turn of her fate—the heavy rumble of a travelling carriage appearing above the crest.

The noses of the leaders come first, it advances

upon them with all the speed of a cracking whip and
four horses;—and within it sits Arthur Aboyne.

We have seen him before, face to face—and but
just lately too,—for he is our Englishman with the
benevolent eyes—with the willing eyes and the sympathizing heart, whom we made acquaintance with
under the porticoes of the little city.

Just a year gone by—all these had met together
on this spot, even as they do now,—the Abbate Faa di
Bruno, Lady Laure, Mr. Mildew the silent witness,
and Arthur Aboyne; but then——two were to stay,
and one to go ;—now it is all reversed.

Then Aboyne was going—going with infinite regret,
infinite anxiety—going alone !

In the last moment he spoke up—as men are wont
to do with their last words.

He owned to a deep personal feeling, but he said
—he put it far from him ! He said—he would ignore
from that day forth its very existence !

He took higher and broader grounds. He urged
his duty, as a father's substitute, and how it behoved
him to act as the man who received that father's
failing words,—he told how one beloved name was
the last upon that father's lips,—he spoke of the vow
he made to be to his child all that a father could be,—
to watch and guard over her, if needs be, with life

itself, and as long as life should last, and he bade them know and feel, how a firm trust in this vow and its faithful fulfilment, smoothed that last hour of agony, and sent a father smiling to his doom.

And he asked, how—how he is to reconcile this vow —how his conscience is to permit him to turn his back upon his ward, and upon his sworn duty to her!

How is he to leave her thus—barely eighteen years of age—in a foreign land!

"Yes!" cried Aboyne—"Why should I dissemble my fears?—and in the hand of an alien Church!"

"In one year, Arthur!" sighed Lady Laure.——

"Leave to me my year of mourning,—leave me for this year,—in this holy spot—with this holy man—with these friends who have beheld all my sorrows, who have known all my tears! Leave me here in this abode of peace and consolation for this one year—and then—I will come!"

And so he went—condemning his own weakness, and distrusting hers.

And here he is—true to the day, and to the hour— come to claim her promise.

And here is she too, ready to redeem it,—it is more than he has dared to hope for, it is a boon he has only dared to pray for!

There are but few words between these two men—
between the man who would take her—and the man
who would keep her.

They look at each other with misdoubting eyes.
True—each one credits the other with the desire to
befriend this "desolate young girl"—and to see her
befriended. But they do not stop here—it is with
something more than this that they credit each other.

In Aboyne, the abbate sees a possible lover, whose
passion is backed by the power of a guardian, and
whose persuasion is strengthened by the intimacies of
family relations.

In the abbate, Aboyne beholds the champion of
his Church—the propagandist, greedy after human
souls, if after nothing else!—presuming upon the
tenderness of youth, and the sympathies given to
sorrow in the time of need.

There can be but little love lost between the repre-
sentatives of such opposing interests,—and scant enough
is their mutual greeting. They content themselves
with a cold bow of the head, as they meet again this
day,—with the prize or the prey, as they may please to
call it, between their four hands.

Five minutes more, and Aboyne, at least, can afford to smile.

He is nearer to the winning-post than that other now, in spite of all his opportunities, by many a mile.

"Our departure will be for to-morrow," says he. He steadies his voice,—he speaks under it. But if he could have his fling, he would make these rocks and hills resound again and again to his words!

But he is afraid even to give a sign of his joy,—he has a superstitious dread of upsetting all this blessed release and restoration and redemption by some eager word or rash look. He does not even face Lády Laure. He looks at the abbate with all the benevolence he can muster;—it is no hard task for him, for he is endowed by nature with the full power of its kindliest expression. But this time, indeed, he dissembles all his feelings.

The abbate answers his look with his most commanding glance;—he is calm, and cold, and concentrated;—all the majestic power of the man comes out,—and Aboyne recoils before it.

"How—how," he cries to his heart—"how has she withstood him !"

Then the abbate bends his eyes to Lady Laure, and lays his hand upon her.

"You leave us, then, to-morrow!——my poor child!
——to-morrow "——

What an unspoken regret echoes in that last—
" To-morrow "!——and what an unspoken blessing
dwells in those eyes, and in the touch of that hand!

" Ah, no! ah, no!" cries Lady Laure. " I cannot
bear it. To-night—now—all is ready! And I am
ready,—Arthur, I am ready!"

She speaks to Aboyne—but she looks at the
abbate. She takes both his hands—she hides her
face in them—her sobs and tears break out, and she
cries aloud—

" Oh, my friend, my father, how shall I go on without you?—how shall I live in that world again?"

With the last exertions which surround the last
moments of all departures—Lady Laure's composure
returns.

She feels—but her feelings are under her control.

And now, as she had said,—all is ready,—and she
is ready—ready for the start;—the horses are har-
nessed, the carriage is in sight—and stowed away
behind it, is the small amount of luggage she takes
with her.

It raises her at once in the good opinion of Paolo—

the vetturino,—in whom the sight of big baggage invariably excites an ill-disguised contempt for his live cargo.

He is already on the box, his reins gathered up, his long whip in rest,—and in his broad-brimmed hat a bunch of red flowers, which greatly set off the black eyes and curly locks that shine beneath it. At his side sits Mademoiselle Sabine,—yes,—our old acquaintance Mademoiselle Sabine. We will give her a friendly greeting, for to her were addressed the last words spoken, in our hearing, by our dear Lucie!

Convent life has not embellished her *grisette* face, —there are some lines about the mouth and eyes—and the tint of the skin is yellowish. She sits with her face curiously puckered up,—it is difficult to say whether she is laughing or crying; but by the light of her subsequent conversation, when they drive off, addressed partly to the shade of her mother, partly to herself, and partly to Paolo, it is made clear that she is crying—crying for joy!

"Oh! pauvre mère, si tu pouvais pendant quelques instants quitter ton pauvre tombeau, si tu pouvais voir la joie de ta pauvre fille, cela ferait du bien à ton pauvre cœur!—Ah, Dieu!—le bonheur de se sentir hors de cette affreuse prison!——On n'aura pas à chercher l'enfer dans l'autre monde, tant que ce couvent existera dans celui-ci."

And she gives a look of concentrated horror and

hatred back at the receding trees which conceal the
House of Consolation.

Paolo, like his fraternity in these lands, is inclined
to be a bit of a wag, a bit of a cynic, more than a bit
of a "bon Catholique."

He pulls up Mademoiselle Sabine sharply, and tells
her she'd better look out, or else she will get into a
place of this name, not so easy to escape from.

He further remarks that "Pour une femme comme
vous,—who could want to be troubled with you up
there?"—and his whip-handle takes the direction of
Mademoiselle Sabine's looks of aversion.

Upon which she begs him to know that nobody
up there did want to be troubled with her!—that they
had done their best to get rid of her; that it was
"une vraie persecution!" but that they had persecuted
her in vain.

She says that long ago she had told the Signor
Abbate himself that she would go as far as the original
of that place, to serve her white angel, and she had
done so; and she would "never have come away
without her, and that is more!"

Paolo shakes his head. He says, "Il faut vivre, et
pour vivre, il faut travailler,—mais il n'est pas toujours
possible de choisir son genre de travail—voilà, qui est
clair!"

"Dame!" cries Mademoiselle Sabine. "Vous ne
me croyez donc pas! Une coiffeuse, comme moi!—
je ne serais pas embarrassée de trouver une place,

n'importe où!—mais je vous dis, que j'y suis restée
parceque cela me plaisait, en dépit d'eux, et me mo-
quant d'eux tout le temps!"

Paolo gives in; which is the man's proper province
in a war of words.

But certainly the poor nuns ought to come in for
a share of whatever commiseration may be extended to
Mademoiselle Sabine for her voluntary imprisonment
amongst them.

But let us put aside Mademoiselle Sabine, and go
back to the group gathered round Lady Laure.

It is a sweet tableau of parting friends—outside
this modern house, upon the well-kept terraced walk of
this graceful garden.

The sun is just past its meridian height,—its rays
are half screened by the tall trees to the westward,—
the flowers are contributing their brightest colours,
their most fragrant odours,—and half a score of canaries
twitter within a green wired aviary,—they bob up and
down within their narrow boundaries, with the tied
legs of all imprisoned creatures, created for the full
freedoms of life,—just as the sisters do, when recreation
time comes round,—only the voices of the canaries pour
forth their songs all unchecked and unrestrained, for
they have been born behind their bars, and their
hearts are glad, and there is no pining with them for
the liberty they have never known.

What a picture is this group of calm-featured

sisters, in their girdled soft-coloured robes, and snow-white veils.   And in their midst Lady Laure, taller by a head,—attired now in the garb of the world she is going to live in again.

She has lost none of her beauty through her sorrows and her tears.   The matchless calm, the matchless air, and the tranquil hours of the shelter she is leaving, have added to her strength, and to her stature.

Every one would embrace the gentle lady, who is bidding them farewell,—even the lay sisters claim a share in this tender adieu.

To her hands come up the young pupils with a wondering air—they do not understand the transformation ;—nothing is asked—nothing is explained within convent walls.

At her feet, clinging to her knees, are the orphans in their convent dress ;—they have been Lady Laure's especial interest,—many of those coarse linen frocks and pinafores have been put together by her own fair hands.   And there stands the gardener, the recipient of many a franc,—and at his side Féroce, the recipient of many a bone ;—there is no need to tell the secrets of the day to friends of his race—they know what's in the air ;—and Féroce, great fellow, will let them know it too,—he will not be left out—he leaps up—he will lick her face with all the expressive marks of a dog's farewell.

And further down is the mild-eyed ruler of this household, the low-voiced Lady Superior, and—" Bless you, my child ! "—says she. " We will remember you in our prayers."

And further on is a tall, calm, commanding man— his eyes, his voice, his hands have still in them that unspeakable blessing which he is there to bestow ;— and with the bestowal of this benediction, which— who can look in his face and doubt ?—comes from his very soul,—he holds out a small medal of base metal ; —if it were cut out of the heart of a ruby it would not add to its value in the eyes of the giver.

" And wear this ! " he says.

He does not add,—for my sake—but, " For the sake of our Blessed Lady ! "

But just as the whip is lifted for the plunge of the start—another travelling party drives up and appears in their midst ;—the four horses back, and caracole, and are drawn with difficulty to one side,—and the little *calèche* is made room for. Two ladies descend from it, and one holds with intense precaution a covered burden ;—it is not the weight of it, that you see in her careful manner,—it is the preciousness of this burden which attracts all eyes.

These ladies are no strangers to this holy sister-hood. They are pious women,—come to make their temporary retreat from the vexations and vanities of a troublesome world,—and also to get out of the way of the troublesome possibilities of an exposure to the blasts of the mistral, which has presented itself, quite out of season, in the less sheltered places of the coast.

Though nothing is to be asked, or to be explained within,—yet curiosity as to things coming from without, is a quite legitimate indulgence in the religious life,—and our good sisters do not fail to indulge in it. One after another they attempt to relieve the younger lady of the precious burden she is carrying with something more than politeness.

"Ah, mesdames! how good you are!" cries the mild-eyed Superior. "You have brought us again your beautiful flowers for our altar!"

"Mais non," says an aged sister, whose hairs would call down your veneration, if such hairs were visible.

—"Mais non, ma mère," cries she, with the freedom of superior years to superior rank.

"C'est bien le calice d'or, pour la chapelle, que madame nous a promis!"

It is a costly promise,—and at its reminder, a disturbed look crosses the face of the elder lady. With inconsiderate haste she catches the burden out of her daughter's hands,—and depriving it rapidly of its covering she displays—a sick parrot! chained to its perch, hanging down its green head half denuded of its feathers,—blinking its white eyelids,—and presenting a most deplorable spectacle of bird invalidism.

"Vous voyez, mes amis!"—cries the lady, with a helpless look of appeal. "Que faire! c'est elle,"— nodding at her daughter with something of disgust. "C'est elle qui l'a voulu!"

The mild-eyed Superior gives an expressive smile ; —the aged sister clasps her hands for the fun of it ;— and, with the cue given, the inferior ranks begin to laugh merrily—and even loudly.

It is an admirable tableau, could it be fixed with the pencil—and an admirable sample of the mild jests, that these mild-eyed, mild-thoughted communities, are permitted to make merry about.

As for Lady Laure,—this little comedy came altogether opportunely.

It arrived at the very moment when she was near to breaking down again,—and sent her away from her safe retreat amidst a shower of smiles, instead of tears.

One face alone wore no smile amongst this crowd who were bidding her God-speed,—it was the face of the Abbate Faa di Bruno. In truth, his lips were made for all things else, but the smiles of mirth.

He smiled in pity—in kindness—even in condemnation ;—but the smiles of unburdened souls, or of spirits that could be sad and glad by turns, were not the signs of his grave rejoicings.

INTERLUDE.

'Tis night! the tempest howls, the torrent roars.
Ope, pious monk, your still monastic doors.
Here let me rest till summoned from my cell
To prayer and penance by the matin bell.
Give me,—'tis all you can, and all I crave—
Your rule, a sackcloth garment, and a grave.
Death I forestall a little ere I die,
And like the hopes I leave—a ruin lie.

From the French.

THE thick snows are falling fast,—not with the soft fall of low-born winter skies, but with the dreadful strength of the white land of the tourmente and the avalanche.

Whose reckless foot is this which mounts in the declining day, to the ice realm of the Alpine king?

. What intrepid traveller is this, who has dared to face the blinding storm,—who climbs the last ledge of slippery rock, and stands safe in life and limb before the gate of the Grey Fathers.

He rings the rusty bell with a firm hand.

'Tis rusty with disuse, as well as with age and rough weather. But, if some rare chance awakes its hollow clang—it echoes from height to height with so wild an alarm that it scares the chamois from its hiding-place—and sends the affrighted eagles circling round in unwonted disturbance.

To-night it is muffled with the falling snow— muffled like a peal for the dead.

The lay brother who throws back the unwilling doors—heavy and mailed, to keep out, not men, but storms—starts at the tall black figure which comes between him and the white wall behind it.

A majestic figure, and a majestic voice that claims an audience of the Prior himself.

This late traveller has not long to wait,—nor is he received as such chance visitors may expect to be.

Along the uneven courts, and up the rough and narrow steps that lead to the Prior's own cell, the lay brother shows the way.

The door is low;—the traveller must lower his high head almost to his knees to enter in.

It is an act of abasement,—a daily act.

"Good for the soul,"—said the pious anchorite, who raised this solid mass upon the foundation of his fragile hut.

"Father," says the man who has now performed this act for the first time,—who hopes that it will be an act that he will repeat each day, with his daily orisons, until he come to die——

—" Father," says this man,—" I bring a life for
a life—a soul for a soul.   No man can do more."

Long, and very long, does the lamp burn in the
Prior's cell this night ;—and when the first rays of
the morning dawn—this lamp is burning still.

Night is still hovering over the plains, but for this
high world, the sun has risen ; but not as the setting,
is the dawning :—the tourmente has stayed its fury ;—
there is only the stealthy avalanche to fear.   Cloudless
is the lower earth, cloudless is the upper sky.

The giant snowpeak rears its great head, dyed rosy
red—each lesser summit gleams with the kindling
touch of the glorious orb, as it shows its golden face,
across the sea of mountain-tops,—with the white
mantle everywhere.   Out of the dark cells and cloisters
of this dark building, two figures step forth into the
full blaze of this gorgeous scene.   Their sight is dazed
with the sudden glory,—but the eyes of one are, by long
habit, seasoned to this ever-recurring splendour of the
opening day ;—eyes, clear and bright as are the eagle's,
which at this moment is winging its bold flight into
the midst of these fiery rays.

A venerable head !—white with age and penance,
in height and noble carriage, not yielding to the
majestic form of the man who stands beside him, with
his face hid in the folds of his long garment.

A holy man, from a land up in the far North. Maybe for this cause he has chosen this region of snow and ice, to live in—and to die in.

"Brother," says he, "let this thought—this night, pass away out of your mind like the thin vapour up yonder, which has this moment gathered, and which, ere we cease to speak, will have dissolved again before our eyes. Take your life back to its appointed service of our dear Lord. The harvest is still for the reaper. Go in hope,—and go in peace."

CHAPTER X.

THE SPHINX.

"As in caverns of the earth,
  Nature, at the jewel's birth,
  Paints it with a stedfast hue
  That pervades its being through,—
  Lady, such my love to you!
  So your image is combined
  With all thoughts that haunt the mind;
  So pervades and fills my heart,
  That the twain can never part.

"As the jewel's native hue,
    Which doth every part pervade;—
    Time can never dull nor fade,
  Never change nor stain anew :—
  Lady, such my love to you!
  So your image Time nor Fate
  From my heart can separate.

"And though force the jewel split,
  Still as every shattered bit
  Keeps unchanged its early hue,—
  Lady, such my love to you!
  And although my heart may break,
  It can ne'er your love forsake.
  Nor another image take."

                                H.

To place no limit to her trust in the friends that claimed her confidence, was the most supreme gift of Lady Laure's supremely gifted heart;—and this virtue of hers seemed in her case to beget a corresponding candour and integrity.

She could say she had had three sincere friends. How few can do as much!

As for her friend Arthur's sincerity, that indeed was a thing never to be doubted. He was not a man to protest much in words, but his deeds spoke for him. But these deeds were too little on his own side. Candid as was his character, he never showed himself as he was.

All his life he had been playing the cold part of the silent lover,—and all his life he had been making to his heart the most fervid protestations,—and all his life Lady Laure had been the object of them. In poetry, and in sober prose, and when the moon shone—and by the garish light of day—it was always the same vow. Love for ever! Love for ever!

But—melancholy fatality!—when the moment came that he spoke out as he never spoke before,—with a bold avowal of this personal feeling, and before witnesses,—joined to it, came the oath to put it far from him. With one hand he bared his love,—with the other he flung it away. He declared it lived,—only to swear that its very existence should henceforth be for ever utterly ignored.

Does any one suppose that it was in his power—

that it could be in any man's power—to keep such an oath? It is open to him to retire again into his pale abstraction of the silent lover. But—to put his love far from him!—as well require of the living entity to divide the heart from the brain.

Yet by Lady Laure he was readily credited, and with a full belief.

She did not enter into the depths of his love. Her experience of the love of men had not been such as to invest it with any very vigorous vitality. She did not weigh the gravity of the stake he had been throwing for, all his life. She did not fathom, that when he had spoken thus, it was in the fervour of an imperious desire, a desire, which he realized as his first duty in life, to remove all obstacles that could stand in the way of his rescuing her from a near and paramount danger,—a danger which to his mind was the greatest that could menace or befall her. And moreover, she had none of these fears for herself; she did not perceive the full force of his cry—To the rescue!

The cry when the enemy at all costs must be routed, —when all considerations save the battle to be won, vanish from a man's mind.

Lady Laure's sadly serene blue eyes see nothing of all this,—they meet his in the fullest confidence that for all time, this personal feeling was to be looked upon as an extinct volcano.

If indeed in her recollection this volcano had ever been in visible action, even her confiding soul might not have been so trustful.

But as for these silent lovers—these smothered fires—what in the nature of things can they look for, —except that we should tread upon them, if needs be, as if they were nothing but the dead ashes of a buried past?

But not only this,—everything else that was on the surface, helped Lady Laure's woman's confidence in these impossible disclaimers.

What was there to suggest a tender passion, either felt or inspired, in Aboyne's own *personnel?*—it is hard to find another word to express the altogether of a man's appearance;—what was there in that ungainly figure, which overpowered you with its proportions;— what was there in that face and those features, those sandy locks, which would look unkempt, whatever their luckless owner could do to the contrary;—what had the luckless owner of all this in common with the erotic god?

Even the eyes would look nothing but benevolent, do what he could.

There might have been a lurking blessing in the midst of this curse of ugliness—if he had known how to handle it aright.

It gave him the *entrée* without opposition,—it disarmed fear;—but the man was not made for wiles.

He was a simple creature, and was in all things as God made him, and left him.

For Lady Laure herself, these unrestrained relations were full of a blessed balm. To sit thus face to face with a friend, who has sworn to be her friend and nothing more,—who has sworn to be her friend for life,—whom she knows to be the soul of honour, truth, and justice,—whose heart she believes is the temple of all the virtues,—what greater balm than this could she have found at this crisis to mitigate the trial of her lonely lot? She wished that all things but the volcano should be between them as in the old days—days which dated back to the earliest of her life.

"Arthur," says she, "why say 'Lady Laure'? If I am not Laure to you, to whom else can I be Laure? Who else in all the world have I left to me but you?"

They travel slowly. There is indeed no need to hurry. He will have her delay here or there—or whereever there is aught that he knows can distract or divert her mind—or help to bring it back to its old channels.

He has always some ready excuse to offer. "A few days hence," says he, "will be better to arrive there;" and "to go round by that way, we shall find better accommodation."

As for himself, his volcano was never before so near to an eruption in its smothered existence.

But he kept it down,—shut his eyes, and enjoyed with all his soul this brief present hour.

It was a wonderful hour for him. There had never been any hour like to it in all his life ;—and a voice, that by fits and starts tolled like a miserable knell in his ears—said that for him there would never be any hour like it again.

But he would give it no hearing ; he cast it behind him, as if it had been the Evil One himself;—in fact, he treated it very much as he had proposed to treat his personal feeling.

Thus he shut both eyes and ears, and drank off all his life's joy at a draught.

But it was not for many days that he ventured to bring out his fan. With really shut eyes, he had spent many a moment of these days picturing its effect and reception. He was one of those men to whom women— his ideal at least—were of the nature of their great sister of the desert.

They were a wonder and an enigma to him.

It was not with Lorraine's scornful cry, " I know nothing about them," that Arthur Aboyne approached the other half of human-kind.

It was rather in the spirit in which men, imbued with the passion of a past age, approach the shrines which, by the sacrifice of their lives, they have at last unearthed.

They stand in this unfamiliar presence,—wondering by what process they have brought themselves so far.

They stand—still unsatisfied,—trembling, fearing, hoping. They would know all the mysteries of this shrine,—they would behold all its beauty,—they would read all its meaning; and yet they hold back—they fear to find it nothing but the baseless fabric of a dream.

It is the sensitive tribute of the scholar, not of the man whose wits are keener than his tastes.

And such a poor sensitive scholar is Arthur Aboyne,—rich in many sympathies—in much learning; poor in the wisdom of this world—poor in grasping the substantial things which make up the resisting power of life,—a man whose fate from first to last is to exist upon shadows.

It was in the most alive of all the dead cities,—whose antique vitality could not be destroyed, even by the presence of a hated and an alien rule,—a city with so many voices of the past, that even the time-stained marble of its statues rings to the touch with a living note, pitched in the very key of human utterance:—in a garden of cypresses, which reckoned their ages by centuries,—whose boast it was to spring nearest to the sun's eye, and yet to debar mother earth of none of the golden rays:——it was in this garden of cypresses and sunshine that Aboyne brought out his fan.

Lady Laure took it with a kind smile of thanks.
She spread out upon her black dress its snowy glories
of silk and seed pearl, and feathery fringe and ivory ;
and then she looked at him and then at it.

"We are hasting away, Arthur," says she, "from
the land where a fan is something more than the mere
toy of a woman's toilette, and a feeling in my mind
tells me that with such toys I have quite done—done
with altogether."

Then she adds, "When we get back, I shall go to
my dear home. I shall not find it lonely—not more
lonely than it was for me in my childhood—and before
—all these—last things came upon me. You know I
was so often alone—so often alone there ;—and the
dear faces that I shall miss there,—I miss everywhere
—here as much as there !——

At Bellarmine I shall spend the second year of
my mourning. You will come and see me there—you
will live there all you please,—but I shall see no one
else—no one of society, I mean,—and after that "—
says she, turning her blue eyes upon him—"after
that, I shall do what I am called upon to do,—I shall
mix in the world again,—I shall try and make the
name I bear honoured ;—I am the last of my race,—I
will not hide their name under a bushel, Arthur !——

But I shall never quit this black dress,—and I
shall never more put on gold or jewels—or wear all
those pretty things which are for the entirely happy ! "

Such was the programme of her life to be,—laid down by Lady Laure.

It was evoked—nay, it sprang life-size out of her heart, with the sight of Aboyne's snowy gift for beauty.

He had thought long,—before he could fix his mind to it. How many times did he walk up and down under the porticoes of that little jewel of a city —before he could decide which of her jewelled wares was most worthy of the lady of his thoughts! "It must be something to speak to her a little of the world,—but not too much ; " and then he fell to moralizing about the witchery which resides in women and in fans.

To the last he is a little doubtful,—it is his nature to distrust himself;—but lately, as he had watched day by day the fair face which was to look from behind this fan, he was in better heart about his choice.

It came to him with a hope that these serene eyes, which saw all things with a quiet pleasure—that this composure, this gentle expansion, this power of resolution, betokened a returning cheer.

He was fain to think that already the grey veil of time was falling between Lady Laure and those vacant chairs. But he was mistaken.

He was like the man who, finding a treasure—a calm and gleamy moonstone—looks into its tearful petrifaction, and expects to see the sparkling water of the diamond.

No; Aboyne did not read his enigma aright,—and as the years went on, he read it never the more clearly.

He gave her all his patient life, and she gave him all her quiet smiles,—and these smiles bewildered him. Then, one day, the patience took fire,—and the volcano burst forth.

And it burnt as it had never burnt before. It could not be helped,—but it was the end of it all.

For him thereafter, there were neither enigmas nor smiles,—nothing but dust and ashes, covering up an unquenchable volcano,—nothing but a life to be lived —and a death to be found—somewhere!

CHAPTER XI.

THE " TIMON."

> " And I have sworn this sainted sod
>   Shall ne'er by woman's foot be trod."

WE have not quite done with solitudes.

There is Lorraine with his solitude of the *Timon*. A breezy sort of solitude to be sure, with its—

> " Sweep through the deep,
>   While the stormy winds do blow ; "

but still a solitude—an absolute solitude as far as woman-kind are concerned.

Yes ; Lorraine still sticks to the *Timon*, and as the years go on his adherence is only the firmer.

That good craft has fulfilled all her engagements ; she has neither sprung a leak, nor carried away her masts ; and, what her master prizes yet more highly ; her deck is still guiltless of a woman's foot !

Time indeed flies fast on ship-board. The husband or the lover, who at the end of his three years' commission holds his wife or his betrothed to his heart, cries with a strange wonder, " And can it be three whole years, my love, since we so met ? "

"Three centuries, say," is the quick reply. "Ah! what a long weary time it has been!"

Not that Lorraine—like England's gallant admiral —roamed the seas, with never a sight of her white cliffs to glad his eyes. With the *Timon* to fall back upon, he ventured into every port,—and there were few harbours at home or abroad, which didn't know full well its green pennant, and its master's gay and hearty presence.

Yes; Lorraine is grown gay and hearty. The fickle waves to him have proved the model of all fidelity,—the trustiest of all true friends. They have swept the cobwebs from his brain,—they have opened the floodgates of his heart,—they have intensified his downrightness,—and steadied his instability;—they have made the man of him at last.

It is the softest summer sunrise that ever dawned upon the earth.

The *Timon,* her white sails set, filled by an invisible wind, is borne along upon sparkling waters to a city all of gold—gold at least to the eye, as it sleeps in these amber and ruby lights.

A glittering mass of gilded domes and.polished balls. A wilderness of fantastic roofs and cupolas, too intricate, too bright almost, to rest the eye upon.

It is a relief to look beyond, to the waving branches which sweep down to the waves;—and to the softer confusion of tapering minarets, fairy palaces, and the pointing cypresses of the gloomy gardens of death.

But soon the sleep of the city is over, and with a great heave it awakes,—and as the *Timon* takes the course towards the shore through a forest of masts, and the motliest crowd of vessels ever gathered together— the noise grows distracting.

Every narrow deck has its own hubbub,—big guns are firing, bands are playing,—national anthems to one hand, national volleys to another,—alongside boatmen are clamouring, *commissionaires* are vociferating,—and then at a moment, as the great disc comes fully up, the shrill sweet cry of the muezzin pierces the air,—it follows, and it follows from mosque to mosque,—it comes nearer and nearer,—and then it dies away as it came,—and this is beautiful—it is like an angel's presence in a pandemonium.

On the shore itself the turmoil is indescribable;— men of all skins, all tongues, all costumes,—all crushing, all calling,—all getting out of the way of yelping dogs, of titanic porters with burdens too big for elephants, and of the gay Arabas with tinkling bells, —oxen and black slaves, and eyes full of depth and languor peeping between the silken hangings.

It has all been described before, and of late fast and furiously—*ad nauseam*—and possibly this may prove the last straw that breaks the camel's back.

But it is done with here, for the master of the *Timon* does not set foot on the shore.

He is something of an epicurean still,—he has heard of mean aspects and ill-paved lanes, of evil sights and sounds and smells, of white slaves and black slave-dealers,—of fair women in market pens, and of merry children playing with human skulls.

And he says he will let well alone,—the external enchantments are enough for him, he will not risk the internal disenchantments.

No doubt, indeed he remarks, the stuffs are fine, and fine are the mosques,—and the women's eyes are finer still ; but these things he is not curious in.

There is something more to be said for the tobacco, which is also fine ; but that can be had for the sending,—so he sets no foot within the city of the Golden Horn ;—he will investigate neither its charms nor its chains, neither its beauty nor its bestiality. But he is in no hurry to leave these waters.

When the stores that can be got—or that cannot be got—are laid in, or done without,—the *Timon* sails out again, and rides quietly at anchor on these still waves.

The gilded caiques glide here and there, the warm wind fans the air ;—the sparkling sunshine is over all —save the precious head-piece of the master of the

Timon ;—an awning shelters this, and beneath it this happy individual passes, it must be owned, many idle hours;—stretched at full length he takes his *Kef,*—it is the glorified siesta of this Eastern land. Eyes half closed,—soul and body in complete repose,—the senses just awake enough to keep the rosewater rising and falling in the amber-mouthed *narghilé.*

Every day, however, the cutter is dispatched into port.

Lorraine sends punctually for his letters, though his correspondents are few.

That, in fact, does not seem to make much difference in the diurnal desire of people to fathom the contents of the post-bag.

One day, however, a letter does arrive—its date is New York, and its weight double—due, it appears, to the solidity of the sheet.

Lorraine does not open it—he turns it over and over;—that too is a natural action. Though the solution is in the hand, there is an indescribable pleasure in guessing at an unknown writing—provided the letter doesn't look like a bill or a begging one—and provided you have faith in your destiny, and have not too many irons in the fire.

It was in the midst of his *Kef* that it was de-

livered, and Lorraine took it altogether in the spirit
of *Kef*;—he placed it beside him, and mused drowsily
upon it,—till of a sudden he started up with a most
dangerous energy;—such conduct in the midst of *Kef*
would lead a native to look at once for your last
hour.

But Lorraine, made of much sterner stuff, survived
it, and seizing the letter cries out—" From Harry English, I'll swear ! "

He did not swear falsely;—this double-weighted
letter was from faithful Harry English.

Lorraine tears it open,—his hand positively trembles
with eagerness and suspense—trembles like a girl's.

The handwriting is round and clear; he has only
to read it off.

" HONOURED SIR,
" We——

" We ! " says Lorraine—" We ! " And he looks
about him ;—then he does the reasonable thing of
going on with the letter.

—" We have said so often that we must write and
tell you all about it."

" By all that's good," cries Lorraine. " They !——
but let's go on."

Then he takes up Harry's tale, and does not break
it short again till he gets to the end of it.

" You see, sir, it's all come out, as you said, and we
are got married. It was a long time before I found

her, though, and when I did, the poor thing was as pale
and weak as a willow. It's a long story sir, and I can't
trouble you with it all. Of course, they took all her
money from her before she'd landed a month,—and
she was forced to go into service, first one place and
another and she got the fever—and got into the
hospital, and that's where I found her. I am ashamed
to say that all the time I kept well and hearty; and
I grew quite stout, sir, to what I was,—and the air here,
which is sharp and hot by turns, browned me, so that
my poor girl didn't know me;—and she thought I was
some charitable gentleman come to take pity on her,
and help her to go back to her mother. Well sir, I
won't go over it all, but when my poor dear knew who
it was, and that I'd been searching up and down for
her, for these two years, she put her poor thin arms
about my neck, and cried as if her dear heart would
break. But with me to take care of her, sir, she soon
got well; and now, sir, she's handsomer than ever—
although I say it, as I suppose I shouldn't do, considering that we're one now. We often talk of coming
back again to the old country, but I don't know how
it is, Myrtilla seems to find this place the best now,
now I'm with her, to make all right. And we get on
very well in the money way. You know, sir, I can turn
my hand to most things, and if you can do that, this
is a good place to be in. We've got one boy, sir, and
we hope you won't take it amiss that we've given him
your name, sir. He's a fine little fellow, sir, and very

like his dear mother. We often have a letter from dear mother;—and now she says she shall die happy.

"Please accept, sir, of Myrtilla's duty and mine.

"Your humble servants,

"HARRY AND MYRTILLA ENGLISH.

"To Sir Claude Lorraine, Baronet."

"Bravo! Harry, bravo!" cries Lorraine. "What a brick that fellow is!"

After thus relieving his excited feelings, Lorraine stops for a few minutes, to consider,—but not in the spirit of *Kef* by any means. Then he brings his hand down on the deck with such a hit, that it makes the *narghilé* jump again.

"Things are coming round again," he cries, —"coming round all right. This is step number one."

This was exactly what it was—

Step Number One.

CHAPTER XII.

WAR, HORRID WAR.

Though still earth's guest, of quitting meditate,
When on some morning either soon or late,
The bare lone soul must all it hold forsake,
And its far flight to the veiled region take.

ANOTHER year,—and another.

In what other words can the history of a life be written? So they hurry on to swell the sum of the past,—units in that mighty sum, smaller than the smallest grain of the sands of the ocean,—yet all numbered and taken account of.

This year, which has just been wiped out of Lorraine's life, has been a unit in every sense of the word, —calm, easy, uneventful,—entirely to his mind.

He has still stuck to the *Timon*, his trusty friend ;— if not of all his friends the trustiest, to him the most serviceable.

Since that morning when Lorraine roused up so rashly from his *Kef* under the white awning of her whiter deck,—she—'tis the only she for him—has borne him safely and surely into many a strange port.

To-day she sails once more into the waters of the Golden Horn—sails straight up to the centre bridge, and straight into the midst of the steamers of all nations, and ships of war of all nations too.

There is the same Babel of voices, the same hubbub and crash;—but no, not the same;—to-day it must be multiplied indefinitely. Thereunto must be added also all sorts of extraneous matter, not indigenous to the confusion, and a most pronounced military element.

Solemn human boulders,—if these men do not know how to fight, they look as if they know how to die.

The cutter of the *Timon* is lowered, and the master of the *Timon* goes over the side, and taking his seat in the cutter, points to the crowded shore.

He is going to land, then, upon this soil so blest and so cursed. Has he got over his prejudices? By no means,—but he bears private despatches to the English ambassador, to be delivered by his own hand.

The *Timon* has outsailed herself in the effort to reach this shore by this day.

The Straits take time, and naturally the *Timon* could not make a short course across the Continent, —but she is here to her day.

"It's all right," as Lorraine cries out, when he sights the two capes.

He lands in the midst of it all. Some formalities must be gone through at the custom-house;—they are mere formalities in his case, and soon over,—the crowd make way for him as if he were a hammal with a grand pianoforte on his back. Their obsequiousness is not altogether due to his imposing person,—it is rather to that which covers it,—a British soldier's uniform !—just now the object of the warmest worship in these parts. It was not without a sigh for the dear old pea-jacket, the sou'wester, the loose collar, and all the flowing comfort of his nautical manner of dress, that he has arrayed himself to-day in all this new splendour—splendour of gold, and splendour of silver, and splendour of yellow and blue.

Nor was it the old splendour of days gone by,—he has changed his colours, though not his flag.   He has grown lazier than ever ;—his mimic quarter-deck life— twelve feet up and down the *Timon's* narrow plank—has added to his weight and to his inertiæ ;—for his part, he'd rather ride than walk, so he says, into a battle, or down a lane,—it is an all-sufficient motive to Lorraine ; —and therefore to-day he stands in the most dashing garb of the most dashing horse regiment of the British force.

His despatches delivered, he turns again on his steps by the way he came,—by mosques and palaces, by graveyards and broken ways, by fountains and gutters, till he is in his cutter again, and steering full for the *Timon*.

There he will await the bugle call,—not yet awhile to sound, for it is smiling spring still,—smiling indeed,—all nature smiles, as if no frown could ever come again upon earth or sky.

But as for Lorraine,—he will have no smiles but those of these laughing waters;—and he may well be content,—for they sparkle and dance enough to gladden and satisfy any heart.

For the rest,—he will have nothing to do with it,— neither embassy balls nor embassy dinners,—nor the sweet waters, with their human flower-beds.

The taste of it all will be bitter to him,—at least, he believes so.

The *Timon* drops anchor again;—she takes her moorings between a huge barrack-like building and a sort of fairy tower, which more remotely rises out of the blue water, white as snow.

It is a lighthouse, and bears a classic name.

The master of the *Timon* reverts to his *Kef* under the awning. But it is not for long,—the hours of *Kef* are numbered.

Soon arrives the Division, and this parts these two friends, and converts the master of the *Timon* into a cavalry captain.

So long as the life of the man whose fate and fortunes we may have resolved to record, keeps to its private career, whether it abounds in shocks or in repose, in bitter or in sweet, we can follow it in

peace;—but when his chances take him into the
mêlée of nations, when to speak of him we must meddle
with history, it is a very different affair.

But your fictitious lives, some one will say,—you
are surely at liberty to take these where you like best.

No,—it is not so.

Even in these fictitious lives, there is an involuntary agency,—a fate that drives along,—if not this
fictitious body,—your living brain.

All we can do now is to hurry, in the brief limits
of a page, through the grim years of that grim war,
in which Lorraine took his part, as he was sure to
take it—when in good earnest,—honestly and bravely,
with all the rest;——from that day when the very
first shot fired came from his own brigade;——past
that hour, when, with it, he bore his charmed life in
and out of that dreadful ride,—the ride for life and
death, and for the honour of the British soldier, who
goes where he is sent,—if it be to the cannon's mouth;
——down to that still more dreadful winter,—cold and
wet and weary, which his stamina carried him through
when others sickened and died;——and onward still,
to the moment when, a volunteer for the Redan, he
stands in the pitchy darkness, made light by the fires
of bursting cannon and blazing barriers,—in the midst
of shot and shell, and of a fiendish struggle—hand
to hand, bayonet to bayonet,—men dashing out each
other's brains,—a hellish uproar of yells and rage,
and anguish and frantic curses!

Thus closed in, he sees before him a man fall,—
and straight upon him set a dozen bayonets. The
man is not wounded, he has but stumbled, so he
thinks;—therefore he lives,—and he has some one to
live for—is Lorraine's answering thought.

And then he does what has often been done
before. He leaps into the middle of the bayonets;
two men he knocks over with his spring,—he fells
the third with his sword, the fourth lifts his arm for
a stab,—but the cannon blaze is gone, and under the
cover of the kind darkness, Lorraine drags his man
away.

The little *Timon* has not been idle. Lorraine has
the money, if he can only know what to do with it,
and now it came handy. He sets up a little hospital
just for one or two, on board the little craft; he ap-
points his surgeon, and has his infirmary, everything
in proper rule;—and not one, and not two lives only,
have looked up again to hope and health under her
green pennant.

This is what has been going on all through the
dreary winter in the little *Timon;*—and now, as a
natural step, he sends under safe charge the man he
has rescued from the bayonets to the same sanatarium,
not as whole as he had hoped,—one fatal thrust had
struck before his saving leap.

But for himself, Lorraine must stay by his work.

The city has fallen,—but the work is not over;—and not until the dreary winter is past and gone,—not until the earth and sky smile again in the sweet days of spring,—not till then does Lorraine step on board the *Timon*.

But many are the inquiries he makes after the rescued life. It does not make progress;—the surgeon shakes his head.

" And yet," says he, " I do all I can."

" Of course you do," replies Lorraine. " It's an odd thing you can't find out who he is."

" He's so reserved," says the surgeon.

The moment at last comes for Lorraine to find this matter out for himself. Free again !

Ah ! words could never express the sense of infinite relief which pervades him, mind and body, as he takes his seat in the cutter, and once more steps on to the deck of the little *Timon*.

" The gentleman would like to see you, sir," says the mate, " when it's convenient."

" I'll be down directly," answers Lorraine. " But tell him to keep himself quiet;—there must be no excitement."

Lorraine is quoting from the surgeon, but it's a word for himself as well as for the patient.

His dread of a scene is as great as ever;—it is natural that a man should be a little warm when thanking another for his life, but he wishes it were over.

"The gentleman seems sinking," says the mate again. " There's a great change in him."

Lorraine does not wait for the third summons;—he hurries down to the cabin.

Propped up by pillows, and white as the sheet that covers him, lies the wounded man,—a gaunt, haggard, lifeless face, worn with loss of blood and pain; only the eyes seem still to be alive,—large, kind, brotherly eyes—yet with a sorrow in them,—eyes that would befit a Christian martyr on the verge of his willing martyrdom.

Lorraine is struck with pity,—all sorts of piteous sights have met his eyes during these grim years;— but this, the last example of their horror, touches him as keenly as if it had been the first. And this man is more to him than another,—he seems to belong to him,—did he not save his life?—yes, at the risk of his own;—and now he could have wept to see that this risk has been all in vain.

Something he murmurs, he knows not what;—he goes up to the couch,—what of a sudden can the lips of a stranger find to say to a dying man?

With an effort the large thin hand is held out to him, and the pale lips move, but the voice will not come.

"I had hoped to have found you better," says Lorraine,—and he presses his hand.

The pale lips move again. "Lorraine, Claude Lorraine,—thank God, I have lived—till now to thank you—to thank you."

Lorraine stands bewildered. Who is this that calls him Claude Lorraine ? Something speaks to him in this voice—in those eyes ;—what is it ?—whose are those eyes ?—what voice is this, that seems to come to him from the very back of his life ?

"Who—who are you ?" he says. · He represses with violence the agitation which has seized upon him ;—he is in terror lest a word from him should hasten by a moment the end—so near—so very near.

Then he looks again into the face,—it might have been young six months ago ; but—now—what a wreck it all was !

"Who are you ?" Again he says the word.

But the white lids have dropt over those strangely kind eyes,—and the man has fainted.

Now the surgeon is summoned.

"Better retire, Sir Claude, for to-night ; this has been too much for him."

"Is he—is he——?" Lorraine cannot utter that word which in every language has the ring of a knell even to its sound.

"No," said the surgeon, quietly ; "he is not dead,— he will not die yet ; leave him to me."

Lorraine's first sentence the following day was an inquiry for the wounded man below.

"He has slept better than he has done for many weeks,—and this morning he has revived a good deal."

"He will recover," cries Lorraine.

The surgeon shakes his head. "That," says he, "is impossible."

In an hour Lorraine is again by the sick couch.

The surgeon is right, the man has much revived, —he can converse with a few words now. As he lies there his eyes rest upon Lorraine.

"You do not know me," says he; "and yet I should have known you, Lorraine."

"Have known—me!" stammers Lorraine.

"Yes; you are little changed to my eyes."

Again the voice rings in his ears, like a distant bell, and the eyes chain him.

"You will tell me, then;" but he breaks off,—a sudden light is thrown in.

"Good God!" he cries;—"it is Aboyne."

Yes; it was Arthur Aboyne.

This man, who stood second in his antagonisms,— for whom he has felt a sort of nameless scorn all his life,—lies before him there, on his bed of death.—He stands beside him, hand in hand; he has risked his own life to save his,—his eyes are wet with pity for him.

It is a very sad step—very sad;—but still it is— Step Number Two.

Soon the *Timon* weighs anchor and is off, sailing away for ever from the Golden Horn.

The wind is up, and she skims the transparent waters like a bird.

To-day they are peopled more thickly than ever. Frigates of all nations, and troopships, and steamers, and a huge British three-decker, not yet relegated into the lumber of the past;—and antique feluccas of classic build;—and caiques light as air, shooting here and there, like watery meteors;—and behind, in the silvery mist of the morning, gleams the golden city.

The white mosques and variegated minarets, the scarlet kiosks and gilded palaces, and the deep verdure of the thick massed foliage, are all dissolving away into the distance like a rainbow of many colours,—or like a fantastic dream, with a wild scare in the middle of it.

Nothing of all this life and motion remains with the *Timon;*—she has outstripped the shipping, and now for all company she has only the albatross and the sea-gull, that come and go in hovering flights, and flit around her bows and her masts, like the disembodied spirits of the dead hecatombs left behind.

With the next morning, they are again in the midst of the bright things of the land. They are cruising through the islands,—green spots of loveliness scattered upon the blue sea.

Skiffs and boats again shoot here and everywhere,

—and there is again the stir of human life. There is still the turban and the heavy gait, still the signs of the alien conqueror ;—but there is also the scarlet cap and the tunic, and the unconquerable air, the grace and the noble brows of a people, that tyranny cannot debase.

To the surprise of the surgeon,—and to the great content of Lorraine and of the little crew, the poor patient whose condition engrossed all their thoughts, began perceptibly to revive.

The face seemed to draw together again, and to look less forlornly hollow,—so it seemed to Lorraine's eyes, but it might have been that his eyes had become accustomed to the grievous sight.

"It is this sea voyage," said the surgeon; "it can do wonders,—at least for a time."

So also can the sympathizing cheer of a light and friendly heart.

Every day Lorraine said, "You look better," and "You look better."

And again, when Aboyne would shake his head sadly, Lorraine would say, "That's not fair now, Arthur"—they had got to Claude and Arthur again —"What's the use of it all, if you won't help us a little?"

"I have nothing to live for," sighs Aboyne.

And Lorraine will reply. "Try and live,—try and live;—there's plenty for all of us to live for."

And so by degrees the blessed infection worked,—and Aboyne caught some of the cheer of his friend. And then the doctor gave leave, and the awning was again hoisted over the deck, and under it lay a pallid face, and a long and broken body,—very different indeed to the robust and lazy being who took his *Kef* beneath it a year ago,—all the difference indeed between Prince Fortune and Prince Fatal !

They were just through the Straits. The skies were perfect,—so too was the sea,—so too were the soft airs that stirred between the two.

It was all as near to the mortal picture of the Heavenly Land as ever by mortal painted. That Heavenly Land—which is not of this world,—a land which has nothing to do with earthly things,—and which a blue sea and a blue sky may stand for, as well as anything else.

Aboyne, in a sitting position, is reclining under the awning against the pillows,—and is curiously watching Lorraine's performances with his *narghilé*. The doctor is in the stern-sheet, fishing for the small fry that dart about just under the glassy wave,—an occupation which, though not blessed with much success, is still a God-send for his empty hands.

"It's pleasant, I suppose," says Aboyne, his eyes still on the smoking machine.

"Pleasant enough," replies Lorraine ; "but you

require certain things about you,—quiet, for instance,
and sunshine, and complete repose. When we get into
the Bay, I know I shall give it up in disgust."

" It looks pleasant," repeats Aboyne, still with his
eyes on the *narghilé*.

" I tell you what it is,—you shall try it one of these
days, Arthur ; you breathe a wonderful deal stronger
than you did,—and it's not fatiguing ;—trust its head
man for that ! Over there," nodding eastward, "they
don't like trouble." Then he added, " I had an idea
myself that it might be good for you. I asked the
doctor about it yesterday, but the worst of him is he's
such a negative fellow."

" He knows more about it probably," replies
Aboyne, languidly.

" About what ? " says Lorraine, sharply. Nothing
gave him now a quicker sensation, sometimes of dis-
pleasure, sometimes of alarm, than if any one threw a
doubt upon Aboyne's better condition.

" About my breathing," is the answer.

" Now, why will you try to make everything in
vain ? " cries Lorraine.

" Why then in vain ? " says Aboyne.

" You know," says Lorraine, with some reproach
in his eyes, " how much depends now upon your
spirits."

" Am I low-spirited, Claude ? I think not."—" All
things considered," he could have added.

" And if ever anything was not in vain,—it is "—

Aboyne's voice falters—"it is your heroic action, and your generous friendship for me."

"Nonsense," says Lorraine;—"let's talk of something else."

"No, Claude, it is good to think of these things. You have not only saved my life, you have taught me to desire to keep it. There is little chance of this," says he, smiling sadly; "but still, all you have done will not have been in vain,—and you have given me the happiest hours of my life."

Aboyne holds out his hand, and Lorraine clasps it in both of his.

"Such hours," says Aboyne, "are worth more than learning or ambition."

Then he pauses,—the large brotherly eyes fall full on Lorraine's.

"Or woman's love," he sighs.

"Or woman's love!" cries Lorraine, with all his heart in his voice.

"Yes, yes, worth a million times more,—a million times more!"

The brotherly eyes still meet his,—but the thoughts beneath them are with one fair face:—and then all the soul goes back to Lorraine, and the eyes speak as plainly as eyes ever spoke, and they say—

"You, too, have suffered!"

The bad spirits are at work again with their vile equivoque,—and Lorraine must again stand by and see himself taken for whiter than he is;—for he reads those eyes! Unless he were blind or dipped in Lethe, how could he fail to read them?

It is too much for him, this false part,—and with Aboyne, too.

"Arthur," he says, "you are mistaken,—the fault was not on her side."

A flush of crimson mounts to the thin cheek, and as quickly fades, leaving face and lips white as death; and one by one the large drops of a great agony come out upon the pallid brow, and stand like summer dew upon the flower. But Lorraine sees nothing of it;—his effort to do justice to the absent has plunged him also into discomposure. All this has been so long dead and buried, that even the ghost of it is too substantial a remembrance. He leans forward, and rests his elbows on his knees, and his head on his hands. But a quicker eye than his is on the patient.

It is the doctor, his fishing over, who comes brusquely up.

"You here?" he says, "when you ought to have been below an hour ago. And what's this, too? What have you been about? How's this?" And he lays his finger lightly upon Aboyne's moist brow.

Some word he tries to utter in reply.

"Don't speak," says the doctor. "You've been talking too much already. Come, Sir Claude, we must get our patient to bed at once."

Lorraine starts up from his attitude.

"What a fool I was," he says, "to let you stay talking up here!"

But Aboyne is almost beyond hearing. The doctor
has called his two aids, the mate and a sailor, and they
are moving the patient out of harm's way as fast as is
allowable to him.

But the harm is done.

That justice to the absent—has taken from him the
only ray of comfort that his heart has fed on for many
a year ——.

Lorraine's discomposure did not entirely depart,
nor was he easy in his mind about Aboyne.

He sent one message after another. At last the
doctor, who had his own shrewd way of managing
things, said, " Tell Sir Claude, that some sound sleep
to-night will, I hope, put things where they were."

There was immense relief in the message; and
Lorraine let the ghosts of the past go quickly back to
their graves, and forgot his discomposure in this release from the anxious fear of the moment.

" But," thinks he, " we'll not run any more of these
rigs ! It comes of that fellow's confounded fishing.
Why didn't he come and see about Arthur before ? "

That night, when all but the watch slept, Lorraine
walked the deck. He walked it in all ease,—he had long
gone back to the pea-jacket and sou'wester, to the loose
tie and flowing collar. Up and down he takes his solitary tread ;—and yet he is not alone. There is an inex-

pressible companionship in the measured plunge of
the vessel's bows into the gurgling waves,—as she
heaves forward before the wind. This lullaby of the
sea has no music in it,—it has only a voice—a voice
that says, like the solemn pendulum of time, " Go
forward! go forward!"

The stars are overhead, in the countless millions of
these marvellous skies. The Milky Way in clear out-
line, divides the glittering throng. There is no moon,
—but these myriad fires light up the dusky wave.

There is the spell of a triumphant solitude, as
the lonely vessel bounds over the lonely sea, under
the silent stars. Lorraine feels it in his own way.

"There is no life like it," thinks he. "No life
like it—never alone—and always alone,—that's the
beauty of it!"

And then, with a quick transition, his thoughts go
to Aboyne.

"God grant that poor fellow may be better to-morrow! I shall miss him, whenever we part. He's the
best companion to my taste I've had for many a long
day—strange, that it should take half a lifetime to get
to the bottom of the good that's in a man!"

But Lorraine, with just the present before him, has
forgotten that with half the world between them, and
a whole world of prejudices,—he had not been in a
position to get to the bottom of the good that was
in Arthur Aboyne.

Lorraine got becalmed with his midnight walk, and it was full eight o'clock before he came on deck next day. He was met by the doctor. His face was a little grave.

"He is gone," said he. "I did not call you, for he was not conscious."

"Dead! Don't say he's dead!" cries Lorraine.

"Yes," says the doctor,—"internal bleeding. I knew it must come,—and he talked too much yesterday."

The doctor's voice was without pathos. He was a thoroughly skilful man, and thoroughly devoted;—as he said, "he had done all he could;"—but he had seen too many "last moments" in the course of the years gone by to be affected by this one. He would have been as glad as the rest if his patient could have recovered,—but he knew he couldn't,—and now he's proved to be right.

It is an hour before the sun goes down. The ship is brought to in the golden path. All hands are called on deck, and then they wrap him in the British flag, and they lower the green pennant half-mast high, and with reverent hands and uncovered heads, and some eyes wet with tears, they commit his body to the deep.

I HEARD A VOICE FROM HEAVEN, SAYING UNTO ME —WRITE—FROM HENCEFORTH BLESSED ARE THE DEAD WHICH DIE IN THE LORD : EVEN SO SAITH THE SPIRIT :—FOR THEY REST FROM THEIR LABOURS.

All through the night the sublime Hymn of Hope sounds in Lorraine's ears. The doctor read the Service, and he read it well.

"He suffered much," said the doctor, as next day they paced the deck together. "I took to him from the first,—he had the most benevolent eyes—and voice too;—the fellows aft would do anything for him."

"Ah!" cries Lorraine. "He'll be blest,—no fear of that! And his troubles are over!" And then he gives a great sigh.

"And yet," he cries again, "I would have given the world to save him,—but it was all in vain!"

So his mind confuses this release from mortal trouble, and this vanity of human effort.

That night they were in the Bay. There was no need to take the bearings—the Storm-House of the Ocean spoke for itself.

The wind grew to a hurricane and the sea ran mountains high, and the *Timon* looked like a fly in the depths of each yawning gulf. If it was not a matter of life and death, it was at least a critical moment. The masts were reefed bare—with only the jib set—closed ports, and hatches tightly screwed down, and for safety they must steer wide of their course.

The *Timon* is trimmed to an inch,—she dashes along before the wind as steady as a top.

The darkness is pitchy, and the decks are swimming, and in the midst of it all, a man is washed overboard. It was his shipmate who felt him go. They could see and hear the man, as little as they could help him!

But you must be in it before you can know what it is,—before you can understand these perils of the deep, which the witty Dorset improvised his dashing song upon, in the days when come what may—all the world was merry!

These perils of the deep!—they remain for us amongst the things that eye cannot picture—nor pen describe. Amongst those things that suffer no change —the same yesterday, to-day, and to-morrow. The grandest type of the Divinity. No wonder that the sailor is of all men most moved to belief.

It is astonishing the sort of breathless pause which succeeds to a howling storm,—whether it comes of contrast, or whether this calm is more absolute than any other, it is hard to say.

To use a ship-board phrase, no one had turned in during this night of jeopardy ;—and when the morning dawned, they looked with a touch of passing awe at each other's washed-out figures and faces.

Such a night!—and it was icy cold, too, after the late soft heats; it was enough to blanch the ruddiest cheek for the hour.

This grey morning light reveals to them that they have had companions in the storm,—companions who have met with a more disastrous fate. As they sail on, they come upon much ship-gear,—spars and broken wood, and floating barrels,—a rich harvest of flotsam and jetsam if the coast and the reapers were near.

There is not a wave to be seen. The sea has swallowed up its prey, and now, like an angry child, its strength exhausted, there remains only the sob and the swell of the heaving bosom.

"We begin to find our legs again," says the doctor, taking a trial stride past Lorraine.

Lorraine says, "Yes;" but he speaks with an inattentive eye, looking vaguely about him. He finds his legs better than some other things which he misses this morning;—and the experience of the last night has not been exactly of the best sort to set him right again. He was still in the maze of it all, too. ·

He had often come in for bad weather, and he had called it a jolly storm, and he had laughed with pleasure as as he stood buffeted about by it. There is no saying, if it had not surprised him down at zero, but that he might have laughed last night,—at the mad weather at least.

But still, it was a new experience,—his jolly storms were but the tempest in the duck-pond to the convulsive throes which the *Timon* that night had lived through. The little *Timon*;—where was the little craft that had behaved better than she had done?

And yet the ties were giving way;—there was a screw loose somewhere.

"It's all for the best," says the doctor again. "What should we have done with that poor fellow last night?"

"Ah! What should we have done?" echoes Lorraine.

Then he betakes himself to the little poop. He leans upon his elbows over the gunwale. It is a favourite post,—a familiar attitude.

Many an hour has he so stood, revelling in this wide ocean. Yesterday it was the dear home of his choice, —to-day it is only a great watery grave.

"When the sea shall give up her dead!" he murmurs;—"when the sea shall give up her dead!"

CHAPTER XIII.

HIS NAME IS UP!—HE MAY GO TO BED.

What your ancestry,—God wot!
This, I say, concerns you not;
Nor your merits, for it's plain
Meritorious acts are vain
Fame and fortune to attain.
Withers' words of wisdom were—
" I nor lack, nor have, nor care!"
—You with much security
May say likewise—if you see,
Somewhere in your history,
In the now or in the then,
Fortune's bird—the snow-white hen!

" ENGLAND,—with all thy faults, I love thee still!"

It is a terribly hackneyed phrase;—and yet, to argue from generalities, we may fairly assume that the more hackneyed the sentiment, the more truth is at the bottom of it. And it is a fact past denying that there is something in the white cliffs, which stirs an Englishman's heart! Something in them which makes him— for the time—glad to see them again.

He may behold behind them toil and trouble;— but this has no effect on the nearer prospect.

He may have come from lands which his soul loves

—which his heart yearns after. He may have left behind in them the inspiration of his powers, and, what is more, the life-springs of his existence—the very breath of his nostrils;—but still, his heart bounds to the white cliffs of his native land. It smiles to his eyes as he draws near to its shores. Let it be in the first glow of a June dawn,—it will intensify the feeling. Before him rises the old castle, with its green frowns;—below it, the old city, shut in between the old cliffs,—their heads in the open sky, their feet in the grey, green sea, their sides radiant with their own white hue, and the young beauty of the day.

Nor is this grey, green sea a mean element in the home picture,—with its spirited contrast to the softer colourings of the lands, and seas he has left behind him.

In the case of Lorraine however, he did not take his first step on British soil with such harmonious surroundings;—it was in the fog and draggle, the smoke and heavy traffic of the London Docks; for, having arrived in his own ship, he had to take her to her own place,—at least he preferred doing so.

Let us suppose a fortnight to have passed over since his arrival, and the *Timon* to be safely moored alongside one of the smaller wharves down the river.

It has been a busy week for Lorraine. He still makes the *Timon* his head-quarters, but his days have been spent, for the most part, on shore,—monopolized

by a variety of things,—pleasant things, all of them.
In the great city he has found much to hear, much
to say, and many things to begin again.   And, when
did Fortune ever fail him?   He has arrived in the
nick of time, to receive in person his allotted honour,
—and to come in, with the rest of the picked band of
war heroes, for his decoration, at the gracious hands
of his Sovereign,—and for the admiring eyes and
tongues of a smiling and sympathizing mass of
observers.

It was an august and moving ceremonial—somewhat sad, and somewhat solemn—and Lorraine forgot,
in the mixed feelings it called up, to find the con-
spicuous part he had to play in it, either a tax or a
bore!   Like the great actors on the mimic stage, he
was too much carried away by his part, to have any
thought for the crowd of lookers-on.   Yet, if he had
seen a little further into this emotional gathering,
there was a pair of glistening blue eyes on the out-
skirts, which followed his every movement, and which,
had they met his, might have stirred a tender chord
in his heart;—might have,—or might not have;—who
can say?

These things gone through, Lorraine proceeds to
another personal matter,—purely personal this time;
namely, the winding-up of his actual relations with the
little *Timon*.   It is a little hard, perhaps, to have to
say it, but it cannot be denied that Lorraine sets himself to this business without regret, and contemplates

his final step off her white decks, without so much as
a sigh.

If a third party could have spoken in the confidence of both, the remark would probably have been
that the *Timon's* part in Lorraine's life was pretty well
played out. She had been to him all that her consol-
ing sex can be, of cheer and charm and companionship, but the tie was loosened. Happily for him, as
he takes such ties,—with this " she "—the tie *could* be
loosened ;—whether he was likely to fall in with that
other hitherto impossible she, who would take her
place,—this Lorraine was not likely to trouble himself
about one way or another.

He had never been in the habit of this sort of
forecasting. In fact, he was not given to forecasting of
any sort ;—he would tell you that in his opinion it was
an idle waste of time,—and probably he would add, that
in his experience, you never know what's coming next.

Generalities—yes ;—they are quite Lorraine's affair.
It is his way of conversing,—not, perhaps, the most
brilliant, but it does not provoke contradiction.

Lorraine had lost no time in getting to England.

After that day of doom and dread in mid-Atlantic,
when the awful veil was lifted for him, just so far as to
bewilder with its darkness and its doubts,—he felt no
inclination to linger on his course.

Once again the winds grew soft, and the suns were
bright,—and the moon's light silvered the water ; but

not once did he think as in days gone by of lay-
ing to, and lowering the little cutter, and enjoying
the delights of a row upon this shoreless sea;—the
inspiration was past!

But what Lorraine did do—was to make straight
for his port, and not to slacken sail till he found himself off the Thames.

Fine weather, in fact, they had to the end;—but it
had not been a cheerful cruise.

It was that vacant couch which depressed him;—he
could never get away from it.

All through the day it stared at him with such a
blank appeal;—but in the half lights, or by the
flickerings of the swinging lamp, he could fancy its
empty space shaped itself into a semblance of its
patient burden.

Then once more he seemed to see the haggard face,
and the gaunt and broken form,—and the benevolent
eyes, looking at him as through a glass darkly.

But it is hard upon the little *Timon*, that, because
of this vacant couch, and because of that wreck-strewn
ocean, and because of the inscrutable wheels upon
which men's lives do move, Lorraine should turn his
back upon her to-day without regret.

Yet—if she can avail herself of it there remains
to her a quiet consolation.

And she is so near to a thing of life, that for the
moment we may well suppose her a little further

endowed;—and with this consolation in view, let us
believe that she sees her master depart, and her green
pennant hauled down, with the modest conviction that
she has done her work,—and done it well—done it so
well, in her master's interests, that there is nothing left
for her to do now, but to pass him on to the next stage
of his career, for which she has so well prepared him.

On Lorraine's side, there may be some inconstancy
—it is human nature—but he has done with the
capricious cynicisms, born of an isolated lot. He takes
no longer for his motto the burden of that jolly miller's
song, who lived by the river Dee.

But still, he is Claude Lorraine, himself and no
other,—and if he could bring himself to speak upon
the sorest sorrow of his soul, he would still tell you
that in all the world he has had but one friend—one
friend, whose image, ever at his heart's recall, lies
embalmed in the starlit vaults of memory.

He is still Claude Lorraine, a man incapable of
cherishing an unappeased regret for a woman,—however
brave and true and tender,—however gentle and innocent and devoted. But there is nothing left in him
of that inert disgust at the existing state of things,
which once ruled his words and ways.

He steps forward to-day with a reasonable content,
—and with things tangible about him,—if not with a
goal, at least with something right and left to turn to.

He is no longer the lay figure in his profession.
That lazy devil!—which he had startled Lady Laure's

innocent ears with, in the old days of his enchantments, has been finally exorcised, and by the very means he put up his prayer for.

And the old isolation, which was half boast, half bugbear,—that, also, is modified.

Far from him, indeed, has it been to form new friendships,—but there are friends and friends, and there are those that he neither can nor will shut out of his life.

There are the comrades with whom he has shared the perils and privations of this grim war, which, God be praised, with its muddle and mire, its blood and misery, and its scant glory, is over at last! and there is the poor brotherly eyed ghost of the little *Timon*, whose life he saved in vain!—who had pointed to a few brief hours and called them "happiest"!—who had sighed out, "Not in vain," with the ring in his voice of the near death-note echoing back to him—"in vain, in vain!"

Yes—in vain for this poor ghost, but not for Lorraine, to him there remains a most undoubted "Not in vain." Henceforth he will go up and down in the company of an heroic deed,—upon his breast he will bear the cross For Valour!—and on its bar will be read the day in which he saved this poor ghost's life—in vain—and not in vain!

The fulness of years is not to the strongest,—the fulness of success is not to the worthiest;—The survival of the fittest is the only law we know of. Alas! poor ghost! Quartâ Lunâ nati.

CHAPTER XIV.

"HÉLAS! JE DEVRAIS LE HAÏR!"

'Tis hate, alas! I ought to feel.
Such sorrow has he caused my heart,
So full of tears and wounding smart,
So desolate, so slow to heal.
'Tis hate, alas! I ought to feel.

In the kiss claimed on his return,
When all his soul came back to me,
My own,—which fain would hidden be,
Saw how his love began to burn
In the kiss claimed at his return.

He says we ne'er shall part again!
What fear is mingled with delight!
Fate wills our hearts should reunite,—
To struggle further is in vain,
He says we ne'er shall part again!

After the French.

IT was in this exhilarating company—*i.e.* of the afore-said heroic deed—that Lorraine stept off the *Timon*,—walking briskly away, or rather getting quickly into the cab that was waiting for him by a kerbstone off the Docks,—with the words, " Drive fast."

It was latish in the evening ;—as yet he had not domiciled himself on shore.

He was bound for a West End reception—a Minis-
terial reception,—not a thing for him just now con-
veniently to refuse, even if he wished to do so ;—but he
had no desire to avoid it.   On the contrary, he looked
forward to some pleasant meetings this evening with
old acquaintances.

It is a sufficiently dreary drive east to west.   The
evening is rainy and dark, and the wind westerly, and
the showers drive due east,—so the drop glasses of the
hansom must be let down, which does not add to the
cheerfulness of the situation.

The street lamps flicker and fade as the cab threads
in and out—one street after another, in an endless sort
of way, wheels and windows shaking and rattling with
a correspondingly ceaseless monotony.

Lorraine starts with plenty in his mind,—and he
turns it over and over ;—but gradually the roll and the
din and the flicker are too much for him, and he falls
into a sleep-and-awake sort of lethargy, till he is
aroused, still only semi-conscious, in the middle of a
regular hullabaloo.

The rain falls thicker than ever, and he peers
through the dripping glasses into the stark look-out,
with the vaguest ideas as to where he is, where he is
going, where he is come from,—and with the remnants
of the feeling still upon him, that as he was moving
so he would move on for ever.

Let any one try it, and see, if on a night like this,
a two hours' solitary course through London streets, in

a London cab, does not land him at his destination in much the same condition.

But Lorraine has not reached his destination.

The street police are bawling to his cabby to fall into line, and this individual, having an ardent mind in a drenched body, is howling back imprecations at the strong hand of this pull-up.

There are still twenty vehicles and more ahead,—plenty of time for Lorraine to wake up and be himself again,—and for cabby to meditate upon the vanity of slanging the police.

But everything comes to an end. Lorraine hears the report of the whip on the roof,—feels the swing of cabby, still indignant, as he leaps to the ground,—and himself prepares, with complete self-possession, so to descend as to save his head, and to keep his epaulettes clear of the muddy wheels.

The house he has drawn up before has nothing of the imposing in it. It stands alone, inside a palisading a little withdrawn from the great thoroughfare in which it is placed;—a long frontage, of which the first floor windows, neither large nor lofty, lighted to-night from end to end, just reveal, between the festooned curtains, the crowded figures moving to and fro.

In those days small groups of gay flower-pots were to be seen in the alcoves of the palisading flanking the gates;—this bright and simple adornment gave a refined home-i-ness to the exterior,—which was a good conductor to the cultivated and graceful ease that ruled the interior.

Lorraine follows up the announcement of his name. And many turn to look, as he bears his broad shoulders and his badge—For Valour, on his breast, into the room.

There is no lack of stars and orders in this august assembly,—the rooms are positively dazzling with them; —but this badge For Valour, a simple thing to look at, to-night is the mark to attract all eyes.

Amongst other things, it is, in the way of honourable decorations, the latest, and the newest.

Lorraine has not far to make his way through the groups about the doorway, to find the hostess of these *salons.*

Salons they are!—or rather, a *salon* it is, in the most cultivated sense of that word,—the nearest approach in the English metropolis to its old Paris prototypes.

She meets him with something more than the gracious welcome accorded to all arriving guests. He is one of the expected lions of the evening;—but much more than this, is the ancient kinship between their families which had made this house familiar to him during his one brief London season.

"Ah, Sir Claude!" says she; "you have come

back to us at last! How many years is it since you disappeared?"

And she gives him a soft questioning look.

"It is hard to count up time," says he, with an inclination of his head, and a smile to the lady,—"when there is nothing before us to mark its flight!"

The lady laughs, and says, "You have been away to some purpose, I see! You have learnt to pay us compliments at last!"

It has been a brilliant evening,—but the rooms are now beginning to thin; the most notable personages have taken their departure, and Lorraine is thinking of following their example,—when his attention is caught by the statuesque figure of a woman some yards to the right of him,—standing alone,—dressed in flowing folds of sable gauze,—with gently folded arms, and a grave sweet face,—a face of regal beauty,—a matchless serenity on the brow,—and with her large quiet eyes fixed full upon him.

He returns the look with the same abstracted air, —it might be, in very fact, two statues gazing at each other,—so absent is all expression of admiration, curiosity, or any human feeling.

Then,—she always, with the same sweet tranquil gravity, moves away into a small boudoir behind her.

Lorraine moves too,—and comes right against a

man, who had joined one of the knots of talkers, of which Lorraine had played the part chiefly of listener, earlier in the evening.

It is a sufficient excuse, however, for addressing this stranger.

"Can you tell me," says he, "who is that distinguished-looking woman standing alone in that little room there?"—and he points to the boudoir.

Something begins to stir within him, and prompts the sudden question.

"Don't you know her?" says the man. "She is the most remarkable woman here this evening,—and she has the most remarkable fortune, too.—She is Lady Laure Lucie, a most singular person;—you must have heard of her!—extremely handsome, as you see,—with enormous wealth, too, and yet never appears except in these dark weeds:—Queen of the Night! Queen of the Night! But not with her stars!—not a jewel—not an ornament!—only on one finger an old seal ring. A countess, too, in her own right,—and yet doesn't assume the title;—and yet she's not mad,—not moody enough for that!—but odd—remarkably odd!——

As to the men,—they're afraid, they say, to go near her,—at least with any request of more importance than, 'How do you do?' She is one of those unapproachably calm women, who inspire us men with the most terror."

And the man, who is about up to Lorraine's elbow, looks up at him with a chuckle at his joke.

But here he is checked, in the midst of his flow of communication,—for the ears it is intended for, seem sealed.

Half turned from him, motionless and without speech, Lorraine stands as if in a trance, his eyes fastened upon the boudoir and its occupant.

" You find it remarkable," says the man.

But his words still excite no reply.

He hunches up his shoulders and his eyebrows,— draws down the corners of his mouth, and turns on his heel.

Crossing his path he sees a *vieux militaire* of his acquaintance, and accosts him with—

" You'll hardly believe it, general, but I've suddenly developed something of the mesmerist in me. It's extremely alarming.   I wouldn't if I knew it touch that sort of thing with my little finger,—nor with a pair of tongs either ! "

" Very incredible indeed ! " says the general, beginning to move off,—but a finger is laid on his arm.

" Stop, let me put you in possession of the facts.   I was talking just now to a tall man in uniform.   I don't know his face or his name.   I was chatting away to him the merest gossip, when all of a sudden I perceived that he was not attending to me,—he didn't seem to hear a word I said,—his eyes were fixed—his tongue tied—body and arms stiff "—and the gossip-monger dropped his own with a jerk—" in fact, rigid, sir, rigid! I positively trembled with apprehension at the obscure cause of this phenomenon."

The general smiles.

"Ah! I see you are incredulous. However, you can judge for yourself. Just cast your eyes behind me —I won't look that way again myself—close by a small plaster cast of a fawn and Bacchus."

The general's eyes follow the directions.

"Your bird is flown," says he.

"Oh, you're not looking in the right direction— the man's big enough to be seen,—he's six feet, if he is an inch."

"Look for yourself," rejoins the general. "You may venture—you'll mesmerize nothing but Bacchus and his fawn."

"But stop," says the general quickly, with a laugh. "I suspect I see your mesmeric subject, with his back to us, talking to Lady Laure Lucie."

"Bless me! So it is! What can he have to say to her? Five minutes ago he didn't know her name! Clearly he had never set eyes on her before!"

"Well," says the general, "they seem to have plenty to say to each other now! I have been observing them all the time you have been talking, and I think I saw him take her hand in his."

The gossip is struck dumb; his eyes devour the scene.

"I never saw Lady Laure Lucie vouchsafe so long a *tête-à-tête* to any man before," remarks the general, himself a little taken by surprise.

But the gossip-monger is not to be foiled; he awakes with a start to the true situation.

"I'll tell you what it is," says he, lowering his voice. "It's her fortune he's after;—I was telling him how tremendous it was."

"That won't do!" says the general. "Now I see who it is;—it's Sir Claude Lorraine,—he's got fortune enough for himself and for you and me too!"

The gossip-monger shakes his head.

"Sir Claude Lorraine," repeats he. "Well, I tell you, it's her fortune he's after! those Irishmen are such fortune-hunters!"

The gossip-monger has made up for his former reticence in the matter of looking behind him;—he has never taken his eyes off the couple.

"He's a remarkably fine-looking fellow," says he. "I shouldn't be surprised if he were to be the right man at last!"

"He's quite one of the best men we've turned out in the war, I can tell you," says the general;—"brave as a lion. He's got the new cross; and if there were any other orders of merit for saving life, he deserves them,—for the beds he set up on board his yacht pulled many a poor fellow through who must have died otherwise."

"Ah," says the gossip-monger, "do you know where he is to be found? I must leave my card on him to-morrow."

"Do you think it will be safe?" says the general,

with a quizzical smile, as he makes a determined advance to the doorway.

The gossip laughs too.

"I'm quite satisfied about my part in the affair," says he; "and I think I see his as well."

"Well, that's satisfactory," says the general, "at any rate;" and finally escapes from his button-holder.

"He's a funny fellow, that!" says the general to himself;—then he looks towards the boudoir.

"No chance of getting a word from Lorraine to-night," thinks he. "Upon my word, I am inclined to think the funny fellow was not so far out."

As for the funny fellow, as far as he could give it notoriety, the next character in which Lorraine appeared in public was, The Irish Fortune-hunter!

But what is going on in the boudoir?

What is Lorraine saying and doing with this broken thread of his life taken up thus unawares, and put into his hands with such abruptness?

It might have been made a matter of very even betting what he would do, and what he would not do. And if Fate had not lain in wait for him with such a combination of fortuitous influences, he might as likely as not have got no further than his favourite

dictum,—You never know what's going to happen
next!

But this involuntary homage he has so uncon-
consciously given,—this unwitting gossip's very per-
tinent chatter,—the novelty of these brilliant social
surroundings,—the proud allurement of this imposing
central figure,—and the proud certainty, that if he
pleases he can go in and win,—he, the only man out
of all men;—all this moves him quite away from the
region of his prosaic generalities,—and invests this
tardy meeting with something that is altogether beyond
the simply unlooked-for.

It lays him under a spell,—and this spell, which
has at first transfixed him, and then has sent him with
three strides up to Lady Laure, works with no diminished effect when he stands in the full lustre of
this most queenly presence.

He is taken by storm,—it becomes a crisis,—and it
leads him at once to one of his sudden resolves.

But he is no longer mute,—and with this happy
restoration of his powers of speech, he becomes himself
again;—himself, with the addition of his sudden
resolve——this remains.

Lorraine's resolves once made partake of the un-
alterable. They have nothing to do with that sort of
impulse which blinds the eyes, and bewilders the
head,—that unreasoning rashness, followed after in
haste, to be repented of at leisure. To conduct such

as this, with all his prudence, Lorraine is personally
no stranger;—he will tell you, that once upon a time
this kind of impetuous folly upset his own common
sense,—to his subsequent and great bewailing.

No,—Lorraine's sudden resolves are of quite a
different nature to this:—they are few and far between;—but when they do come, they have the force
of an inspiration for him;—they have the value of
deliberate action,—they are based upon an instinctive
conviction of the best thing to be done for himself
in particular, and generally for every one else.

No doubt, there was something headlong in the
mastering feelings which impelled him into the
boudoir, but now that he is come to himself, his
spoken expression of these feelings is quiet enough;
and he breaks the silence of years with—

"Laure, I am here—here at last."

For a moment—for one moment she hesitates;—
and then, both white hands go out to meet him.

It is the very movement, the very action of her
old despair,—the despairing action that he so remorse-
lessly put aside.

But now, there is neither despair nor remorseless-
ness,—nor indeed, remorse.

He takes the two white hands, and says, "I am
come, for my wife at last, Laure."

CHAPTER XV.

MARRIED.

In the joyous noontide day,
    Who can night remember?
Or amid the flowers of May,
    Think of drear December?
So no cloud of sorrow past
Can the present joy o'ercast.

Love springs not, nor shares of earth
    Its mortality.
'Tis a seed of heavenly birth,
    And can never die.
Where it mingles, naught can sever;
Lighted once, it burns for ever.

Angry storms perchance may rend,
    Winter's frosts may chill it;
Here their baneful powers end,—
    They can never kill it.
Genial breezes, sun and rain,
Soon shall make it bloom again!

                                        H.

YES ;—they are married,—married, if not settled ;—
and Lorraine sits down beside Lady Laure, and watches
her white fingers weaving always their pretty mysteries
of silk and lace just with the old half-lazy stretch.

Only, to-day there is the expression of absolute
content in every word and look and movement.

He has at last found the end he had to consider.

And he starts anew, with the good little *Timon's* fair and fond and faithful successor, for life's final goal;—with always his easy conscience in the past,—and with abundance of faith in the future.

"Con miglior corso e con migliore stella," and thus he arrives at Step Number Three.

As for the gossip-monger—the general's "funny fellow," he ran about for a week after the event—which, indeed, created a singular sensation in society—with a "I told you so!"—"I told you so!"

But the old general's verdict was—

"I have myself not the smallest doubt in the world, but that it was an old engagement."

After all—with poor Mr. Mildew left out,—and one or two necessary differences,—it was astonishing how much the life of this married pair resembled the life of that pair of lovers eight years before.

With Lorraine there never could be sentiment at any time of his life,—or under any circumstances;—and he sits now, talking his generalities and his common sense, just as he did then;—just as if they had never been parted;—he rallies her, and laughs

at her,—and amuses himself with all the grand
emotions—as he called them one day—left out as
much as ever.

One emotion excepted.

Alike for one and for the other, there exists one
profound dolor—one unhealed scar,—one deathless
regret,—one undying memory,—one name breathed
not again till now.

"Grief itself is mortal,"—but to die well, it must
have vent;—and this sore sorrow of their souls has
prevailed in silence.

But now it can speak out;—and now the scar that
has seared both their hearts may begin to heal.

Now once more, as of old, they sit together
through the long summer morning, with Lucie's name
upon their lips,—with Lucie's winning ways, with
Lucie's wayward worshipped self before them.

He stands the very same,—the radiant hair and
eyes,—the tender transports,—the paroxysms of pain,
—the inexpressible gentleness,—all are there.

His image—

> "Like a star;
> Beacons from the abode where the eternal are."

All through these years—from then till now—
the rending pathos, the intense appeal of his latest
words,—fired with the prophetic passion of a soul

strung with the supreme agonies of life and death and suffering,—of fate and love and sacrifice,—have swept like unfathomable echoes through her heart.

All through these years,—the wail of "this poor Lucie,"—of "Claude, my brother,"—has rung with a never-ending knell through his soul.

What a boon, after these long years of voiceless echoes,—of soundless knells,—of pent-up saddest loss, —to say, heart to heart, and eyes looking into each other's troubled depths—

"His will has been strong as Fate. His wish is fulfilled;—he is our brother;—we will mourn for him together"!

And there is yet another memory,—yet another regret,—yet another name, to summon up from the past of their divided lives, and to unite them in a common sympathy. Lady Laure listens with as much pride as pity to Lorraine's unvarnished tale of the last cruise of the little *Timon*.

Pride in the *Timon's* master,—pity for the *Timon's* poor ghost.

Lady Laure will hear all about the heroic deed,— but it is the fate of the poor ghost that Lorraine has in his mind.

Again he calls him "a good fellow." And again

he says, "I would have given all the world to bring him back alive." And again he sighs. "I saved his life in vain, Laure; I saved his life in vain!"

Then a tear glistens in her eyes. And then she takes the Badge for Valour from its case, with a smile.

"And let me look at it, Claude, let me look at it," she cries.

And so, with smiles and sighs,—but without a fear or a frown, they begin their married life.

Nor let some one prone to cavilling say that they are all too old for Love's young dream.

If they had not begun to count time so early, they would not have had such a long look back now.

Reckon up their joint years as one, and you will have a good round sum; take them singly, and with the balance well to his side, and you will find that for wedded folk they are still in Life's green leaf.

As Lorraine said one day with one of his old laughs, "It was all for the best, Laure. If it had come about then, we should have been an old married couple by this time,—while now, we're nothing, but a pair of young lovers."

The sun of the dog days was beginning to make the town unendurably hot, and Lorraine's new-born patience was straining to its limits,—when he cried out one stifling morning—

"Since roasting on a slow spit is not to my mind, Laure, what do you say to our taking to-morrow that break-neck adventure, which, if I remember right, I set down myself in our programme, for this appropriate season?

What do you say? Shall this be carried out like all the rest of it,—finally, fully, and to the very letter?"

Lady Laure laughs and says, "Yes," and "yes." "And—let us . go to-morrow!" she cries. "Sabine and I don't want much preparation!"

Lady Laure was still, when back in her happy self, prone to her pretty impulses.

But Lorraine replies, "To-morrow? — whoever thought of getting off by to-morrow? Haven't I a week's affairs to get through? And there's the *Timon*. I must see about sending her round to Loughmore Bay!"

Then Lady Laure laughs—laughs as in old days, with her large blue eyes surprised and smiling.

"And how could I tell," cries she, "that you didn't mean what you said?"

But the break-neck adventure came to pass in due time, and the bridal pair set off for the high Alps,— with Sabine—the faithful Sabine—as sole suite and attendant.

"You have got that Frenchwoman still for your

maid," said Lorraine to Lady Laure. "She didn't take to me in those days. I don't know how she'll fancy me in these, for your master and hers."

"Ah!" cries Lady Laure, "Sabine is like her mistress;—she understands things better now."

"What things?" says Lorraine, with malice.

Then Lady Laure is embarrassed.

"You know what I mean, Claude,—the world and its ways!"

"The world and its ways!" says he, still with his pleasure in persiflage.

"So, I see, I represent to you and to the discriminating Sabine—the world and its ways!"

Then Lady Laure begins, with all the gravity of her sweet face, to enter into her explanation—

"She has learnt, as I have," says she, "who to accuse,—and where to excuse."

"Upon my word, Laure," cries Lorraine, "you and she have learnt to talk very wisely. We have changed places, my dear,—I am growing the Simpleton, and you the Sage. You see I share the force of both the epithets;—but don't be learning too much of the ways and the wisdom of this world you have taken to studying. It's a very corrupting world at best, I can tell you; and you were just as well off, Laure, when you understood nothing about it."

Lorraine's argumentative strains are as apt as ever to fall off into their old inconsequences!

Let us suppose the break-neck adventure well in hand,—and with neither broken necks nor shattered limbs.

Lady Laure revives her old accomplishments taught her by her Grey Squire with distinguished success. She goes up a real mountain; she sets up her stone on the top; and Lorraine cuts an L on the flag-staff for both,—and they devour their hunch of bread and bottle of milk with an exuberance of appetite and high spirits.

Lady Laure's pale serenity is put to flight.

Auburn tresses are all a-flowing,—cheeks and eyes are all aglow,—she is breathless with the proud exertion;—she is radiant in the cloudless sun and sky of this clear upper earth.

Lorraine, himself a little breathless, has still eyes for these new charms.

"Let me look at you," he cries. "Why, I don't know you! I'll tell you what it is, Laure. We'll build a châlet somewhere in these high parts. This milk-maid style becomes you a deal better than your milk-and-water one, you may believe me!"

They were immensely happy.

But pleasures purely as such, if they are to remain pleasures, must be partaken of sparingly,—and one day, when the beds were particularly hard, and the partitions between them and their neighbours particu-larly thin,—when the wine was thin too,—and the

bread was like stale seed-cake without the sweet,—
when the mutton was goat, and the chickens were
sparrows, and everything else in accordance, then
Lorraine said—

"For the present we have had enough of it;—we
will go down."

"And why?" said Lady Laure, after sundry more
ups and downs,—and when they were near unto the
direct home route—"And why shall we go round that
way, Claude?"

"Because," says Lorraine—with something between
a smile and a sigh—"because

> 'There I spent some happy hours,
> Which live in memory yet.'

That's the poetical way to put it, isn't it, Laure?" and
he turns the smile into a laugh.

"Ah! when?" cries she.

"Ah! when, indeed! Ah, woeful when!" says he,
and the smile and the sigh come back.

"Listen, Laure; can you bear to hear the truth?"

"You know I can," is her ready reply.

Lorraine half laughs again. "You've caught your
hare! Well, that's the essential point to sensible
people like you!

It was full eight years ago,"—and then he stops to consider,—and then he looks curiously at his companion.

"You've not forgotten, Laure, have you, the day I bounded away from you like a bullet off a—a—— ? You see, I can't find any simile for you, but an alligator—I might say rhinoceros, but there's not the slightest affinity to you in either of these mailed beasts,—the metaphor is too forced. I—do very well for the bullet—but as for you—— "

"Oh, never mind," says Lady Laure, laughing at his absurdities—"you are tantalizing me."

"Laure," says Lorraine, with seriousness real or affected, "you have not the gift of observation,—do you not perceive that I am making the time out, and that I can't come to the point exactly?"

"Then do come to the point," says she; "why shouldn't you?"

"Well," he answers, "I am not so clear why I don't,—whether it is because of you sitting there, or whether it is because of—— However, here it is. In that old city, which we shall reach one of these evenings, I came upon the greatest consolation of my past life;—a consolation that was all consolation,—no vexation, no distrust, and it came in the shape of a woman!"

Lady Laure has caught her hare, and holds it well in hand, and further than this, she has no fears that it will turn restive.

But still she colours up.

"Of course," she says, with an awkward pause.

"Of course!" repeats Lorraine. "But why of course?"

"Of course," says she, with a little firmness, "you would not go through all these years without something of that——" And she stops.

"Something of what?" repeats he again.

"Something of that sort of thing, Claude."

Lorraine laughs.

"Well, as to that sort of thing, to come no nearer to its particularity than you do Laure, I have had precious little of it in my life, but quite as much as I wanted——————, but now your question is answered, and you know the reason why we have, as you say, come all this way round."

If Time in our century had no other landmarks, the changeful locomotion of the age would alone be sufficient to show its strides.

But with the ancient city Lorraine is going round by, not even the modes of reaching it had suffered any change.

It is all just as it was, when he and Mufti, and the flower-pot, and their bright little mistress, and the sour old *grognon* filled the *rotonde* of the rumbling big diligence, and arrived at its gates,—pretty well a decade before.

"Laure," says Lorraine, "did you ever travel in a diligence?"

She shakes her head.

"You know," says she, "I have really travelled very little."

"Well," he rejoins, "it's not exactly the traveller's experience most to be coveted."

"Why did you ask me, then?" is the answer;— and Lady Laure rests her blue eyes upon him, with one of her old, quiet, wondering looks.

"Why?—of course, there's a why to everything, Laure;—and this why is, that if you've no objection, we'll take the *rotonde* of the diligence to ourselves to-morrow, and go on, that way to the spot of my consolation."

"How can I object?" says she. "I dare say it's very comfortable in its way."

"And I dare to say it's very uncomfortable in its way!" is his quick reply.

"What do you mean, Claude? Why do you go by it, then?"

"That's just the mystery of it, Laure, for you and for me too, I begin to think. How do you like the idea of going about the world with a husband who has a mystery in his sleeve?—— Why do we do this or that, or anything? I've often asked myself these questions, and I never could get a satisfactory reply."

To Lorraine, Lady Laure could never be more than the half-child she began by being.

But yesterday is not to-day. Yesterday her eyes would have filled with tears at his wayward remarks; to-day she sits down at his feet, takes his two hands prisoners,—looks up at him with her sweet blue eyes, and says—

"Kiss me."

"I object to tears" was the rebuff those blue eyes met with in the old times.

In these new times, the corresponding rebuff—"I object to kisses"—has yet to be given.

CHAPTER XVI.

SANS L'OUBLIER.

Without forgetting—we our love may fly,
And banish far the lover's name and speech;
From absence we may strength and hope beseech,
To 'scape the thraldom of his mastery,—
Without forgetting.

Without forgetting—streams there are that course
And carry life far off to other flowers;
I quit the fields that hueless death devours,
And wander like the stream that quits its source,—
Without forgetting.

Without forgetting—a soft voice and dear;
What ages born and dead I since have known!
Not yet untroubled could I bear its tone.
It is a voice that I have ceased to hear,—
Without forgetting.

After the French.

LORRAINE'S plan for the next day's travelling was completely carried out.

The vetturino who had brought them thus far agrees to take carriage and horses back again with him. It was not the arrangement they started with, but the omnipotent napoleon conquers all difficulties.

"It's all right," says Lorraine, coming in with the

air of a man who has achieved his object. "I've talked the fellow over, and he's off;—but we shall have to be stirring early, you know,—sharp five, Laure, sharp five!"

Sharp five found every one ready, and shivering somewhat, as they stand waiting for the word to mount, in the courtyard of the office of the diligence.

It is the small capital of the district, not placed to perfection, and the clammy chill of the early morning fills the level valley.

Lorraine walks to and fro and stamps his feet. "I wish we were off, Laure; it's cold for you!"

Sabine looks pinched and cross. She is beginning to distrust the late signs of amendment in her old aversion.

There are plenty of diligences, half a dozen or more, and all about to depart;—and there is the risk, if you act precipitately, that you may move off in the opposite direction to your baggage and your intentions.

Lorraine is too old a soldier to fall into any such trap as this, and though his patience is still not what it might be, he awaits the word of command.

With time it comes, and he and Lady Laure and Sabine—Sabina, as Lorraine, for some occult reason, insists upon calling her—take their seats in the *rotonde*, and endeavour to fill it.

It is still the twilight of the dawn.

Lorraine, with a striking repetition of a former era, proceeds to take a peaceful nap.

But with the nap the similarity abruptly ends. He opens his eyes to the sun's awakening rays, but he beholds no Mufti,—no flower-pot,—no bright little mistress,—no *vieux grognon.*

What he does see is,—Lady Laure and Sabine, with their veils down, asleep in their respective angles.

It was Lorraine's first attempt at a sentimental journey, and it was his last.

Shut yourself up for a twelve hours' spell in the *rotonde* of a diligence, with your wife and her lady's-maid,—with an atrocious smell of tobacco,—with your head, do what you will, encountering the roof at every roll and jerk of the ill-built vehicle,—with no stretch for your legs, and nothing to speak of, to sit upon,—and you will appreciate Lorraine's specific against sentimental journeys.

" Here at last ! " cries Lorraine. " Whatever form of thanksgiving, Laure, you like to put up, I'll join in it."

" Oh ! there's nothing to complain of ! " says she.

" Well, all I've got to say," says he, " the next time you're bent upon another edition of it, you'll have to leave me out of your expedition."

Lady Laure is on the point of saying, " Why, it was you, Claude, who were bent upon it ! "

But Lady Laure has grown wise and wary,—as her husband said.

"You shall never do anything of the kind if you don't like," says she, with a happy laugh.

And so they roll through the gates, and into the highways of the old city.

Lorraine might have quitted it yesterday. The streets are just as dull, the lake is just as fair, the gloomy old minster stands where it did,—and so does the quaint old inn.

"It looks small," says Lady Laure, trying to take a general view of it as they draw up.

Lorraine is thinking just the same thing. It is the first perceptible difference that occurs to him, in the external look of things here.

But he rejects the admission with—"What in the world would you have, Laure? Meurice's or Claridge's! Women raise their expectations so wildly!"

"Not quite that," says she, laughing. "But for a town it certainly looks a little place." And so it did.

Lady Laure was correct, and Lorraine was not candid.

When he last looked up at those windows, what a breadth and depth there was about them!

How is their light departed! and how are their proportions dwarfed and diminished!

So the world goes round,—with flourish and fade,—with fancy and fact,—with old spells and new;—and

Lorraine makes the best of it,—chooses their rooms—
first floor rooms, rooms farthest from his old sky par-
lour—farthest from a well-remembered door ;—leads
Lady Laure thither by the well-known flight of stairs :
—sets Sabine to work to provide her with tea and all
available solaces, and turns off himself to take his cigar
and to refresh his associations.

"I was a fool," thinks he, "for coming! I've let it
rest so long,—what was the use of bringing it all up
to my mind, just at this moment, too ? "

Lady Laure also addressed one word to herself—

"What an odd place this seems for Claude to have
met any one ! I wonder who it was ? "

The journey was of twelve hours. These antique
lumber-waggons were for the most part punctual, and
having started, at sharp five A.M. they arrive almost
to the moment, at sharp five P.M.

The sun has not set. There is the old glory upon
the lake,—"l'ombre du bois" is to a shadow the
same,—and the pavilion—it too stands unchanged—the
frescoed nymphs are untouched by time,—the water
laps the steps with its old tranquillizing monotony.
And Lorraine himself,—he stands in the midst of all
these stationary memorials,—to look at him, as stationary as any of them,—the very incarnation of fair and
fortunate manhood. But there is a flaw for this brief

moment in the smooth inner man,—the old scar is half inclined to bleed,—an old sigh bursts out again,—and he is driven to cry aloud, " All gone! all gone!"

The lake is still gorgeous. There are the little towns, set in the golden lights. There are the black-bearded mountains. The scene is lovely as ever, but it gives him more pain than pleasure,—and he turns away—turns up the serpentine path beneath the trees, so often trod, so well remembered,—and going in by the glass doors he is taking his way to his wife, —but, what does he see at the other end of the covered corridor—the corridor along which he and a pair of velvety eyes have so often watched for an unwieldy body with a halting step to appear,—or better far, to disappear?

What is that curly wig and cropped coat and tufted tail that he catches sight of?

" Mufti, Mufti, poor fellow!" cries Lorraine.

And with a spring, a white poodle is crouching at his feet.

The world may laugh, but as for Lorraine, he could have wept for joy!

Yes; it is Mufti,—if not that Mufti—this Mufti; —always Mufti.

Waking him out of his sudden transport comes the rumble of grating wheels on the tiled floor advancing

behind him,—and starting out of the way, he falls
into the midst of a yet dearer surprise.

Can he believe his senses? Is that, indeed, the
vieux grognon muffled up in a wheeled chair?—and are
those the sweet velvety eyes that he catches sight of
in the distance? Yes, it is all a fact. The eluding
shadows of the *rotonde*,—of the pavilion,—and of his
unforgetting heart, take shape and substance, and stand
before him.

"Ah! I see you again; I see you again!" And
this is Valérie's greeting.

What does he say? It were hard to set down.

He holds her hands, and he looks into her velvety
eyes and he says, soft and low—

"Valérie! Valérie!"

.

Eight years! Well, if not eight, seven. Who
could credit it? Who, to look into that bright,
speaking face, into those velvety eyes;—who could
credit that all these years stretch out between this
moment, and those long-past happy hours?

These years, that have transformed Lady Laure
from a shrinking girl into a stately woman,—have left
Valérie de Keradec the same sweet woman still,—to
the very quivering smile of the soft, red lips,—to the
very sparkle that comes through the dark fringed
lashes.

"Valérie, Valérie! My brave and tender Valérie!"

He has no other words. He has no other thought,—no other memory.

From his dilating eyes—eyes that tell the strong joy that swells the heart beneath them—all things vanish but one form, one memory,—all things fade and fall away: wedded ties and wedding tours and wedded life. He sees only Valérie de Keradec. He remembers only the happy hours they passed together.

But the Present has at hand a sure and swift memento,—and spinning along with her flapper, to keep him alive to the things that concern him, comes Mademoiselle Sabine.

Kind Heaven! Is this,—are these tumultuous joys, nothing but the dead Past? And does the living Present exist alongside of that pert lady's-maid?

Even so.

Sabine's round eyes have again the old malice in them.

This journey!—this caprice! Lorraine is again *lourd*, again "vrai Anglais!"

"Miladi," says she—when Sabine is on her high horse, she invariably reverts to her mother tongue—"Miladi ne pourra jamais supporter la fatigue de pareils voyages! Monsieur elle se meurt, je vais la coucher de suite."

Miladi!

The whole force of the awakening,—the whole history of the situation lies, in that word.

Madame de Keradec sees—hears—and comprehends. She does not draw back. She does not start —nor weep—nor frown—nor even sigh. She is the complete mistress of herself.

"All right," says Lorraine,—head, heart, thought, all still whirling, swimming, throbbing.

"Avec son,—all right! Toujours son,—all right!" and with the hiss of a stage whisper, Sabine departs.

Madame de Keradec follows her with her eyes. Sabine is truly *du pays*. She appreciates her so perfectly—malice and all—and then the velvety eyes meet Lorraine's.

"I find you married."

"Yes,—married, Valérie!" He speaks with one of his old, dogged tones.

"Married—to your too-good woman,—your angel, your child,—your statue,—your queen!"

The velvety eyes drop with the last word.

"You have a good memory, Valérie," says Lorraine, bitterly.

"Ah! Je vous l'ai dit," murmurs she,—the eyes still down.

"Yes;—and I didn't believe it," is his reply.

"Ah! quel bonheur pour elle!"

And the eyes go up, glistening now with the bright tears that will not overflow.

"Take me to her, my friend, and let me learn to love her also!"

And then the tears flow freely down.

"Valérie, Valérie!" cries Lorraine. "It is you who are an angel. My good angel, if ever mortal had one!"

In all his life, Lorraine never spoke a truer word. In this moment, all things are again trembling in the scales. And in this moment,—Valérie, brave, true, and tender,—throws herself, with all her weight, on the side of Honour and Truth.

There he stands before her,—weaker than he has ever been;—even the soft companionship of his few wedded days makes him the more easy prey to the old passion, which has sprung up so fiercely.

She has only to put the match to these fires, which have but slumbered, and she can make the old passion burst into such a blaze as his heart has never yet been scorched by.

She can break up his life with a vengeance; and she can turn the honied bliss of her happy rival to gall of the bitterest dye.

But Madame de Keradec's heart has changed as little as her face. She understands now more than ever the absoluteness of love once given;—and more than ever she is capable of making the sacrifice of it with the calm and simple courage of a true and tender mind. It costs her a tear ;—it may cost her many more, for she is tender and constant ;—but, she can forget herself,—she can think only of another,—she can accept her own sacrifice, she can love,—and not forget. She is an alchemist, and can convert the dead weights of life into soaring pinions. She is brave and true and pure. She is the very woman of all others to be a man's good angel. But of such there are not many! They are like the visits of the angels themselves,— few, and far between.

"Et mon pauvre père, comment le trouvez vous ?"

It was the question of all others, that was the most calculated to bring Lorraine back to himself. What was he to reply ?

Le vieux grognon was still to be recognized,—though swelled in face and body and legs, with watery eyes and palsied hands,—he is a sad specimen of what may be in store for the most valiant of us.

Lorraine endeavours to express all his sympathy for this state of suffering.

"But I hope Monsieur Le Brun will soon be on his feet again," he says, addressing Madame de Keradec.

But the invalid breaks in with a voice thicker than ever.

"Monsieur le colonel,—Monsieur le colonel."

There is a vain attempt to lift the swollen eyebrow, but Lorraine catches the eye glaring with all its old ferocity from beneath it.

" Ah ! certainly," he answers ; " I ought not to forget that you have fought for your country, Monsieur le colonel ! "

As of old, for Valérie's sake, he will humour the old man.

" Ah, la patrie ! " is the appeased reply, " vous l'avez bien dis ! Ces blessures, monsieur,—you may now judge of what they were—now that you see what they have made of me ! Ces blessures ! que j'ai reçues, le cœur rempli d'une fierté guerrière, en combattant pour ma patrie, ces blessures me meneront au tombeau ! "

Colonel Le Brun had talked so long, and so valiantly about his wounds, that whoever else was sceptical, his own convictions in them were not to be shaken.

But with the next turn of the chair the concierge came out of the glass doors ; he had the house porter with him,—quite a different concierge to the democratic one—affable, and condescending, he might have been the *ober kellner* himself.

Colonel Le Brun is under his especial charge—and he intimates, with a profound obeisance, that the supper prepared for Monsieur le colonel " vient d'etre servi," and he proposes, with the assistance of the house porter, to conduct him to it.

The colonel waves his shaky hand, or tries to do so —with a corresponding condescension, and gives a sort of snort of satisfaction ;—it is made up of the anticipation of the supper, and of the gratification given to him by the respectful manners of the concierge.

The colonel has two passions—to inspire terror, and to extract homage.

So left, these two friends—friends and nothing more —look at each other silently and sadly,—not with the sadness of sorrow, but with the sadness of all those things that touch the heart.

"The sunset is on the lake, Valérie," says Lorraine ; —"let us look at it once again together. Let us go to the pavilion."

He takes her hand for a moment, to induce her ; but she has the full will to do what he wishes, and so says frankly—

"De tout, mon cœur ! "

"Ah! mon Dieu," she says to her heart,—"can I refuse to stand there once more with him? Is it not for us the spot sacred as the Temple of Heaven ? "

And then, without more thoughts or words, they thread together the shade of the plane trees, and the

serpentine walk,—and stand once more side by side in
the pavilion by the lake.

Once more—once more!—the words have that
" dying fall " which goes with sweet music at night;—
they have a pathos which can only chime in with—
Never again.

" Valérie," says Lorraine, " it was the merest
chance,—the merest chance ! "

Madame de Keradec has no affectation ; she does
not pretend not to know what this—it—stands for.

" Ah, no ! " says she.   " It was always to be,—one
of the days to come."

And then she goes a step forward.   She rests her
arms against the low pillar of the steps,—and looks
down at the lapping water.

It is the very spot he stood upon, on one dark
dreary night-fall, awaiting the fate that was to part
them,—as friends, for years,—as lovers, for ever.

So she stands, thinking perhaps of that Past, and
that parting—of this Present, and this meeting ;—and
perhaps driving it all from her heart, and gathering up
her strength for the future.

Lorraine is glib enough of tongue, and perhaps
something too much of it,—when matters, whether good
or bad, go no further than skin-deep.

But in those rare moments when his heart is touched,
he is of all men the poorest in words.

Madame de Keradec has thought out her thoughts, and she turns her brave tender face to this silent man.

"My friend," says she, "you see well how it was all meant to be. Your fiancée—the sister of your friend bien aimé,—tant pleuré. She is your wife. We are friends,—we end as we began—friends—à jamais!"

The tears glisten again in the soft eyes,—they even stand on the fringed eyelashes.

But she will not have them overflow this time.

"And ah!" she cries, "is it not so much better like this? If you had come to me, and had said what you said to her,—what could I have done?——

I could never have left mon pauvre père; and I could never have given to you that cruel No."

With "that cruel No," one rebellious tear brims over on to the oval cheek.

Lorraine, with a sort of dumb helpless action, holds out his hand, as if to say—Make of it what you will.

Madame de Keradec accepts the sign;—she advances to him,—she takes his hand, offered not indeed to her—but as it were to the winds,—takes it with that inimitable fascination in voice, look, and movement, which is her unalienable charm.

"It is agreed," she says; "you give me your hand upon it. We are friends—three friends;—vous me comprenez bien, n'est ce pas?"

"Three friends," echoes Lorraine.

"And now," says she, leading him off to other thoughts, just in the old way,—just with the old power, —just with the old generous sympathy, which would spare him one pang the more,—which would at all costs spare him——

—"And now," she says, "will you not hear some news of Louis—Louis, who owes his life to you, my friend?"

"It was the best day's work in my life!" cries Lorraine, with a profound sigh,—not the sigh of grief, but of relief—from the thraldom of being tongue-tied: —he has found a word to utter at last.

"I never knew how it all happened!" says she— with a look in her face, which says, "Tell it to me now."

"It's just as well that you didn't," says Lorraine.

"Ah! I could never bring him to speak of it."

"No wonder!" His eyes are fixed upon Madame de Keradec, but he sees the shock head of Bijou, and the cadaverous countenance of the red-haired Russ.

"It was revolting," says he,—"revolting."

Madame de Keradec, as she once was fain to own, had her little curiosity about her friends,—and she could exercise it skilfully, to the unravelling of their mysteries. But she lays aside her talent now. The curiosity still remains,—but she does not even say to herself, "pour une autre fois!"

She goes back to her brother.

"Louis,—he too is married," says she. "I was so glad, and so sorry,—that is always the way, is it not?" and she looks up in his face.

"With women, perhaps," says Lorraine;—"not with men, Valérie."

He stops with his hand to his forehead.

"What do you think of?" she asks.

"I was regretting;"—and then he stops, and considers her. He looks at her, as she stands there with her typical face, and typical character,—typical of all that comes the nearest to his highest standard of woman as she should be.

What was Lorraine regretting? A mixture of all things, perhaps,—but the predominant regret was one not unworthy of him;—it was the regret that this woman,—so bright and winning,—with the tact and tenderness of unselfishness decked in smiles,—should be condemned, either by his fatality or hers, or both,— never to make the happiness of some man, if not of himself, of another,—should die a flower ungathered, for what can "le pauvre Hégésippe" count for?— should be chained through all her *beaux jours* to the Juggernaut car of the *vieux grognon's* wheeled chair!

"Parlez donc," says she, gently.

"I was thinking, Valérie," says he, "of the difference your brother's marriage must make."

"His wife is charming," says she, quickly. "Elle fut mon amie d'enfance."

"I was not thinking of him," says he.

"They have not long been married," she answers; "but soon we shall begin to see each other very much."

"Ah!" says Lorraine. "Somehow or other, men always belong to their wives!"

He speaks with the brother and the *belle sœur* solely in his view, and by the inadvertence of a pre-occupied mind, he does not even perceive the application to his own position.

But she does.

It is getting dusk, and the flush of the damask cheek—and the so near to pallor of the retreating flood,—are hidden from all eyes.

But the flat truism has stabbed her heart,—not with its utterance, but with its truth.

Then suddenly comes a rustling through the leaves, —and a whine and a dash.

It is Mufti,—he has sniffed them out.

"Poor Mufti! poor fellow!" Lorraine is already making an alliance.

"We must take him in," says Madame de Keradec. "The hotel people are in despair if the poor animal is loose in the garden,—and for him too it is safer—we are so near to the lake."

"But he can swim," remarks Lorraine.

"Yes, I dare say; but he was nearly drowned in that

place where there is that waterfall. We tried it this
year,—but it was 'detestable!'"—The "detestable"
takes the pronunciation "du pays."—"We are so much
more happy here!" she cries.

"Are you happy, Valérie?"

"Oui, mon ami!" says she,—the velvety eyes
opening wider than they have ever done, with the
courage of the moment. "N'en doutez point! Il est
heureux,—celui qui croit l'être!" and she gives him a
bright smile.

And then they address themselves to keeping
guard over Mufti's high spirits and capers;—just as if
his good behaviour was, of all serious things, the most
serious they had now to consider. Once passed
through the glass doors, they give him his liberty;
—but he dashes out by the hall into the road.

"Shall we follow him?" says Lorraine.

"We had perhaps better," says she, in return. "He
is young, he may get lost;"—and she looks anxiously
through the window.

Lorraine whistles in vain.

This Mufti is unacquainted with his call.

So they walk up and down. Suddenly Lorraine
stops.

"What are those booths," says he, "that they are
setting up to-night?"

"It is the fair to-morrow;—you do not forget, we
saw it together!"

Lorraine does not forget.

"And will they come," says he, "Zephirina and Cherubino and the uncle?"

He sees them only as memory paints them,—still the two merry elfs, with white curls, and tumbled frocks;—he can see even the back of the rawboned chestnut horse.

"Hélas! non," says she. "It is a too sad tale. I always asked for them;—you know that I was to take Zephirina! Ah! all that was a dream. It was the second year, I think, they came as usual. She was no bigger,—just the same; always la petite fée. Well, it is so sad,—the brother and the sister both took a fever, and died in a week, just over there—in the waggon where it stood,—and the rough man, perhaps he was the uncle,—he was found drowned in the lake. They said he drank wine to drown his care,—and so fell in."

"Maybe," answers Lorraine, musing over it all, with his eyes fixed upon where the waggon stood,— "and maybe he asked the lake to drown his care, without the go-between of the wine.

I can see their two heads now," he says, "with their kisses and their little hugging arms, all in the dark and the cold of that raw, miserable morning!"

"Mais comment," asks she, "how was that?"

"Didn't I ever tell you?" asks he.

"Did you ever write to me?" she cries.

He turns to her, with a world of shame and self-reproach in his eyes.

"Never! Valérie, never! not once! It is as bitter a truth for me as for you!"

And then again, opportunely as before, bounces up the rampaging, rollicking Mufti. He nearly upsets Lorraine's equilibrium.

"He is still so young," says Madame de Keradec. Excusing the dog,—she passes over the man.

What is to be said of his transgression and its consequences—save that it was to be?

"He is so young," says Madame de Keradec,—"and wild still!" Then she adds with a sad voice—

"Hélas! no Mufti has been like that Mufti!" and the voice grows sadder still, as she relates how that Mufti came to an early grave.

"I always thought," she says, "that he pined to death for the loss of you!"

Poor Mufti! he was a dog of fine feelings,—it was quite a possible dog-tragedy;—but there was also that kick of the democratic concierge delivered in the intention of them all;—Mufti's heart and ribs may both have been broken together.

"Only one short week,—one short week after I saw you depart!"

Lorraine looks up at the windows.

"You were not there, Valérie,—not even at your own windows;—they stared so blankly that morning!"

"I saw you," she whispers, half shyly;—"I saw you." And then she speaks out. "Can you think I should let you get up and be driven away from me, without my sending after you un—un—adieu, mon ami?"

The play of his old raillery comes into Lorraine's eyes—when the jest of the thing strikes him;—it is a clear proof that he is becoming master of himself.

"Un baiser, Valérie! Why not say the word? There was no harm in it then, and I don't know that there would be any harm in it now!" Then he looks down at her, frankly and fearlessly, and with steady and honest eyes.

"This friendship footing," says he, "remains to be arranged. But one thing I am sure of,—that I have found you, and that I don't mean to lose you again! Whatever you may think of me,—you *know* you can trust yourself! We have got our lives,—and we are going to make the best of them, and, by God's help, Valérie, we are going to do as we'd be done by, all round!"

One more word winds up the scene.

"To-morrow, Valérie, you and Laure must make acquaintance."

CHAPTER XVII.

THE CURTAIN DROPS.

" Farewell ! a word that must be . . .
A sound that makes us linger . . ."

THERE are certain persons who are never contented
with their pleasures till they have drained them to
the dregs. They sit up through the small hours
talking over the play when it is done ;—they insist
upon stopping for the wind-up of the tragedy, though
they know it is likely to turn the pathos to bathos ;—
they are the self-elected claqueurs of encores ;—they
cork up their claret, and put away their melon to the
next day ;—they will utilize all the dross ;—they will
even read their newspapers a day old rather than not
read them to the full ;—they cannot bring themselves
to fling away any of the husks of their mortal coil ;—
they eat their oysters with pleasure, but behold with a
pang the shells lying on the dust-heap. It is a dark
saying to them, that the half is better than the whole.

They arrive at your house the first, and leave it
the last ;—they are the staying bores of morning
visitors.

They are fidgety people to live with, bent upon destroying the aroma of everything in life by the necessity which exists for them,—to *exploiter* all their opportunities to the uttermost,—a strain which even reacts upon themselves;—for they are mostly persons of bilious habit, with little to say for themselves,—dreary in countenance, and prone to yawning.

But of all these *exploiteurs*, the long-winded story-teller is perhaps as great a sinner as any,—he even sins when he knows better:—that "invincible igno-rance" which is not answerable for its state, is not for him,—nor does he, like the rest of these sinners, escape the penalty of his misdemeanours,—one way or another, he rarely goes unwhipped!

One single plea may be advanced for him,—his sin is not a grovelling one. If there is a spark of vitality in his characters, it is because they have interested him, if they interest no one else,—and when the moment comes to bid them farewell, he is fain to linger over it,—to put off by a few words or a few pages, that melancholy "must be;"—a hazardous indulgence, like all unlawful pleasures, for his next leaf may see him floundering in the abject miseries of anti-climax.

If you are down upon him, it is only what he deserves, not for his feelings—but for the way he has mismanaged his expression of them. The sentiment itself is one hallowed by all time.

It must have been from pure affection for their creations, not from paucity of imagination, that the story-tellers of all ages have clung to the figures already upon their canvas,—have reproduced the same impersonations in one grouping after another, with merely the connection and sequence that cotemporary or advancing life suggests,—advancing so far as to bring even the children's children upon the scene.

But it belongs only to the few master hands to do this with success;—the smaller folk must do it at their own peril.

It may be all a very lame excuse, seized upon by one of this latter tribe;—but it must serve the purpose of an apology for bringing up Prince Fortune and his friends again, in a final chapter.

It is so soon to draw the curtain over this career.

Lorraine has barely got through the half of the years allotted to man;—the fruits of his life are barely maturing.

We left him taking one of his strong resolves;— it might be better art to leave its fulfilment with a doubt;—but since it is nigh upon a quarter of a century since that resolve was taken,—as far as the unities go, there need be no doubt attached to it;— and there is a satisfaction in setting down that he did not vary in this from his former precedents.

His strong resolve once taken, he kept to it—to the letter,—and in its entire spirit.

He made the best of his life,—and did as he would be done by, all round.

He kept Friendship at his left hand, and Love at his right;—and if he did not say, "How happy could I be with either!" he did say, "How happy I am with both!"

He lived in an old-fashioned way,—and he had an old-fashioned family,—plenty of sons and daughters.

"Room for all,"—as he was given to say with the arrival of each little stranger!

Plenty of money,—too much;—they were too rich, —they had too much to dispose of:—three great fortunes, and as many and more great places. And with Lady Laure's persistent disregard of the jeweller's counter,—and Lorraine's own personal difficulty in spending,—their abundance was the only crushing thing in their lives.

"You see, Laure," says Lorraine, "it mayn't be a fault, but it's true, there's nothing of the spendthrift in you, or of the fine miser in me—and there's a limit to the setting up of Almshouses and Hospitals—in fact, it's admitted on all hands, that too much of a good thing is a nuisance!"

Then Lady Laure laughs and tells him "not to be unhappy—by-the-by, the boys will make it quite easy for him."

There were all the old names over again,—ringing new peals of Youth and Joy in their ears. Lucie and Arthur, and Louis and Valérie;—but this Lucie who romps with his father—his first-born and his darling,—who climbs his back, and shrieks for joy,—is no inheritor of the radiant hair and eyes that once went with this dear name;—he is the very image of his father, with his robust beauty;—and it is better so;—long ago, Lorraine had said, "There can be but one Lucie in the world!"

There is even a Myrtilla;—and Myrtilla herself, staid and full-blown, acts as sponsor and head nurse at the christening. Once more the Lough Beg gates are unbarred;—and once more she sits with the lodge door flung wide open now,—with half a dozen rosy urchins of her own, running in and out of it.

And Harry English, in a still more unfeeling state of breadth and weight, making almost two of Lorraine himself, is head mate again of the pinnace, and man-of-all-trades on board the *Timon*.

Castle Loughmore and the old château of Keradec compare notes,—and summer suns see a living freight of old friends and young faces, arriving upon the shores of La Vielle Bretagne;—and to receive them, Madame de Keradec, always less changed than any one,—and Louis and the *belle sœur*,—and the *vieux grognon*, in his chair, who cannot die,—and *la chère tante*, with her weird tales for the young ones, who continues to live.

Thus around Lorraine all good things group and
gather;—there is but one jar left,—and that, he would
tell you again,—is none of his own seeking!

None the less, it is of his own making,—at least,
you might say so—at the first glance.

How far we do or do not lead up to the occult
things of our own lives, it will never be given to us to
know.

How this came about was simple enough.

It was Lady Laure who laid the first stone of it,—
it was not wise of her—for she ought to have known
her husband by this time.

But, as we said long ago—to unite the wisdom of
the serpent to the harmlessness of the dove, was the
one human perfection in which Lady Laure was found
wanting.

It was at the birth of the third son.

" We will call him Horace," says Lady Laure.

" With all my heart "—answers Lorraine, offhand.
" But—wasn't that the name of your old Fungus?
Take care, don't bring the boy up on that food, my
dear,—anyhow ! "

He laughs at his joke. There is not the shadow of
a frown upon his brow at this ill-starred revival of the
old jarring topic.

And as to Lady Laure—she is not so sensitive—not
so easily wounded now. Moreover, her strategy of
married life was laid down in her honeymoon, and she
has kept to it unwaveringly.

But the worst of it was—that it was not—"With all my heart."

Lorraine never took to the boy, and the thing grew upon him. There is no romping with Horace—no high games here! The child is the youngest of three,—but he does not always remain in his petticoats,—and when the time comes for him to take his place with his brothers—with his father—there is no place for him.

Children have such an instinct, such a preternatural insight into these things. They do not know whether it is for their own sins—or for another's—they do not connect it with offence,—but they feel in a mute bewildered way, the icy difference there is between those who are loved, and the one who is not loved.

Some well-merited cuffs do the other youngsters come in for,—but not once has Lorraine lifted his hand against Horace.

And yet Horace is the only one who does not—who cannot rush up to him, asking for all he wants—or dragging him away to his revels, with the fearless confidence which a father's indulgence inspires.

So the boy takes to his mother, nestling at her knees,—following her steps,—watching for her opening door,—telling her all his troubles,—confiding to her all his pleasures,—clinging to her with all the kindling love of a child-heart, that knows what it is to be left out in the cold.

And as the boy grows older and can no longer sit all day at his mother's knee, he quits the noisy rounds of his brothers' sports, and betakes himself to the wild company of the birds and the beasts,—he wanders alone in the lovely wildernesses of these moors and lakes.

Not with the sombre eye of Sir Loftus, but with the quick ken of Nature's elected child. The dumb creatures are his playfellows,—they come at his call,—the birds sit on his hands,—the beasts crouch at his feet,—he grows learned in their ways and wiles,—and he grows healthy and happy apace.

His mother's eye marks it all, and is glad.

Day by day he brings his armfuls of wild blossoms to her lap;—she takes them tenderly,—she will not throw one away,—she parts his brown wavy locks, and kisses his broad boy's forehead,—and looks at his large grey eyes speaking their innocent language through their curly lashes,—and listens with rapt attention to his eager histories of his birds, and of his beasts,—of his races with the butterflies, and his rambles after the flowers,—and calls him her darling Horace,—and thinks of her Grey Squire!

She thinks that she sees his mantle descending upon her boy!

She thinks of him with the chastened pleasure of a memory that has lost its pang.

Thinks of the smiling days before it all began :—

Of that sunlight everywhere, of that land where it was a bliss to live!—thinks of those days, when she was young and he was strong,—and they took their way together—by hill and dell—by rock and shore,—thinks of the joys of those long wanderings,—of the delights of those long teachings,—of the charm of that companion,—of the tenderness of that true friend.

"Ah! poor Mr. Mildew!" sighs Lady Laure,—her hand still amongst her boy's brown curls.

"Who was that, mother?"

"A wise good man, Horace, who loved all birds and beasts and flowers,—just as you do."

"Where is he, mother?" cries the boy.

She turns the bright young face up to her's, and gives it again a mother's kiss.

"He is with God, my child," says Lady Laure; "and you have his name,—he too was Horace."

Poor Mr. Mildew!—poor generous soul! Did he not feel it? did he not know it?—know—that Lady Laure's first love was her Grey Squire!——

A gentle love, which had no meaning beyond the burst of the rosebud to its new-found world,—which had no passion but its own sweet gratitude,—a glow-worm flame, which prepared her maiden heart for the fiercer fires, which too soon were to come by.

From the first, a dim instinct of this may have been at the bottom of Lorraine's implacable resentment at the man's name, and at everything concerning him.

For all his indifference, and in spite of his own Friendship and Love, Lorraine was the last man to endure his rivals with patience;—rivals with any success,—rivals who unknown to him, had broken up the ground before him;—a more unpardonable offence, possibly, than trenching upon territory that he had been the first to appropriate, and appraise.

With such men, the thought is the thing!

Lorraine could take the poor loveless ghost of the little *Timon* by the hand, and to his heart. But never Mr. Mildew!

"Laure," says Lorraine, "why do you let that boy of yours run wild as he does? He grows as solitary as Uncle Loftus;—there is not a spark of spirit in him!"

"Ah, Claude!" cries Lady Laure, forgetting all her married tactics; "you do not love Horace,—why is it?"

"Why," says Lorraine, with a frown—"why did you give him that name?"

FINIS.

LONDON: PRINTED BY WILLIAM CLOWES AND SONS, LIMITED,
STAMFORD STREET AND CHARING CROSS.

A Catalogue of American and Foreign Books Published or Imported by MESSRS. SAMPSON LOW & CO. *can be had on application.*

Crown Buildings, 188, *Fleet Street, London,*
April, 1880.

𝔄 𝔖election from the 𝔏ist of 𝔅ooks

PUBLISHED BY

SAMPSON LOW, MARSTON, SEARLE, & RIVINGTON.

ALPHABETICAL LIST.

A CLASSIFIED Educational Catalogue of Works published in Great Britain. Demy 8vo, cloth extra. Second Edition, revised and corrected to Christmas, 1879, 5*s.*

About (Edmond). See "The Story of an Honest Man."

About Some Fellows. By an ETON BOY, Author of "A Day of my Life." Cloth limp, square 16mo, 2*s.* 6*d.*

Adventures of Captain Mago. A Phœnician's Explorations 1000 years B.C. By LEON CAHUN. Numerous Illustrations. Crown 8vo, cloth extra, gilt edges, 7*s.* 6*d.* ; plainer binding, 5*s.*

Adventures of a Young Naturalist. By LUCIEN BIART, with 117 beautiful Illustrations on Wood. Edited and adapted by PARKER GILLMORE. Post 8vo, cloth extra, gilt edges, New Edition, 7*s.* 6*d.*

Afghan Knife (The). A Novel. By ROBERT ARMITAGE STERNDALE, Author of "Seonee." Small post 8vo, cloth extra, 6*s.*

Afghanistan and the Afghans. Being a Brief Review of the History of the Country, and Account of its People. By H. W. BELLEW, C.S.I. Crown 8vo, cloth extra, 6*s.*

Alcott (Louisa M.) Jimmy's Cruise in the "Pinafore." With 9 Illustrations. Second Edition. Small post 8vo, cloth gilt, 3*s.* 6*d.*

———— *Aunt Jo's Scrap-Bag.* Square 16mo, 2*s.* 6*d.* (Rose Library, 1*s.*)

———— *Little Men : Life at Plumfield with Jo's Boys.* Small post 8vo, cloth, gilt edges, 3*s.* 6*d.* (Rose Library, Double vol. 2*s.*)

———— *Little Women.* 1 vol., cloth, gilt edges, 3*s.* 6*d.* (Rose Library, 2 vols., 1*s.* each.)

A

Alcott (Louisa M.) Old-Fashioned Girl. Best Edition, small
post 8vo, cloth extra, gilt edges, 3s. 6d. (Rose Library, 2s.)

——— *Work and Beginning Again.* A Story of Experience.
Experience. 1 vol., small post 8vo, cloth extra, 6s. Several Illustrations. (Rose Library, 2 vols., 1s. each.)

——— *Shawl Straps.* Small post 8vo, cloth extra, gilt, 3s. 6d.

——— *Eight Cousins; or, the Aunt Hill.* Small post 8vo,
with Illustrations, 3s. 6d.

——— *The Rose in Bloom.* Small post 8vo, cloth extra,
3s. 6d.

——— *Silver Pitchers.* Small post 8vo, cloth extra, 3s. 6d.

——— *Under the Lilacs.* Small post 8vo, cloth extra, 5s.

——— *Jack and Jill.* Small post 8vo, cloth extra, 5s.
"Miss Alcott's stories are thoroughly healthy, full of racy fun and humour . . .
exceedingly entertaining . . . . We can recommend the 'Eight Cousins.'"—
Athenæum.

Alpine Ascents and Adventures; or, Rock and Snow Sketches.
By H. SCHÜTZ WILSON, of the Alpine Club. With Illustrations by
WHYMPER and MARCUS STONE. Crown 8vo, 10s. 6d. 2nd Edition.

Andersen (Hans Christian) Fairy Tales. With Illustrations in
Colours by E. V. B. Royal 4to, cloth, 25s.

Animals Painted by Themselves. Adapted from the French of
Balzac, Georges Sands, &c., with 200 Illustrations by GRANDVILLE.
8vo, cloth extra, gilt, 10s. 6d.

Art Education. See "Illustrated Text Books."

Art in the Mountains: The Story of the Passion Play. By
HENRY BLACKBURN, Author of "Artists and Arabs," "Breton
Folk," &c. With numerous Illustrations, and an Appendix for
Travellers, giving the Expenses of the Journey, Cost of Living, Routes
from England, &c., Map, and Programme for 1880. 4to, cloth, 10s. 6d.
"Of the many previous accounts of the play, none, we are disposed to think,
recalls that edifying and impressive spectacle with the same clearness and
vividness as Mr. Blackburn's volume."—*Guardian.*
"He writes in excellent taste, and is interesting from the first page to the
last."—*Saturday Review.*

Art of Reading Aloud (The) in Pulpit, Lecture Room, or Private
Reunions. By G. VANDENHOFF, M.A. Crown 8vo, cloth extra, 6s.

Art Treasures in the South Kensington Museum. Published,
with the sanction of the Science and Art Department, in Monthly
Parts, each containing 8 Plates, price 1s. In this series are included
representations of Decorative Art of all countries and all times from
objects in the South Kensington Museum, under the following classes:—
Sculpture: Works in Marble, Ivory, and Terra-Cotta.
Bronzes: Statuettes, Medallions, Plaques, Coins.
Decorative Painting and Mosaic.

Decorative Furniture and Carved Wood-Work.
Ecclesiastical Metal-Work.
Gold and Silversmiths' Work and Jewellery.
Limoges and Oriental Enamels.
Pottery of all Countries.
Glass : Oriental, Venetian, and German.
Ornamental Iron-Work : Cutlery.
Textile Fabrics : Embroidery and Lace.
Decorative Bookbinding.
Original Designs for Works of Decorative Art.
Views of the Courts and Galleries of the Museum.
Architectural Decorations of the Museum.

The Plates are carefully printed in atlas 8vo (13 in. by 9 in.), on thick ivory-tinted paper ; and are included in a stout wrapper, ornamented with a drawing from " The Genoa Doorway " recently acquired by the Museum.

Asiatic Turkey : being a Narrative of a Journey from Bombay to the Bosphorus. By GRATTAN GEARY, Editor of the *Times of India.* 2 vols., crown 8vo, cloth extra, with many Illustrations, and a Route Map, 28s.

Australian Abroad (The). Branches from the Main Routes Round the World. Comprising the Author's Route through Japan, China, Cochin-China, Malasia, Sunda, Java, Torres Straits, Northern Australia, New South Wales, South Australia, and New Zealand. By JAMES HINGSTON (" J. H." of the *Melbourne Argus*). With Maps and numerous Illustrations from Photographs. 2 vols., 8vo, 14s. each.

Autobiography of Sir G. Gilbert Scott, R.A., F.S.A., &c. Edited by his Son, G. GILBERT SCOTT. With an Introduction by the DEAN OF CHICHESTER, and a Funeral Sermon, preached in Westminster Abbey, by the DEAN OF WESTMINSTER. Also, Portrait on steel from the portrait of the Author by G. RICHMOND, R.A. 1 vol., demy 8vo, cloth extra, 18s.

*B*AKER *(Lieut.-Gen. Valentine, Pasha). See* "War in Bulgaria."

THE BAYARD SERIES,

Edited by the late J. HAIN FRISWELL.

Comprising Pleasure Books of Literature produced in the Choicest Style as Companionable Volumes at Home and Abroad.

"We can hardly imagine better books for boys to read or for men to ponder over."—*Times.*

Price 2s. 6d. each Volume, complete in itself, flexible cloth extra, gilt edges, with silk Headbands and Registers.

The Story of the Chevalier Bayard. By M. DE BERVILLE.
De Joinville's St. Louis, King of France.

A 2

The Bayard Series (continued) :—

The Essays of Abraham Cowley, including all his Prose Works.

Abdallah ; or the Four Leaves. By EDOUARD LABOULLAYE.

Table-Talk and Opinions of Napoleon Buonaparte.

Vathek : An Oriental Romance. By WILLIAM BECKFORD.

The King and the Commons. A Selection of Cavalier and Puritan Songs. Edited by Prof. MORLEY.

Words of Wellington : Maxims and Opinions of the Great Duke.

Dr. Johnson's Rasselas, Prince of Abyssinia. With Notes.

Hazlitt's Round Table. With Biographical Introduction.

The Religio Medici, Hydriotaphia, and the Letter to a Friend. By Sir THOMAS BROWNE, Knt.

Ballad Poetry of the Affections. By ROBERT BUCHANAN.

Coleridge's Christabel, and other Imaginative Poems. With Preface by ALGERNON C. SWINBURNE.

Lord Chesterfield's Letters, Sentences, and Maxims. With Introduction by the Editor, and Essay on Chesterfield by M. DE STE.-BEUVE, of the French Academy.

Essays in Mosaic. By THOS. BALLANTYNE.

My Uncle Toby; his Story and his Friends. Edited by P. FITZGERALD.

Reflections ; or, Moral Sentences and Maxims of the Duke de la Rochefoucauld.

Socrates : Memoirs for English Readers from Xenophon's Memorabilia. By EDW. LEVIEN.

Prince Albert's Golden Precepts.

A Case containing 12 Volumes, price 31s. 6d. ; or the Case separately, price 3s. 6d.

Beauty and the Beast. An Old Tale retold, with Pictures by E. V. B. 4to, cloth extra. 10 Illustrations in Colours. 12s. 6d.

Beumers' German Copybooks. In six gradations at 4d. each.

Biart (Lucien). See "Adventures of a Young Naturalist," "My Rambles in the New World," "The Two Friends," "Involuntary Voyage."

Bickersteth's Hymnal Companion to Book of Common Prayer may be had in various styles and bindings from 1*d.* to 21*s.* *Price List and Prospectus will be forwarded on application.*

Bickersteth (Rev. E. H., M.A.) The Reef and other Parables. 1 vol., square 8vo, with numerous very beautiful Engravings, 2*s.* 6*d.*

—— *The Clergyman in his Home.* Small post 8vo, 1*s.*

—— *The Master's Home-Call: or, Brief Memorials of* Alice Frances Bickersteth. 20th Thousand. 32mo, cloth gilt, 1*s.*

—— *The Master's Will.* A Funeral Sermon preached on the Death of Mrs. S. Gurney Buxton. Sewn, 6*d.* ; cloth gilt, 1*s.*

—— *The Shadow of the Rock.* A Selection of Religious Poetry. 18mo, cloth extra, 2*s.* 6*d.*

—— *The Shadowed Home and the Light Beyond.* 7th Edition, crown 8vo, cloth extra, 5*s.*

Bida. *The Authorized Version of the Four Gospels*, with the whole of the magnificent Etchings on Steel, after drawings by M. BIDA, in 4 vols., appropriately bound in cloth extra, price 3*l.* 3*s.* each. Also the four volumes in two, bound in the best morocco, by Suttaby, extra gilt edges, 18*l.* 18*s.*, half-morocco, 12*l.* 12*s.*

"Bida's Illustrations of the Gospels of St. Matthew and St. John have already received here and elsewhere a full recognition of their great merits."—*Times.*

Biographies of the Great Artists, Illustrated. This Series is issued in the form of Handbooks. Each is a Monograph of a Great Artist, and contains Portraits of the Masters, and as many examples of their art as can be readily procured. They are Illustrated with from 16 to 20 Full-page Engravings. Cloth, large crown 8vo, 3*s.* 6*d.* per Volume.

Titian.	**Rubens.**	**Tintoret and Veronese.**
Rembrandt.	**Leonardo.**	**Hogarth.**
Raphael.	**Turner.**	**Michelangelo.**
Van Dyck and Hals.	**The Little Masters.**	**Reynolds.**
Holbein.	**Delaroche & Vernet.**	**Gainsborough.**
	Figure Painters of Holland.	

"A deserving Series, based upon recent German publications."—*Edinburgh Review.*
"Most thoroughly and tastefully edited."—*Spectator.*

Black (Wm.) Three Feathers. Small post 8vo, cloth extra, 6*s.*

—— *Lady Silverdale's Sweetheart, and other Stories.* 1 vol., small post 8vo, 6*s.*

—— *Kilmeny: a Novel.* Small post 8vo, cloth, 6*s.*

—— *In Silk Attire.* 3rd Edition, small post 8vo, 6*s.*

—— *A Daughter of Heth.* 11th Edition, small post 8vo, 6*s.*

—— *Sunrise.* 15 Monthly Parts, 1*s.* each.

Blackmore (*R. D.*) *Lorna Doone.* 10th Edition, cr. 8vo, 6s.

—— — *Alice Lorraine.* 1 vol., small post 8vo, 6th Edition, 6s.

—— — *Clara Vaughan.* Revised Edition, 6s.

—— — *Cradock Nowell.* New Edition, 6s.

—— — *Cripps the Carrier.* 3rd Edition, small post 8vo, 6s.

—— — *Mary Anerley.* 3 vols., 31s. 6d.

—— — *Erema; or, My Father's Sin.* With 12 Illustrations, small post 8vo, 6s.

Blossoms from the King's Garden : Sermons for Children. By the Rev. C. BOSANQUET. 2nd Edition, small post 8vo, cloth extra, 6s.

Blue Banner (*The*); *or, The Adventures of a Mussulman, a* Christian, and a Pagan, in the time of the Crusades and Mongol Conquest. Translated from the French of LEON CAHUN. With Seventy-six Wood Engravings. Imperial 16mo, cloth, gilt edges, 7s. 6d.; plainer binding, 5s.

Boy's Froissart (*The*). 7s. 6d. *See* "Froissart."

Brave Janet: A Story for Girls. By ALICE LEE. With Frontispiece by M. ELLEN EDWARDS. Square 8vo, cloth extra, 3s. 6d.

Brave Men in Action. By S. J. MACKENNA. Crown 8vo, 480 pp., cloth, 10s. 6d.

Brazil : the Amazons, and the Coast. By HERBERT H. SMITH. With 115 Full-page and other Illustrations. Demy 8vo, 650 pp., 21s.

Brazil and the Brazilians. By J. C. FLETCHER and D. P. KIDDER. 9th Edition, Illustrated, 8vo, 21s.

Breton Folk : An Artistic Tour in Brittany. By HENRY BLACKBURN, Author of "Artists and Arabs," "Normandy Picturesque," &c. With 171 Illustrations by RANDOLPH CALDECOTT. Imperial 8vo, cloth extra, gilt edges, 21s.

British Goblins : Welsh Folk-Lore, Fairy Mythology, Legends, and Traditions. By WIRT SYKES, United States Consul for Wales. With Illustrations by J. H. THOMAS. This account of the Fairy Mythology and Folk-Lore of his Principality is, by permission, dedicated to H.R.H. the Prince of Wales. Second Edition. 8vo, 18s.

British Philosophers.

Buckle (*Henry Thomas*) *The Life and Writings of.* By ALFRED HENRY HUTH. With Portrait. 2 vols., demy 8vo.

Burnaby (*Capt.*) *See* "On Horseback."

Burnham Beeches (*Heath, F. G.*). With numerous Illustrations and a Map. Crown 8vo, cloth, gilt edges, 3s. 6d. Second Edition. "Writing with even more than his usual brilliancy, Mr. HEATH here gives the public an interesting monograph of the splendid old trees. . . . This charming little work."—*Globe.*

Butler (W. F.) The Great Lone Land; an Account of the Red River Expedition, 1869-70. With Illustrations and Map. Fifth and Cheaper Edition, crown 8vo, cloth extra, 7s. 6d.

———— *The Wild North Land; the Story of a Winter Journey* with Dogs across Northern North America. Demy 8vo, cloth, with numerous Woodcuts and a Map, 4th Edition, 18s. Cr. 8vo, 7s. 6d.

———— *Akim-foo: the History of a Failure.* Demy 8vo, cloth, 2nd Edition, 16s. Also, in crown 8vo, 7s. 6d.

CADOGAN (Lady A.) Illustrated Games of Patience. Twenty-four Diagrams in Colours, with Descriptive Text. Foolscap 4to, cloth extra, gilt edges, 3rd Edition, 12s. 6d.

Caldecott (R.). See "Breton Folk."

Carbon Process (A Manual of). See LIESEGANG.

Ceramic Art. See JACQUEMART.

Changed Cross (The), and other Religious Poems. 16mo, 2s. 6d.

Chant Book Companion to the Book of Common Prayer. Consisting of upwards of 550 Chants for the Daily Psalms and for the Canticles; also Kyrie Eleisons, and Music for the Hymns in Holy Communion, &c. Compiled and Arranged under the Musical Editorship of C. J. VINCENT, Mus. Bac. Crown 8vo, 2s. 6d.; Organist's Edition, fcap. 4to, 5s.

Of various Editions of HYMNAL COMPANION, *Lists will be forwarded on application.*

Child of the Cavern (The); or, Strange Doings Underground. By JULES VERNE. Translated by W. H. G. KINGSTON. Numerous Illustrations. Sq. cr. 8vo, gilt edges, 7s. 6d.; cl., plain edges, 5s.

Child's Play, with 16 Coloured Drawings by E. V. B. Printed on thick paper, with tints, 7s. 6d.

———— *New.* By E. V. B. Similar to the above. *See* New.

Children's Lives and How to Preserve Them; or, The Nursery Handbook. By W. LOMAS, M.D. Crown 8vo, cloth, 5s.

Children's Magazine. Illustrated. *See* St. Nicholas.

Choice Editions of Choice Books. 2s. 6d. each, Illustrated by C. W. COPE, R.A., T. CRESWICK, R.A., E. DUNCAN, BIRKET FOSTER, J. C. HORSLEY, A.R.A., G. HICKS, R. REDGRAVE, R.A., C. STONEHOUSE, F. TAYLER, G. THOMAS, H. J. TOWNSHEND, E. H. WEHNERT, HARRISON WEIR, &c.

Bloomfield's Farmer's Boy.	Milton's L'Allegro.
Campbell's Pleasures of Hope.	Poetry of Nature. Harrison Weir.
Coleridge's Ancient Mariner.	Rogers' (Sam.) Pleasures of Memory.
Goldsmith's Deserted Village.	Shakespeare's Songs and Sonnets.
Goldsmith's Vicar of Wakefield.	Tennyson's May Queen.
Gray's Elegy in a Churchyard.	Elizabethan Poets.
Keat's Eve of St. Agnes.	Wordsworth's Pastoral Poems.

" Such works are a glorious beatification for a poet."—*Athenæum.*

Christ in Song. By Dr. PHILIP SCHAFF. A New Edition,
Revised, cloth, gilt edges, 6s.

Cobbett (William). A Biography. By EDWARD SMITH. 2
vols., crown 8vo, 25s.

Comedy (The) of Europe, 1860—1890. A retrospective and
prospective Sketch. Crown 8vo, 6s.

Conflict of Christianity with Heathenism. By Dr. GERHARD
UHLHORN. Edited and Translated from the Third German Edition
by G. C. SMYTH and C. J. H. ROPES. 8vo, cloth extra, 10s. 6d.

Continental Tour of Eight Days for Forty-four Shillings. By
a JOURNEY-MAN. 12mo, 1s.
        "The book is simply delightful."—*Spectator.*

Corea (The). See "Forbidden Land."

Covert Side Sketches: Thoughts on Hunting, with Different
Packs in Different Countries. By J. NEVITT FITT (H.H. of the *Sporting
Gazette,* late of the *Field*). 2nd Edition. Crown 8vo, cloth, 10s. 6d.

Crade-Land of Arts and Creeds; or, Nothing New under the
Sun. By CHARLES J. STONE, Barrister-at-law, and late Advocate,
High Courts, Bombay, 8vo, pp. 420, cloth, 14s.

Cripps the Carrier. 3rd Edition, 6s. See BLACKMORE.

Cruise of H.M.S. "Challenger" (The). By W. J. J. SPRY, R.N.
With Route Map and many Illustrations. 6th Edition, demy 8vo, cloth,
18s. Cheap Edition, crown 8vo, some of the Illustrations, 7s. 6d.

Curious Adventures of a Field Cricket. By Dr. ERNEST
CANDÈZE. Translated by N. D'ANVERS. With numerous fine
Illustrations. Crown 8vo, cloth extra, gilt edges, 7s. 6d.

DANA (R. H.) Two Years before the Mast and Twenty-Four
years After. Revised Edition with Notes, 12mo, 6s.

Daughter (A) of Heth. By W. BLACK. Crown 8vo, 6s.

Day of My Life (A); or, Every Day Experiences at Eton.
By an ETON BOY, Author of "About Some Fellows." 16mo, cloth
extra, 2s. 6d. 6th Thousand.

Day out of the Life of a Little Maiden (A): Six Studies from
Life. By SHERER and ENGLER. Large 4to, in portfolio, 5s.

Diane. By Mrs. MACQUOID. Crown 8vo, 6s.

Dick Cheveley: his Fortunes and Misfortunes. By W. H. G.
KINGSTON. 350 pp., square 16mo, and 22 full-page Illustrations.
Cloth, gilt edges, 7s. 6d.

Dick Sands, the Boy Captain. By JULES VERNE. With
nearly 100 Illustrations, cloth extra, gilt edges, 10s. 6d.

Dodge (Mrs. M.) Hans Brinker; or, the Silver Skates. An entirely New Edition, with 59 Full-page and other Woodcuts. Square crown 8vo, cloth extra, 5*s.* ; Text only, paper, 1*s.*

Dogs of Assize. A Legal Sketch-Book in Black and White. Containing 6 Drawings by WALTER J. ALLEN. Folio, in wrapper, 6*s.* 8*d.*

EIGHT Cousins. See ALCOTT.

Eldmuir: An Art-Story of Scottish Home-Life, Scenery, and Incident. By JACOB THOMPSON, Jun. Illustrated with Engravings after Paintings of JACOB THOMPSON. With an Introductory Notice by LLEWELLYNN JEWITT, F.S.A., &c. Demy 8vo, cloth extra, 14*s.*

Elinor Dryden. By Mrs. MACQUOID. Crown 8vo, 6*s.*

Embroidery (Handbook of). By L. HIGGIN. Edited by LADY MARIAN ALFORD, and published by authority of the Royal School of Art Needlework. With 16 page Illustrations, Designs for Borders, &c. Crown 8vo, 5*s.*

English Catalogue of Books (The). Published during 1863 to 1871 inclusive, comprising also important American Publications. 30*s.*

*** Of the previous Volume, 1835 to 1862, very few remain on sale ; as also of the Index Volume, 1837 to 1857.

—— *Supplements,* 1863, 1864, 1865, 3*s.* 6*d.* each ; 1866 to 1880, 5*s.* each.

English Writers, Chapters for Self-Improvement in English Literature. By the Author of "The Gentle Life," 6*s.* ; smaller edition, 2*s.* 6*d.*

English Philosophers. A Series of Volumes containing short biographies of the most celebrated English Philosophers, designed to direct the reader to the sources of more detailed and extensive criticism than the size and nature of the books in this Series would permit. Though not issued in chronological order, the series will, when complete, constitute a comprehensive history of English Philosophy. Two Volumes will be issued simultaneously at brief intervals, in square 16mo, price 2*s.* 6*d.*

The following are already arranged :—

Bacon. Professor FOWLER, Professor of Logic in Oxford.

Berkeley. Professor T. H. GREEN, Professor of Moral Philosophy, Oxford.

Hamilton. Professor MONK, Professor of Moral Philosophy, Dublin.

J. S. Mill. Miss HELEN TAYLOR, Editor of "The Works of Buckle," &c.

Mansel. Rev. J. H. HUCKIN, D.D., Head Master of Repton.

Adam Smith. Mr. J. A. FARRER, M.A., Author of "Primitive Manners and Customs."

English Philosophers, continued :—

Hobbes.   Mr. A. H. GOSSET, B.A., Fellow of New College, Oxford.
Bentham.   Mr. G. E. BUCKLE, M.A., Fellow of All Souls', Oxford.
Austin.   Mr. HARRY JOHNSON, B.A., late Scholar of Queen's College, Oxford.
Hartley.   ⎱ Mr. E. S. BOWEN, B.A., late Scholar of New College,
James Mill.   ⎰   Oxford.
Shaftesbury.   ⎱ Professor FOWLER.
Hutcheson.   ⎰

Erchomenon ; or, The Republic of Materialism.   Small post 8vo, cloth, 5s.

Erema ; or, My Father's Sin.   See BLACKMORE.

Eton.   See "Day of my Life," "Out of School," "About Some Fellows."

Evans (C.) Over the Hills and Far Away.   By C. EVANS. One Volume, crown 8vo, cloth extra, 10s. 6d.

——— *A Strange Friendship.*   Crown 8vo, cloth, 5s.

F *AMILY Prayers for Working Men.*   By the Author of "Steps to the Throne of Grace."   With an Introduction by the Rev. E. H. BICKERSTETH, M.A.   Cloth, 1s. ; sewed, 6d.

Fern Paradise (The): A Plea for the Culture of Ferns.   By F. G. HEATH.   New Edition, entirely Rewritten, Illustrated with Eighteen full-page, numerous other Woodcuts, including 8 Plates of Ferns and Four Photographs, large post 8vo, cloth, gilt edges, 12s. 6d.   Sixth Edition.   In 12 Parts, sewn, 1s. each.

   " This charming Volume will not only enchant the Fern-lover, but will also please and instruct the general reader."—*Spectator.*

Fern World (The).   By F. G. HEATH.   Illustrated by Twelve Coloured Plates, giving complete Figures (Sixty-four in all) of every Species of British Fern, printed from Nature ; by several full-page Engravings.   Cloth, gilt, 6th Edition, 12s. 6d.   In 12 parts, 1s. each.

   " Mr. HEATH has really given us good, well-written descriptions of our native Ferns, with indications of their habitats, the conditions under which they grow naturally, and under which they may be cultivated."—*Athenæum.*

Few (A) Hints on Proving Wills.   Enlarged Edition, 1s.

First Steps in Conversational French Grammar.   By F. JULIEN. Being an Introduction to "Petites Leçons de Conversation et de Grammaire," by the same Author.   Fcap. 8vo, 128 pp., 1s.

Five Years in Minnesota.   By MAURICE FARRAR, M.A. Crown 8vo, cloth extra, 6s.

Flooding of the Sahara (The).   See MACKENZIE.

Food for the People ; or, Lentils and other Vegetable Cookery. By E. E. ORLEBAR.   Third Thousand.   Small post 8vo, boards, 1s.

A Fool's Errand. By ONE OF THE FOOLS. Crown 8vo, cloth extra, 5s.

Footsteps of the Master. *See* STOWE (Mrs. BEECHER).

Forbidden Land (A): Voyages to the Corea. By G. OPPERT. Numerous Illustrations and Maps. Demy 8vo, cloth extra, 21s.

Four Lectures on Electric Induction. Delivered at the Royal Institution, 1878-9. By J. E. H. GORDON, B.A. Cantab. With numerous Illustrations. Cloth limp, square 16mo, 3s.

Foreign Countries and the British Colonies. Edited by F. S. PULLING, M.A., Lecturer at Queen's College, Oxford, and formerly Professor at the Yorkshire College, Leeds. A Series of small Volumes descriptive of the principal Countries of the World by well-known Authors, each Country being treated of by a Writer who from Personal Knowledge is qualified to speak with authority on the Subject. The Volumes will average 180 crown 8vo pages, will contain Maps, and, in some cases, a few typical Illustrations.

The following Volumes are in preparation :—

Denmark and Iceland.	Russia.	Canada.
Greece.	Persia.	Sweden and Norway.
Switzerland.	Japan.	The West Indies.
Austria.	Peru.	New Zealand.

Franc (Maude Jeane). The following form one Series, small post 8vo, in uniform cloth bindings :—

——— *Emily's Choice.* 5s.

——— *Hall's Vineyard.* 4s.

——— *John's Wife : a Story of Life in South Australia.* 4s.

——— *Marian ; or, the Light of Some One's Home.* 5s.

——— *Silken Cords and Iron Fetters.* 4s.

——— *Vermont Vale.* 5s.

——— *Minnie's Mission.* 4s.

——— *Little Mercy.* 5s.

——— *Beatrice Melton.* 4s.

*Friends and Foes in the Transkei : An Englishwoman's Experi-*ences during the Cape Frontier War of 1877-8. By HELEN M. PRICHARD. Crown 8vo, cloth, 10s. 6d.

Froissart (The Boy's). Selected from the Chronicles of England, France, Spain, &c. By SIDNEY LANIER. The Volume will be fully Illustrated. Crown 8vo, cloth, 7s. 6d.

Funny Foreigners and Eccentric Englishmen. 16 coloured comic Illustrations for Children. Fcap. folio, coloured wrapper, 4s.

*G*A*MES of Patience.* See CADOGAN.

Gentle Life (Queen Edition). 2 vols. in 1, small 4to, 10s. 6d.

THE GENTLE LIFE SERIES.

Price 6s. each ; or in calf extra, price 10s. 6d. ; Smaller Edition, cloth extra, 2s. 6d.

A Reprint (with the exception of "Familiar Words" and "Other People's Windows") has been issued in very neat limp cloth bindings at 2s. 6d. each.

The Gentle Life. Essays in aid of the Formation of Character of Gentlemen and Gentlewomen. 21st Edition.

"Deserves to be printed in letters of gold, and circulated in every house."—*Chambers' Journal.*

About in the World. Essays by Author of "The Gentle Life."

"It is not easy to open it at any page without finding some handy idea."—*Morning Post.*

Like unto Christ. A New Translation of Thomas à Kempis' "De Imitatione Christi." 2nd Edition.

"Could not be presented in a more exquisite form, for a more sightly volume was never seen."—*Illustrated London News.*

Familiar Words. An Index Verborum, or Quotation Handbook. Affording an immediate Reference to Phrases and Sentences that have become embedded in the English language. 3rd and enlarged Edition. 6s.

"The most extensive dictionary of quotation we have met with."—*Notes and Queries.*

Essays by Montaigne. Edited and Annotated by the Author of "The Gentle Life." With Portrait. 2nd Edition.

"We should be glad if any words of ours could help to bespeak a large circulation for this handsome attractive book."—*Illustrated Times.*

The Countess of Pembroke's Arcadia. Written by Sir PHILIP SIDNEY. Edited with Notes by Author of "The Gentle Life." 7s. 6d.

"All the best things are retained intact in Mr. Friswell's edition."—*Examiner.*

The Gentle Life. 2nd Series, 8th Edition.

"There is not a single thought in the volume that does not contribute in some measure to the formation of a true gentleman."—*Daily News.*

The Silent Hour: Essays, Original and Selected. By the Author of "The Gentle Life." 3rd Edition.

"All who possess 'The Gentle Life' should own this volume."—*Standard.*

Half-Length Portraits. Short Studies of Notable Persons. By J. HAIN FRISWELL. Small post 8vo, cloth extra, 6s.

Essays on English Writers, for the Self-improvement of Students in English Literature.

"To all who have neglected to read and study their native literature we would certainly suggest the volume before us as a fitting introduction."—*Examiner.*

The Gentle Life Series (*continued*) :—

Other People's Windows. By J. HAIN FRISWELL. 3rd Edition.
"The chapters are so lively in themselves, so mingled with shrewd views of human nature, so full of illustrative anecdotes, that the reader cannot fail to be amused."—*Morning Post.*

A Man's Thoughts. By J. HAIN FRISWELL.

German Primer. Being an Introduction to First Steps in German. By M. T. PREU. 2s. 6d.

Getting On in the World ; or, Hints on Success in Life. By W. MATHEWS, LL.D. Small post 8vo, cloth, 2s. 6d.; gilt edges, 3s. 6d.

Gilpin's Forest Scenery. Edited by F. G. HEATH. Large post 8vo, with numerous Illustrations. Uniform with "The Fern World" and "Our Woodland Trees." 12s. 6d.
"Those who know Mr. HEATH's Volumes on Ferns, as well as his 'Woodland Trees,' and his little work on 'Burnham Beeches,' will understand the enthusiasm with which he has executed his task. . . . The Volume deserves to be a favourite in the boudoir as well as in the library."—*Saturday Review.*

Gordon (J. E. H.). See "Four Lectures on Electric Induction," "Physical Treatise on Electricity," &c.

Gouffé. *The Royal Cookery Book.* By JULES GOUFFÉ ; translated and adapted for English use by ALPHONSE GOUFFÉ, Head Pastrycook to her Majesty the Queen. Illustrated with large plates printed in colours. 161 Woodcuts, 8vo, cloth extra, gilt edges, 2l. 2s.

—— Domestic Edition, half-bound, 10s. 6d.
"By far the ablest and most complete work on cookery that has ever been submitted to the gastronomical world."—*Pall Mall Gazette.*

Gouraud (Mdlle.) Four Gold Pieces. Numerous Illustrations. Small post 8vo, cloth, 2s. 6d. See also Rose Library.

Government of M. Thiers. By JULES SIMON. Translated from the French. 2 vols., demy 8vo, cloth extra, 32s.

Great Artists. See Biographies.

Greek Grammar. See WALLER.

Guizot's History of France. Translated by ROBERT BLACK. Super-royal 8vo, very numerous Full-page and other Illustrations. In 5 vols., cloth, gilt, each 24s.
"It supplies a want which has long been felt, and ought to be in the hands of all students of history."—*Times.*

—— —— —— —— *Masson's School Edition.* The History of France from the Earliest Times to the Outbreak of the Revolution ; abridged from the Translation by Robert Black, M.A., with Chronological Index, Historical and Genealogical Tables, &c. By Professor GUSTAVE MASSON, B.A., Assistant Master at Harrow School. With 24 full-page Portraits, and many other Illustrations. 1 vol., demy 8vo, 600 pp., cloth extra, 10s. 6d.

Guizot's History of England. In 3 vols. of about 500 pp. each, containing 60 to 70 Full-page and other Illustrations, cloth extra, gilt, 24s. each.
> " For luxury of typography, plainness of print, and beauty of illustration, these volumes, of which but one has as yet appeared in English, will hold their own against any production of an age so luxurious as our own in everything, typography not excepted."—*Times.*

Guyon (Mde.) Life. By UPHAM. 6th Edition, crown 8vo, 6s.

*H*ANDBOOK *to the Charities of London.* See LOW's.

—— *of Embroidery ; which see.*

——— *to the Principal Schools of England.* See Practical.

Half-Hours of Blind Man's Holiday ; or, Summer and Winter Sketches in Black & White. By W. W. FENN. 2 vols., cr. 8vo, 24s.

Half-Length Portraits. Short Studies of Notable Persons. By J. HAIN FRISWELL. Small post 8vo, 6s. ; Smaller Edition, 2s. 6d.

Hall (W. W.) How to Live Long; or, 1408 *Health Maxims,* Physical, Mental, and Moral. By W. W. HALL, A.M., M.D. Small post 8vo, cloth, 2s. Second Edition.

Hans Brinker ; or, the Silver Skates. See DODGE.

Have I a Vote ? A Handy Book for the Use of the People, on the Qualifications conferring the Right of Voting at County and Borough Parliamentary Elections. With Forms and Notes. By T. H. LEWIS, B.A., LL.B. Paper, 6d.

Heart of Africa. Three Years' Travels and Adventures in the Unexplored Regions of Central Africa, from 1868 to 1871. By Dr. GEORG SCHWEINFURTH. Numerous Illustrations, and large Map. 2 vols., crown 8vo, cloth, 15s.

Heath (Francis George). See " Fern World," " Fern Paradise," " Our Woodland Trees," " Trees and Ferns;" " Gilpin's Forest Scenery," " Burnham Beeches," " Sylvan Spring," &c.

Heber's (Bishop) Illustrated Edition of Hymns. With upwards of 100 beautiful Engravings. Small 4to, handsomely bound, 7s. 6d. Morocco, 18s. 6d. and 21s. An entirely New Edition.

Hector Servadac. See VERNE. 10s. 6d. and 5s.

Heir of Kilfinnan (The). New Story by W. H. G. KINGSTON, Author of " Snoe Shoes and Canoes," " With Axe and Rifle," &c. With Illustrations. Cloth, gilt edges, 7s. 6d.

History and Handbook of Photography. Translated from the French of GASTON TISSANDIER. Edited by J. THOMSON. Imperial 16mo, over 300 pages, 70 Woodcuts, and Specimens of Prints by the best Permanent Processes. Second Edition, with an Appendix by the late Mr. HENRY FOX TALBOT. Cloth extra, 6s.

History of a Crime (The) ; Deposition of an Eye-witness. By
VICTOR HUGO. 4 vols., crown 8vo, 42s. Cheap Edition, 1 vol., 6s.

—— *England. See* GUIZOT.

—— *France. See* GUIZOT.

—— *of Russia. ee* RAMBAUD.

—— *Merchant Shipping. See* LINDSAY.

—— *United States. See* BRYANT.

—— *Ireland.* STANDISH O'GRADY. Vols. I. and II., 7s. 6d.
each.

—— *American Literature.* By M. C. TYLER. Vols. I.
and II., 2 vols, 8vo, 24s.

History and Principles of Weaving by Hand and by Power. With
several hundred Illustrations. By ALFRED BARLOW. Royal 8vo,
cloth extra, 1l. 5s. Second Edition.

Hitherto. By the Author of "The Gayworthys." New Edition,
cloth extra, 3s. 6d. Also, in Rose Library, 2 vols., 2s.

Home of the Eddas. By C. G. LOCK. Demy 8vo, cloth, 16s.

How to Live Long. See HALL.

How to get Strong and how to Stay so. By WILLIAM BLAIKIE.
A Manual of Rational, Physical, Gymnastic, and other Exercises.
With Illustrations, small post 8vo, 5s.

"Worthy of every one's attention, whether old or young."—*Graphic.*

Hugo (Victor) "Ninety-Three." Illustrated. Crown 8vo, 6s.

—— *Toilers of the Sea.* Crown 8vo. Illustrated, 6s. ; fancy
boards, 2s. ; cloth, 2s. 6d. ; On large paper with all the original
Illustrations, 10s. 6d.

——. *See* "History of a Crime."

Hundred Greatest Men (The). 8 vols., containing 15 to 20
Portraits each, 21s. each. See below.

"Messrs. SAMPSON LOW & Co. are about to issue an important 'International'
work, entitled, 'THE HUNDRED GREATEST MEN;' being the Lives and
Portraits of the 100 Greatest Men of History, divided into Eight Classes, each Class
to form a Monthly Quarto Volume The Introductions to the volumes are to be
written by recognized authorities on the different subjects, the English contributors
being DEAN STANLEY, Mr. MATTHEW ARNOLD, Mr. FROUDE, and Professor MAX
MÜLLER: in Germany, Professor HELMHOLTZ; in France, MM. TAINE and
RENAN; and in America, Mr. EMERSON. The Portraits are to be Reproductions
from fine and rare Steel Engravings."—*Academy.*

Hygiene and Public Health (A Treatise on). Edited by A. H.
BUCK, M.D. Illustrated by numerous Wood Engravings. In 2
royal 8vo vols., cloth, one guinea each.

Hymnal Companion to Book of Common Prayer. See
BICKERSTETH.

*I*LLUSTRATED *Text-Books of Art-Education.* A Series
of Monthly Volumes preparing for publication. Edited by EDWARD
J. POYNTER, R.A., Director for Art, Science and Art Department.

The first Volumes, large crown 8vo, cloth, 3s. 6d. each, will be issued in the
following divisions :—

PAINTING.

Classic and Italian. | French and Spanish.
German, Flemish, and Dutch. | English and American.

ARCHITECTURE.

Classic and Early Christian. | Gothic, Renaissance, & Modern.

SCULPTURE.

Classic and Oriental. | Renaissance and Modern.

ORNAMENT.

Decoration in Colour. | Architectural Ornament.

Illustrations of China and its People. By J. THOMPSON
F.R.G.S. Four Volumes, imperial 4to, each 3*l*. 3*s*.

In my Indian Garden. By PHIL ROBINSON. With a Preface
by EDWIN ARNOLD, M.A., C.S.I., &c. Crown 8vo, limp cloth, 3*s*. 6*d*.

Involuntary Voyage (An). Showing how a Frenchman who
abhorred the Sea was most unwillingly and by a series of accidents
driven round the World. Numerous Illustrations. Square crown
8vo, cloth extra, 7*s*. 6*d*.

Irish Bar. Comprising Anecdotes, Bon-Mots, and Biographical Sketches of the Bench and Bar of Ireland. By J. RODERICK
O'FLANAGAN, Barrister-at-Law. Crown 8vo, 12*s*. Second Edition.

*J*ACK *and* J*ill.* By Miss ALCOTT. Small post 8vo, cloth,
gilt edges, 5*s*.

Jacquemart (A.) History of the Ceramic Art. By ALBERT
JACQUEMART. With 200 Woodcuts, 12 Steel-plate Engravings, and
1000 Marks and Monograms. Translated by Mrs. BURY PALLISER.
Super-royal 8vo, cloth extra, gilt edges, 28*s*.

Jimmy's Cruise in the Pinafore. See ALCOTT.

*K*AFIRLAND : *A Ten Months' Campaign.* By FRANK N.
STREATFIELD, Resident Magistrate in Kaffraria, and Commandant
of Native Levies during the Kaffir War of 1878. Crown 8vo, cloth
extra, 7*s*. 6*d*.

Keble Autograph Birthday Book (The). Containing on each left-
hand page the date and a selected verse from Keble's hymns.
Imperial 8vo, with 12 Floral Chromos, ornamental binding, gilt edges,
15*s*.

Khedive's Egypt (The); or, The old House of Bondage under New Masters. By EDWIN DE LEON. Illustrated. Demy 8vo, 8*s.* 6*d.*

King's Rifle (The): From the Atlantic to the Indian Ocean; Across Unknown Countries; Discovery of the Great Zambesi Affluents, &c. By Major SERPA PINTO. With 24 full-page and about 100 smaller Illustrations, 13 small Maps, and 1 large one. Demy 8vo.

Kingston (W. H. G.). See "Snow-Shoes."

—— *Child of the Cavern.*

—— *Two Supercargoes.*

—— *With Axe and Rifle.*

—— *Begum's Fortune.*

—— *Heir of Kilfinnan.*

—— *Dick Cheveley.*

LADY Silverdale's Sweetheart. 6*s. See* BLACK.

Lenten Meditations. In Two Series, each complete in itself. By the Rev. CLAUDE BOSANQUET, Author of "Blossoms from the King's Garden." 16mo, cloth, First Series, 1*s.* 6*d.* ; Second Series, 2*s.*

Lentils. See "Food for the People."

Liesegang (Dr. Paul E.) A Manual of the Carbon Process of Photography. Demy 8vo, half-bound, with Illustrations, 4*s.*

Life and Letters of the Honourable Charles Sumner (The). 2 vols., royal 8vo, cloth. Second Edition, 36*s.*

Lindsay (W. S.) History of Merchant Shipping and Ancient Commerce. Over 150 Illustrations, Maps and Charts. In 4 vols., demy 8vo, cloth extra. Vols. 1 and 2, 21*s.* ; vols. 3 and 4, 24*s.* each.

Lion Jack: a Story of Perilous Adventures amongst Wild Men and Beasts. Showing how Menageries are made. By P. T. BARNUM. With Illustrations. Crown 8vo, cloth extra, price 6*s.*

Little King; or, the Taming of a Young Russian Count. By S. BLANDY. 64 Illustrations. Crown 8vo, gilt edges, 7*s.* 6*d.* ; plainer binding, 5*s.*

Little Mercy; or, For Better for Worse. By MAUDE JEANNE FRANC, Author of "Marian," "Vermont Vale," &c., &c. Small post 8vo, cloth extra, 4*s.* Second Edition.

Long (Col. C. Chaillé) Central Africa. Naked Truths of Naked People : an Account of Expeditions to Lake Victoria Nyanza and the Mabraka Niam-Niam. Demy 8vo, numerous Illustrations, 18*s.*

Lost Sir Massingberd. New Edition, crown 8vo, boards, coloured wrapper, 2*s.*

Low's German Series—

1. **The Illustrated German Primer.** Being the easiest introduction to the study of German for all beginners.   1s.
2. **The Children's own German Book.** A Selection of Amusing and Instructive Stories in Prose. Edited by Dr. A. L. MEISSNER. Small post 8vo, cloth, 1s. 6d.
3. **The First German Reader, for Children from Ten to Fourteen.** Edited by Dr. A. L. MEISSNER. Small post 8vo, cloth, 1s. 6d.
4. **The Second German Reader.** Edited by Dr. A. L. MEISSNER. Small post 8vo, cloth, 1s. 6d.

   Buchheim's Deutsche Prosa.   Two Volumes, sold separately : —

5. **Schiller's Prosa.** Containing Selections from the Prose Works of Schiller, with Notes for English Students. By Dr. BUCHHEIM, Small post 8vo, 2s. 6d.
6. **Goethe's Prosa.** Selections from the Prose Works of Goethe, with Notes for English Students. By Dr. BUCHHEIM. Small post 8vo, 3s. 6d.

Low's International Series of Toy Books.   6d. each ; or Mounted on Linen, 1s.

1. **Little Fred and his Fiddle,** from Asbjörnsen's "Norwegian Fairy Tales."
2. **The Lad and the North Wind,**   ditto.
3. **The Pancake,**   ditto.

Low's Standard Library of Travel and Adventure.   Crown 8vo, bound uniformly in cloth extra, price 7s. 6d.

1. **The Great Lone Land.** By Major W. F. BUTLER, C.B.
2. **The Wild North Land.** By Major W. F. BUTLER, C.B.
3. **How I found Livingstone.** By H. M. STANLEY.
4. **The Threshold of the Unknown Region.** By C. R. MARK-HAM. (4th Edition, with Additional Chapters, 10s. 6d.)
5. **A Whaling Cruise to Baffin's Bay and the Gulf of Boothia.** By A. H. MARKHAM.
6. **Campaigning on the Oxus.** By J. A. MACGAHAN.
7. **Akim-foo: the History of a Failure.** By MAJOR W F. BUTLER, C.B.
8. **Ocean to Ocean.** By the Rev. GEORGE M. GRANT. With Illustrations.
9. **Cruise of the Challenger.** By W. J. J. SPRY, R.N.
10. **Schweinfurth's Heart of Africa.** 2 vols., 15s.
11. **Through the Dark Continent.** By H. M. STANLEY. 1 vol., 12s. 6d.

Low's Standard Novels. Crown 8vo, 6*s.* each, cloth extra.

My Lady Greensleeves. By HELEN MATHERS, Authoress of " Comin' through the Rye," " Cherry Ripe," &c.

Three Feathers. By WILLIAM BLACK.

A Daughter of Heth. 13th Edition. By W. BLACK. With Frontispiece by F. WALKER, A.R.A.

Kilmeny. A Novel. By W. BLACK.

In Silk Attire. By W. BLACK.

Lady Silverdale's Sweetheart. By W. BLACK.

History of a Crime: The Story of the Coup d'État. By VICTOR HUGO.

Alice Lorraine. By R. D. BLACKMORE.

Lorna Doone. By R. D. BLACKMORE. 8th Edition.

Cradock Nowell. By R. D. BLACKMORE.

Clara Vaughan. By R. D. BLACKMORE.

Cripps the Carrier. By R. D. BLACKMORE.

Erema ; or My Father's Sin. By R. D. BLACKMORE.

Innocent. By Mrs. OLIPHANT. Eight Illustrations.

Work. A Story of Experience. By LOUISA M. ALCOTT. Illustrations. *See also* Rose Library.

The Afghan Knife. By R. A. STERNDALE, Author of " Sconee."

A French Heiress in her own Chateau. By the author of " One Only," "Constantia," &c. Six Illustrations.

Ninety-Three. By VICTOR HUGO. Numerous Illustrations.

My Wife and I. By Mrs. BEECHER STOWE.

Wreck of the Grosvenor. By W. CLARK RUSSELL.

Elinor Dryden. By Mrs. MACQUOID.

Diane. By Mrs. MACQUOID.

Poganuc People, Their Loves and Lives. By Mrs. BEECHER STOWE.

A Golden Sorrow. By Mrs. CASHEL HOEY.

Low's Handbook to the Charities of London. Edited and revised to date by C. MACKESON, F.S.S., Editor of " A Guide to the Churches of London and its Suburbs," &c. 1*s.*

MACGAHAN (J. A.) Campaigning on the Oxus, and the Fall of Khiva. With Map and numerous Illustrations, 4th Edition, small post 8vo, cloth extra, 7*s.* 6*d.*

Macgregor (John) " Rob Roy " on the Baltic. 3rd Edition, small post 8vo, 2*s.* 6*d.*

—— *A Thousand Miles in the "Rob Roy" Canoe.* 11th Edition, small post 8vo, 2*s.* 6*d.*

Macgregor (John) Description of the "Rob Roy" Canoe, with Plans, &c, 1s.

—— *The Voyage Alone in the Yawl "Rob Roy."* New Edition, thoroughly revised, with additions, small post 8vo, 5s.; boards, 2s. 6d.

Mackenzie (D). The Flooding of the Sahara. By DONALD MACKENZIE. 8vo, cloth extra, with Illustrations, 10s. 6d.

Macquoid (Mrs.) Elinor Dryden. Crown 8vo, cloth, 6s.

—— *Diane.* Crown 8vo, 6s.

Magazine (Illustrated) for Young People. See "St. Nicholas."

Markham (C. R.) The Threshold of the Unknown Region. Crown 8vo, with Four Maps, 4th Edition. Cloth extra, 10s. 6d.

Maury (Commander) Physical Geography of the Sea, and its Meteorology. Being a Reconstruction and Enlargement of his former Work, with Charts and Diagrams. New Edition, crown 8vo, 6s.

Memoirs of Madame de Rémusat, 1802—1808. By her Grandson, M. PAUL DE RÉMUSAT, Senator. Translated by Mrs. CASHEL HOEY and and Mr. JOHN LILLIE. 4th Edition, cloth extra. This work was written by Madame de Rémusat during the time she was living on the most intimate terms with the Empress Josephine, and is full of revelations respecting the private life of Bonaparte, and of men and politics of the first years of the century. Revelations which have already created a great sensation in Paris. 8vo, 2 vols. 32s.

Men of Mark: a Gallery of Contemporary Portraits of the most Eminent Men of the Day taken from Life, especially for this publication, price 1s. 6d. monthly. Vols. I., II., III., and IV., handsomely bound, cloth, gilt edges, 25s. each.

Michael Strogoff. 10s. 6d. and 5s. See VERNE.

Mitford (Miss). See "Our Village."

Montaigne's Essays. See "Gentle Life Series."

My Brother Jack; or, The Story of Whatd'yecallem. Written by Himself. From the French of ALPHONSE DAUDET. Illustrated by P. PHILIPPOTEAUX. Imperial 16mo, cloth extra, gilt edges, 7s. 6d.; plainer binding, 5s.

My Lady Greensleeves. By HELEN MATHERS, Authoress of "Comin' through the Rye," "Cherry Ripe," &c. 1 vol. edition, crown 8vo, cloth, 6s.

My Rambles in the New World. By LUCIEN BIART, Author of "The Adventures of a Young Naturalist." Numerous full-page Illustrations. Crown 8vo, cloth extra, gilt edges, 7s. 6d.; plainer binding, 5s.

Mysterious Island. By JULES VERNE. 3 vols., imperial 16mo. 150 Illustrations, cloth gilt, 3s. 6d. each; elaborately bound, gilt edges, 7s. 6d. each. Cheap Edition, with some of the Illustrations, cloth, gilt, 2s.; paper, 1s. each.

NARES (Sir G. S., K.C.B.) Narrative of a Voyage to the Polar Sea during 1875-76, in H.M.'s Ships "Alert" and "Discovery." By Captain Sir G. S. NARES, R.N., K.C.B., F.R.S. Published by permission of the Lords Commissioners of the Admiralty. With Notes on the Natural History, edited by H. W. FEILDEN, F.G.S., C.M.Z.S., F.R.G.S., Naturalist to the Expedition. Two Volumes, demy 8vo, with numerous Woodcut Illustrations, Photographs, &c. 4th Edition, 2l. 2s.

National Music of the World. By the late HENRY F. CHORLEY. Edited by H. G. HEWLETT. Crown 8vo, cloth, 8s. 6d.

"What I have to offer are not a few impressions, scrambled together in the haste of the moment, but are the result of many years of comparison and experience."—*From the Author's "Prelude."*

New Child's Play (A). Sixteen Drawings by E. V. B. Beautifully printed in colours, 4to, cloth extra, 12s. 6d.

New Guinea (A Few Months in). By OCTAVIUS C. STONE, F.R.G.S. With numerous Illustrations from the Author's own Drawings. Crown 8vo, cloth, 12s.

New Ireland. By A. M. SULLIVAN, M.P. for Louth. 2 vols., demy 8vo, 30s. Cheaper Edition, 1 vol., crown 8vo, 8s. 6d.

New Novels. Crown 8vo, cloth, 10s. 6d. per vol. :—

Mary Anerley. By R. D. BLACKMORE, Author of "Lorna Doone," &c. 3 vols.

The Sisters. By G. EBERS, Author of "An Egyptian Princess." 2 vols., 16mo, 2s. each.

Countess Daphne. By RITA, Authoress of "Vivienne" and "Like Dian's Kiss." 3 vols.

Sunrise. By W. BLACK. In 15 Monthly Parts, 1s. each.

Wait a Year. By HARRIET BOWRA, Authoress of "A Young Wife's Story." 3 vols.

Sarah de Beranger. By JEAN INGELOW. 3 vols.

The Braes of Yarrow. By C. GIBBON. 3 vols.

Elaine's Story. By MAUD SHERIDAN. 2 vols.

Prince Fortune and His Friends. 3 vols.

Noble Words and Noble Deeds. Translated from the French of
E. MULLER, by DORA LEIGH. Containing many Full-page Illustrations by PHILIPPOTEAUX. Square imperial 16mo, cloth extra, 7s. 6d.

North American Review (The). Monthly, price 2s. 6d.

Notes on Fish and Fishing. By the Rev. J. J. MANLEY, M.A.
With Illustrations, crown 8vo, cloth extra, leatherette binding, 10s. 6d.

Nursery Playmates (Prince of). 217 Coloured pictures for
Children by eminent Artists. Folio, in coloured boards, 6s.

*O*BERAMMERGAU *Passion Play.* See "Art in the
Mountains."

Ocean to Ocean: Sandford Fleming's Expedition through
Canada in 1872. By the Rev. GEORGE M. GRANT. With Illustrations. Revised and enlarged Edition, crown 8vo, cloth, 7s. 6d.

Old-Fashioned Girl. See ALCOTT.

Oliphant (Mrs.) Innocent. A Tale of Modern Life. By Mrs.
OLIPHANT, Author of "The Chronicles of Carlingford," &c., &c.
With Eight Full-page Illustrations, small post 8vo, cloth extra, 6s.

On Horseback through Asia Minor. By Capt. FRED BURNABY,
Royal Horse Guards, Author of "A Ride to Khiva." 2 vols.,
8vo, with three Maps and Portrait of Author, 6th Edition, 38s.;
Cheaper Edition, crown 8vo, 10s. 6d.

Our Little Ones in Heaven. Edited by the Rev. H. ROBBINS.
With Frontispiece after Sir JOSHUA REYNOLDS. Fcap., cloth extra,
New Edition—the 3rd, with Illustrations, 5s.

Our Village. By MARY RUSSELL MITFORD. Illustrated with
Frontispiece Steel Engraving, and 12 full-page and 157 smaller Cuts
of Figure Subjects and Scenes. Crown 4to, cloth, gilt edges, 21s.

Our Woodland Trees. By F. G. HEATH. Large post 8vo,
cloth, gilt edges, uniform with "Fern World" and "Fern Paradise,"
by the same Author. 8 Coloured Plates (showing leaves of every
British Tree) and 20 Woodcuts, cloth, gilt edges, 12s. 6d. Third
Edition.

"The book, as a whole, meets a distinct need; its engravings are excellent, its
coloured leaves and leaflets singularly accurate, and both author and engraver
appear to have been animated by a kindred love of their subject."—*Saturday
Review.*

PAINTERS of All Schools. By LOUIS VIARDOT, and other
Writers. 500 pp., super-royal 8vo, 20 Full-page and 70 smaller
Engravings, cloth extra, 25*s.* A New Edition is issued in Half-
crown parts, with fifty additional portraits, cloth, gilt edges, 31*s.* 6*d.*

Palliser (Mrs.) A History of Lace, from the Earliest Period.
A New and Revised Edition, with additional cuts and text, upwards
of 100 Illustrations and coloured Designs. 1 vol. 8vo, 1*l.* 1*s.*

"One of the most readable books of the season ; permanently valuable, always interesting, often amusing, and not inferior in all the essentials of a gift book."—*Times.*

—— *Historic Devices, Badges, and War Cries.* 8vo, 1*l.* 1*s.*

—— *The China Collector's Pocket Companion.* With upwards of 1000 Illustrations of Marks and Monograms. 2nd Edition,
with Additions. Small post 8vo, limp cloth, 5*s.*

Petites Leçons de Conversation et de Grammaire: Oral and
Conversational Method ; being Lessons introducing the most Useful
Topics of Conversation, upon an entirely new principle, &c. By
F. JULIEN, French Master at King Edward the Sixth's School,
Birmingham. Author of "The Student's French Examiner," "First
Steps in Conversational French Grammar," which see.

Phillips (L.) Dictionary of Biographical Reference. 8vo,
1*l.* 11*s.* 6*d.*

Photography (History and Handbook of). *See* TISSANDIER.

Physical Treatise on Electricity and Magnetism. By J. E. H.
GORDON, B.A. · With about 200 coloured, full-page, and other
Illustrations. Among the newer portions of the work may be
enumerated : All the more recent investigations on Striæ by Spottis-
woode, De la Rue, Moulton, &c. An account of Mr. Crooke's recent
researches. Full descriptions and pictures of all the modern Magnetic
Survey Instruments now used at Kew Observatory. Full accounts of
all the modern work on Specific Inductive Capacity, and of the more
recent determination of the ratio of Electric units (v). It is believed
that in respect to the number and beauty of the Illustrations, the work
will be quite unique. 2 vols., 8vo, 36*s.*

Picture Gallery of British Art (The). 38 Permanent Photographs after the most celebrated English Painters. With Descriptive
Letterpress. Vols. 1 to 5, cloth extra, 18*s.* each. Vols. 6, 7, and 8,
commencing New Series, demy folio, 31*s.* 6*d.*

Pinto (Major Serpa). *See* "King's Rifle."

Placita Anglo-Normannica. The Procedure and Constitution of
the Anglo-Norman Courts (WILLIAM I.—RICHARD I.), as shown by
Contemporaneous Records. With Explanatory Notes, &c. By M. M.
BIGELOW. Demy 8vo, cloth, 21*s.*

Plutarch's Lives. An Entirely New and Library Edition. Edited by A. H. CLOUGH, Esq. 5 vols., 8vo, 2*l.* 10*s.*; half-morocco, gilt top, 3*l.* Also in 1 vol., royal 8vo, 800 pp., cloth extra, 18*s.*; half-bound, 21*s.*

—— *Morals.* Uniform with Clough's Edition of "Lives of Plutarch." Edited by Professor GOODWIN. 5 vols., 8vo, 3*l.* 3*s.*

Poems of the Inner Life. A New Edition, Revised, with many additional Poems. Small post 8vo, cloth, 5*s.*

Poganuc People: their Loves and Lives. By Mrs. BEECHER STOWE. Crown 8vo, cloth, 6*s.*

Polar Expeditions. *See* KOLDEWEY, MARKHAM, MACGAHAN, and NARES.

Practical (A) Handbook to the Principal Schools of England. By C. E. PASCOE. New Edition, crown 8vo, cloth extra, 3*s.* 6*d.*

Prejevalsky (N. M.) From Kulja, across the Tian Shan to Lob-nor. Translated by E. DELMAR MORGAN, F.R.G.S. Demy 8vo, with a Map. 16*s.*

Prince Ritto ; or, The Four-leaved Shamrock. By FANNY W. CURREY. With 10 Full-page Fac-simile Reproductions of Original Drawings by HELEN O'HARA. Demy 4to, cloth extra, gilt, 10*s.* 6*d.*

Publishers' Circular (The), and General Record of British and Foreign Literature. Published on the 1st and 15th of every Month, 3*d.*

RAMBAUD (Alfred). History of Russia, from its Origin to the Year 1877. With Six Maps. Translated by Mrs. L. B. LANG. 2 vols., demy 8vo, cloth extra, 38*s.*

Recollections of Writers. By CHARLES and MARY COWDEN CLARKE. Authors of "The Concordance to Shakespeare," &c. ; with Letters of CHARLES LAMB, LEIGH HUNT, DOUGLAS JERROLD, and CHARLES DICKENS ; and a Preface by MARY COWDEN CLARKE. Crown 8vo, cloth, 10*s.* 6*d.*

Reminiscences of the War in New Zealand. By THOMAS W. GUDGEON, Lieutenant and Quartermaster, Colonial Forces, N.Z. With Twelve Portraits. Crown 8vo, cloth extra, 10*s.* 6*d.*

Rémusat (Madame de). *See* "Memoirs of."

Robinson (Phil). *See* "In my Indian Garden."

Rochefoucauld's Reflections. Bayard Series, 2*s.* 6*d.*

Rogers (S.) Pleasures of Memory. See " Choice Editions of Choice Books." 2*s.* 6*d.*

Rose in Bloom. See ALCOTT.

Rose Library (The). Popular Literature of all countries. Each volume, 1*s.* ; cloth, 2*s.* 6*d.* Many of the Volumes are Illustrated—

1. **Sea-Gull Rock.** By JULES SANDEAU. Illustrated.
2. **Little Women.** By LOUISA M. ALCOTT.
3. **Little Women Wedded.** Forming a Sequel to "Little Women."
4. **The House on Wheels.** By MADAME DE STOLZ. Illustrated.
5. **Little Men.** By LOUISA M. ALCOTT. Dble. vol., 2*s.* ; cloth, 3*s.* 6*d.*
6. **The Old-Fashioned Girl.** By LOUISA M. ALCOTT. Double vol., 2*s.* ; cloth, 3*s.* 6*d.*
7. **The Mistress of the Manse.** By J. G. HOLLAND.
8. **Timothy Titcomb's Letters to Young People, Single and Married.**
9. **Undine, and the Two Captains.** By Baron DE LA MOTTE FOUQUÉ. A New Translation by F. E. BUNNETT. Illustrated.
10. **Draxy Miller's Dowry, and the Elder's Wife.** By SAXE HOLM.
11. **The Four Gold Pieces.** By Madame GOURAUD. Numerous Illustrations.
12. **Work.** A Story of Experience. First Portion. By LOUISA M. ALCOTT.
13. **Beginning Again.** Being a Continuation of "Work." By LOUISA M. ALCOTT.
14. **Picciola; or, the Prison Flower.** By X. B. SAINTINE. Numerous Graphic Illustrations.
15. **Robert's Holidays.** Illustrated.
16. **The Two Children of St. Domingo.** Numerous Illustrations.
17. **Aunt Jo's Scrap Bag.**
18. **Stowe (Mrs. H. B.) The Pearl of Orr's Island.**
19. —— **The Minister's Wooing.**
20. —— **Betty's Bright Idea.**
21. —— **The Ghost in the Mill.**
22. —— **Captain Kidd's Money.**
23. —— **We and our Neighbours.** Double vol., 2*s.*
24. —— **My Wife and I.** Double vol., 2*s.* ; cloth, gilt, 3*s.* 6*d.*
25. **Hans Brinker; or, the Silver Skates.**
26. **Lowell's My Study Window.**
27. **Holmes (O. W.) The Guardian Angel.**
28. **Warner (C. D.) My Summer in a Garden.**

The Rose Library, continued :—

29. **Hitherto.** By the Author of "The Gayworthys." 2 vols., 1s. each.
30. **Helen's Babies.** By their Latest Victim.
31. **The Barton Experiment.** By the Author of "Helen's Babies."
32. **Dred.** By Mrs. BEECHER STOWE. Double vol., 2s. Cloth, gilt, 3s. 6d.
33. **Warner (C. D.) In the Wilderness.**
34. **Six to One.** A Seaside Story.

Russell (W. H., LL.D.) The Tour of the Prince of Wales in India. By W. H. RUSSELL, LL.D. Fully Illustrated by SYDNEY P. HALL, M.A. Super-royal 8vo, cloth extra, gilt edges, 52s. 6d.; Large Paper Edition, 84s.

SANCTA Christina: a Story of the First Century. By ELEANOR E. ORLEBAR. With a Preface by the Bishop of Winchester. Small post 8vo, cloth extra, 5s.

Scientific Memoirs: being Experimental Contributions to a Knowledge of Radiant Energy. By JOHN WILLIAM DRAPER, M.D., LL.D., Author of "A Treatise on Human Physiology," &c. With Steel Portrait of the Author. Demy 8vo, cloth, 473 pages, 14s.

Scott (Sir G. Gilbert.) See "Autobiography."

Sea-Gull Rock. By JULES SANDEAU, of the French Academy. Royal 16mo, with 79 Illustrations, cloth extra, gilt edges, 7s. 6d. Cheaper Edition, cloth gilt, 2s. 6d. *See also* Rose Library.

Seonee: Sporting in the Satpura Range of Central India, and in the Valley of the Nerbudda. By R. A. STERNDALE, F.R.G.S. 8vo, with numerous Illustrations, 21s.

The Serpent Charmer: a Tale of the Indian Mutiny. By LOUIS ROUSSELET, Author of "India and its Native Princes." Numerous Illustrations. Crown 8vo, cloth extra, gilt edges, 7s. 6d. , plainer binding, 5s.

Shakespeare (The Boudoir). Edited by HENRY CUNDELL. Carefully bracketted for reading aloud ; freed from all objectionable matter, and altogether free from notes. Price 2s. 6d. each volume, cloth extra, gilt edges. Contents :—Vol I., Cymbeline—Merchant of Venice. Each play separately, paper cover, 1s. Vol. II., As You Like It—King Lear—Much Ado about Nothing. Vol. III., Romeo and Juliet—Twelfth Night—King John. The latter six plays separately, paper cover, 9d.

Shakespeare Key (The). Forming a Companion to "The Complete Concordance to Shakespeare." By CHARLES and MARY COWDEN CLARKE. Demy 8vo, 800 pp., 21s.

Shooting: its Appliances, Practice, and Purpose. By JAMES DALZIEL DOUGALL, F.S.A., F.Z.A. Author of "Scottish Field Sports," &c. Crown 8vo, cloth extra, 10s. 6d.
"The book is admirable in every way. . . . . We wish it every success."—*Globe.*
"A very complete treatise. . . . . Likely to take high rank as an authority on shooting."—*Daily News.*

Silent Hour (The). *See* "Gentle Life Series."

Silver Pitchers. *See* ALCOTT.

Simon (Jules). *See* "Government of M. Thiers."

Six to One. A Seaside Story. 16mo, boards, 1s.

Smith (G.) Assyrian Explorations and Discoveries. By the late GEORGE SMITH. Illustrated by Photographs and Woodcuts. Demy 8vo, 6th Edition, 18s.

———— *The Chaldean Account of Genesis.* By the late G. SMITH, of the Department of Oriental Antiquities, British Museum. With many Illustrations. Demy 8vo, cloth extra, 6th Edition, 16s.

Snow-Shoes and Canoes ; or, the Adventures of a Fur-Hunter in the Hudson's Bay Territory. By W. H. G. KINGSTON. 2nd Edition. With numerous Illustrations. Square crown 8vo, cloth extra, gilt edges, 7s. 6d. ; plainer binding, 5s.

Songs and Etchings in Shade and Sunshine. By J. E. G. Illustrated with 44 Etchings. Small 4to, cloth, gilt tops, 25s.

South Kensington Museum. Monthly 1s. *See* "Art Treasures."

Stanley (H. M.) How I Found Livingstone. Crown 8vo, cloth extra, 7s. 6d. ; large Paper Edition, 10s. 6d.

———— *"My Kalulu," Prince, King, and Slave.* A Story from Central Africa. Crown 8vo, about 430 pp., with numerous graphic Illustrations, after Original Designs by the Author. Cloth, 7s. 6d.

———— *Coomassie and Magdala.* A Story of Two British Campaigns in Africa. Demy 8vo, with Maps and Illustrations, 16s.

———— *Through the Dark Continent,* which see.

St. Nicholas Magazine. 4to, in handsome cover. 1s. monthly. Annual Volumes, handsomely bound, 15s. Its special features are, the great variety and interest of its literary contents, and the beauty and profuseness of its Illustrations, which surpass anything yet attempted in any publication for young people, and the stories are by the best living authors of juvenile literature. Each Part contains, on an average, 50 Illustrations.

Story without an End. From the German of Carové, by the late Mrs. SARAH T. AUSTIN. Crown 4to, with 15 Exquisite Drawings by E. V. B., printed in Colours in Fac-simile of the original Water Colours; and numerous other Illustrations. New Edition, 7s. 6d.

—— square 4to, with Illustrations by HARVEY. 2s. 6d.

Stowe (Mrs. Beecher) Dred. Cheap Edition, boards, 2s. Cloth, gilt edges, 3s. 6d.

—— *Footsteps of the Master.* With Illustrations and red borders. Small post 8vo, cloth extra, 6s.

—— *Geography*, with 60 Illustrations. Square cloth, 4s. 6d.

—— *Little Foxes.* Cheap Edition, 1s.; Library Edition, 4s. 6d.

—— *Betty's Bright Idea.* 1s.

—— *My Wife and I; or, Harry Henderson's History.* Small post 8vo, cloth extra, 6s.*

—— *Minister's Wooing.* 5s.; Copyright Series, 1s. 6d.; cl., 2s.*

—— *Old Town Folk.* 6s.; Cheap Edition, 2s. 6d.

—— *Old Town Fireside Stories.* Cloth extra, 3s. 6d.

—— *Our Folks at Poganuc.* 10s. 6d.

—— *We and our Neighbours.* 1 vol., small post 8vo, 6s. Sequel to "My Wife and I."*

—— *Pink and White Tyranny.* Small post 8vo, 3s. 6d.; Cheap Edition, 1s. 6d. and 2s.

—— *Queer Little People.* 1s.; cloth, 2s.

—— *Chimney Corner.* 1s.; cloth, 1s. 6d.

—— *The Pearl of Orr's Island.* Crown 8vo, 5s.*

—— *Little Pussey Willow.* Fcap., 2s.

* *See also* Rose Library.

Stowe (Mrs. Beecher) Woman in Sacred History. Illustrated with 15 Chromo-lithographs and about 200 pages of Letterpress. Demy 4to, cloth extra, gilt edges, 25*s.*

Student's French Examiner. By F. JULIEN, Author of " Petites Leçons de Conversation et de Grammaire." Square crown 8vo, cloth, 2*s.*

Studies in German Literature. By BAYARD TAYLOR. Edited by MARIE TAYLOR. With an Introduction by the Hon. GEORGE H. BOKER. 8vo, cloth extra, 10*s.* 6*d.*

Studies in the Theory of Descent. By Dr. AUG. WEISMANN, Professor in the University of Freiburg. Translated and edited by RAPHAEL MELDOLA, F.C.S., Secretary of the Entomological Society of London. Part I.—" On the Seasonal Dimorphism of Butterflies," containing Original Communications by Mr. W. H. EDWARDS, of Coalburgh. With two Coloured Plates. Price of Part. I. (to Subscribers for the whole work only) 8*s* ; Part II. (6 coloured plates), 16*s.* ; Part III., 6*s.*

Sugar Beet (The). Including a History of the Beet Sugar Industry in Europe, Varieties of the Sugar Beet, Examination, Soils, Tillage, Seeds and Sowing, Yield and Cost of Cultivation, Harvesting, Transportation, Conservation, Feeding Qualities of the Beet and of the Pulp, &c. By L. S. WARE. Illustrated. 8vo, cloth extra, 21*s.*

Sullivan (A. M., M.P.). *See* " New Ireland."

Sulphuric Acid (A Practical Treatise on the Manufacture of). By A. G. and C. G. LOCK, Consulting Chemical Engineers. With 77 Construction Plates, and other Illustrations.

Sumner (Hon. Charles). *See* Life and Letters.

Sunrise: A Story of These Times. By WILLIAM BLACK, Author of " A Daughter of Heth," &c. To be published in 15 Monthly Parts, commencing April 1st, 1*s.* each.

Surgeon's Handbook on the Treatment of Wounded in War. By Dr. FRIEDRICH ESMARCH, Professor of Surgery in the University of Kiel, and Surgeon-General to the Prussian Army. Translated by H. H. CLUTTON, B.A. Cantab, F.R.C.S. Numerous Coloured Plates and Illustrations, 8vo, strongly bound in flexible leather, 1*l.* 8*s.*

Sylvan Spring. By FRANCIS GEORGE HEATH. Illustrated by 12 Coloured Plates, drawn by F. E. HULME, F.L.S., Artist and Author of " Familiar Wild Flowers;" by 16 full-page, and more than 100 other Wood Engravings. Large post 8vo, cloth, gilt edges, 12*s.* 6*d.*

TAUCHNITZ'S English Editions of German Authors.
Each volume, cloth flexible, 2*s.* ; or sewed, 1*s.* 6*d.* (Catalogues post free on application.)

—————— (*B.*) *German and English Dictionary.* Cloth, 1*s.* 6*d.;* roan, 2*s.*

—————— *French and English.* Paper, 1*s.* 6*d.* ; cloth, 2*s.* ; roan, 2*s.* 6*d.*

—————— *Italian and English.* Paper, 1*s.* 6*d.* ; cloth, 2*s.* ; roan, 2*s.* 6*d.*

—————— *Spanish and English.* Paper, 1*s.* 6*d.* ; cloth, 2*s.* ; roan, 2*s.* 6*d.*

—————— *New Testament.* Cloth, 2*s.* ; gilt, 2*s.* 6*d.*

Taylor (*Bayard*). *See* "Studies in German Literature."

Textbook (*A*) *of Harmony.* For the Use of Schools and Students. By the late CHARLES EDWARD HORSLEY. Revised for the Press by WESTLEY RICHARDS and W. H. CALCOTT. Small post 8vo, cloth extra, 3*s.* 6*d.*

Through the Dark Continent : The Sources of the Nile ; Around the Great Lakes, and down the Congo. By HENRY M. STANLEY. 2 vols., demy 8vo, containing 150 Full-page and other Illustrations, 2 Portraits of the Author, and 10 Maps, 42*s.* Seventh Thousand. Cheaper Edition, crown 8vo, with some of the Illustrations and Maps. 1 vol., 12*s.* 6*d.*

Tour of the Prince of Wales in India. See RUSSELL.

Trees and Ferns. By F. G. HEATH. Crown 8vo, cloth, gilt edges, with numerous Illustrations, 3*s.* 6*d.*
"A charming little volume."—*Land and Water.*

Turkistan. Notes of a Journey in the Russian Provinces of Central Asia and the Khanates of Bokhara and Kokand. By EUGENE SCHUYLER, Late Secretary to the American Legation, St. Petersburg. Numerous Illustrations. 2 vols, 8vo, cloth extra, 5th Edition, 2*l.* 2*s.*

Two Friends. By LUCIEN BIART, Author of "Adventures of a Young Naturalist," "My Rambles in the New World," &c. Small post 8vo, numerous Illustrations, gilt edges, 7*s.* 6*d.* ; plainer binding, 5*s.*

Two Supercargoes (*The*) ; *or, Adventures in Savage Africa.* By W. H. G. KINGSTON. Numerous Full-page Illustrations. Square imperial 16mo, cloth extra, gilt edges, 7*s.* 6*d.* ; plainer binding, 5*s.*

UP and Down ; or, Fifty Years' Experiences in Australia, California, New Zealand, India, China, and the South Pacific. Being the Life History of Capt. W. J. BARRY. Written by Himself. With several Illustrations. Crown 8vo, cloth extra, 8*s.* 6*d.*

" Jules Verne, that Prince of Story-tellers."—TIMES.

BOOKS BY JULES VERNE.

LARGE CROWN 8VO . . .	Containing 550 to 600 pp. and from 50 to 100 full-page illustrations.		Containing the whole of the text with some illustrations.	
WORKS.	In very handsome cloth binding, gilt edges.	In plainer binding, plain edges.	In cloth binding, gilt edges, smaller type.	Coloured Boards.
	s. d.	*s. d.*	*s. d.*	
Twenty Thousand Leagues under the Sea. Part I. Ditto. Part II.	10 6	5 0	3 6	2 vols., 1s. each.
Hector Servadac . . .	10 6	5 0		
The Fur Country . . .	10 6	5 0	3 6	2 vols., 1s. each.
From the Earth to the Moon and a Trip round it	10 6	5 0	2 vols., 2s. each.	2 vols., 1s. each.
Michael Strogoff, the Courier of the Czar . .	10 6	5 0		
Dick Sands, the Boy Captain	10 6			*s. d.*
Five Weeks in a Balloon .	7 6	3 6	2 0	1 0
Adventures of Three Englishmen and Three Russians	7 6	3 6	2 0	1 0
Around the World in Eighty Days	7 6	3 6	2 0	1 0
A Floating City	7 6	3 6 *	2 0	1 0
The Blockade Runners .			2 0	1 0
Dr. Ox's Experiment . .			2 0	1 0
Master Zacharius . . .	7 6	3 6	2 0	1 0
A Drama in the Air . .			2 0	1 0
A Winter amid the Ice .			2 0	1 0
The Survivors of the " Chancellor ". . . .	7 6	3 6	2 0	2 vols. 1s. each.
Martin Paz			2 0	1 0
THE MYSTERIOUS ISLAND, 3 vols. :—	22 6	10 6	6 0	3 0
Vol. I. Dropped from the Clouds	7 6	3 6	2 0	1 0
Vol. II. Abandoned . .	7 6	3 6	2 0	1 0
Vol. III. Secret of the Island	7 6	3 6	2 0	1 0
The Child of the Cavern .	7 6	3 6		
The Begum's Fortune. .	7 6			
The Tribulations of a Chinaman	7 6			

CELEBRATED TRAVELS AND TRAVELLERS. 3 vols. Demy 8vo, 600 pp., upwards of 100 full-page illustrations, 12s. 6d.; gilt edges, 14s. each :—
  (1) THE EXPLORATION OF THE WORLD.
  (2) THE GREAT NAVIGATORS OF THE EIGHTEENTH CENTURY.
  (3) THE EXPLORERS OF THE NINETEENTH CENTURY. (*In the Press.*)

WALLER (Rev. C. H.) The Names on the Gates of Pearl, and other Studies. By the Rev. C. H. WALLER, M.A. Second edition. Crown 8vo, cloth extra, 6*s.*

—— *A Grammar and Analytical Vocabulary of the Words in* the Greek Testament. Compiled from Brüder's Concordance. For the use of Divinity Students and Greek Testament Classes. By the Rev. C. H. WALLER, M.A. Part I., The Grammar. Small post 8vo, cloth, 2*s.* 6*d.* Part II. The Vocabulary, 2*s.* 6*d.*

—— *Adoption and the Covenant.* Some Thoughts on Confirmation. Super-royal 16mo, cloth limp, 2*s.* 6*d.*

Wanderings in the Western Land. By A. PENDARVES VIVIAN, M.P. With many Illustrations from Drawings by Mr. BIERSTADT and the Author, and 3 Maps. 1 vol., demy 8vo, cloth extra, 18*s.*

War in Bulgaria: a Narrative of Personal Experiences. By LIEUTENANT-GENERAL VALENTINE BAKER PASHA. Maps and Plans of Battles. 2 vols., demy 8vo, cloth extra, 2*l.* 2*s.*

Warner (C. D.) My Summer in a Garden. Rose Library, 1*s.*

—— *Back-log Studies.* Boards, 1*s.* 6*d.*; cloth, 2*s.*

—— *In the Wilderness.* Rose Library, 1*s.*

—— *Mummies and Moslems.* 8vo, cloth, 12*s.*

Weaving. See " History and Principles."

Whitney (Mrs. A. D. T.) Hitherto. Small post 8vo, 3*s.* 6*d.* and 2*s.* 6*d.*

—— *Sights and Insights.* 3 vols., crown 8vo, 31*s.* 6*d.*

—— *Summer in Leslie Goldthwaite's Life.* Cloth, 3*s.* 6*d.*

Wills, A Few Hints on Proving, without Professional Assistance. By a PROBATE COURT OFFICIAL. 5th Edition, revised with·Forms of Wills, Residuary Accounts, &c. Fcap. 8vo, cloth limp, 1*s.*

With Axe and Rifle on the Western Prairies. By W. H. G. KINGSTON. With numerous Illustrations, square crown 8vo, cloth. extra, gilt edges, 7*s.* 6*d.*; plainer binding, 5*s.*

Witty and Humorous Side of the English Poets (The). With a variety of Specimens arranged in Periods. By ARTHUR H. ELLIOTT. 1 vol., crown 8vo, cloth, 10*s.* 6*d.*

Woolsey (C. D., LL.D.) Introduction to the Study of International Law; designed as an Aid in Teaching and in Historical Studies. 5th Edition, demy 8vo, 18*s.*

Words of Wellington: Maxims and Opinions, Sentences and Reflections of the Great Duke, gathered from his Despatches, Letters, and Speeches (Bayard Series). 2*s.* 6*d.*

Wreck of the Grosvenor. By W. CLARK RUSSELL. 6*s.* Third and Cheaper Edition.

London:

SAMPSON LOW, MARSTON, SEARLE, & RIVINGTON,

CROWN BUILDINGS 188, FLEET STREET.